THE FLOWER SHOP ON SERENDIPITY LANE

SARAH HOPE

B

Boldwood

First published in 2021. This edition first published in Great Britain in 2024 by Boldwood Books Ltd.

Cover Design by Head Design Ltd

Cover Illustration: Shutterstock

A CIP catalogue record for this book is available from the British Library.

Paperback ISBN 978-1-80549-140-8

Large Print ISBN 978-1-80549-141-5

Hardback ISBN 978-1-80549-139-2

Ebook ISBN 978-1-80549-142-2

Kindle ISBN 978-1-80549-143-9

Audio CD ISBN 978-1-80549-134-7

MP3 CD ISBN 978-1-80549-135-4

Digital audio download ISBN 978-1-80549-137-8

Boldwood Books Ltd
23 Bowerdean Street
London SW6 3TN
www.boldwoodbooks.com

For my children,
Let's change our stars
xXx

1

Sadie Locke pulled the front door shut and listened to the all too familiar click as it locked. The click which used to wake her up when her ex-husband, Max, stumbled through the door in the early hours of the morning, and more recently, reassured her that her daughter, Lily, had arrived home from musing around the shops with her friends safely on a Saturday afternoon.

She'd miss that click.

'Sadie, hi. How are you, love?'

Turning around, Sadie watched as her neighbour of fifteen years, Anna, walked down the driveway towards her, a sympathetic smile predictably plastered on her face. 'I'm good, thanks. Looking forward to getting into our new place now.'

'Of course.' Anna pulled her bulging canvas shopping bag higher up her shoulder. 'You're ever so brave. I couldn't imagine just upping and leaving and heading somewhere completely unknown. And starting your own business as well?'

'Oh, it's not brave. I should have done it years ago.'

'Well, in my book, it's brave. I don't think I'd ever have the courage to do that. Especially with everything Max put you through.'

'That was a long time ago. Five years now.'

'Even so...' Anna looked longingly towards her house before making a point of looking at her watch. 'Anyway, I'd better get back. Lots to do.'

Sadie nodded and pointed the key towards her car. 'Me too.'

Stepping forward, Anna wrapped her arms awkwardly around Sadie's shoulders. 'Good luck.'

'Thanks.' As Anna disappeared through the gap in the hedge dividing their driveways, Sadie turned and posted the house key through the letter box. She should have left it inside. She shrugged. The last thing she wanted to do was go back in and have to face the emptiness again.

Turning, she retreated to the car. For the very last time.

Why had Anna had to bring up Max? She was more than just his ex-wife – she was a person in her own right. She couldn't wait to get settled in their new place, to be known only as Sadie Locke, the florist. To be herself. For too long now, people had been referring to her as Sadie – the single mum whose husband had had an affair for two years behind her back without her realising. Yes, it would be a good feeling to be plain old Sadie again.

Slipping behind the steering wheel, she set up the satnav and waited for the routing system to kick in. Their new place was only a twenty-minute drive, but the few times she'd made the journey she'd always got lost as soon as she'd turned off the main road. She'd have to get used to navigating the small winding country roads which led to the village and their new home.

Resting her hands on the top of the steering wheel, she took in the large three-bed semi in front of her. She could still remember when they'd moved in. It had just been her and Max back then. They'd had to rent a bedsit for two years to scrape the money together for a deposit, and after thinking a place like this would be out of their league, they'd somehow both landed a pay rise at work and thought all their dreams had come true.

Sadie scrunched up her nose. They had. Her dreams had come true, or at least she'd thought they had. It had only been two beautiful girls later, and fourteen years of being together, that she'd learnt the dream she'd been living had been a lie.

Filling her lungs with the sweet scent of the honeysuckle growing in the flowerbed, Sadie released the handbrake and let the car roll down the driveway.

Onwards and upwards, as her mother had always said.

* * *

'The destination is on your right.' The drab tones of the satnav told her the obvious, and Sadie pulled onto the pavement and shut off the engine. The removal crew were already there and had been for quite a while, if the bored expression on the driver's face was anything to go by.

'Hi. Sorry to keep you.' Sadie quickly strode towards the van.

'No problem.' Doug, the driver, nodded curtly.

Rummaging around in her bag, Sadie pulled out the keys, the huge estate agent's generic key ring still attached, and headed toward the door.

After twisting the key, she pushed the door open and breathed in the musty smell of time laced with the scent of old forgotten flowers. Going to the large front window, she pulled up the blind, immediately flooding the shop with the clean sunlight of spring. The pale green walls stood bare, the posters covering them when she'd viewed the property having been torn down. The white floor tiles were murky with the dust and mud of shoes, and the four floral display units and flower buckets, which the previous owner had promised to leave behind, were stacked against the far wall in front of the counter.

Sadie sniffed the air. Some flowers had definitely been left behind and forgotten, and she'd bet a million pounds the smell was coming from wilted lilies.

'Do you want everything taken upstairs?' Doug came in behind her carrying one end of a sideboard she'd upcycled with white chalk paint.

'Not that. Can you pop it over in that corner, please? And the three tub chairs need to stay down here too, please. Apart from that, everything else belongs upstairs. Thanks.'

'Okay.' Doug wrinkled up his nose.

'That's my first job – to find the offending smell.' Sadie grimaced. Placing the key on the counter, she began searching behind and beneath the buckets and floral display units. Nothing. Apart from a thick layer of dust, they were empty and clean.

Making her way behind the counter, she trailed her fingers along the dark wood. Ducking through the beaded curtain strung up in the archway leading to the back room, and minding the shallow step, she gagged. If the sudden strength in smell was anything to go by, the forgotten blooms must be hidden somewhere close.

Bingo! Underneath the large old pine workbench, which stood proudly in the middle of the room and filled most of it, Sadie spotted the offending flowers. She'd been right – they were lilies. Or had been. The bunch of five stems must have been left when the previous owners had moved out two months ago.

Gingerly picking them up, she made a beeline for the back door, unlocked it and stepped out into the small car park behind. Locating the industrial-sized bin, shared by the small row of shops, she lifted the lid and disposed of them. Wiping her hands down her already grubby jeans, Sadie turned back towards The Flower Shop.

Just before returning to the chaos inside, she glanced up at the signage above the small back window. The hand-painted cursive writing really was beautiful. The Flower Shop on Serendipity Lane. From what the previous owners had told her, the name had been passed on through three genera-tions of florists before they had bought it twenty-five years ago. With it steeped in history, along with the positive reputation it held in the local vicinity, Sadie had already decided to keep the name.

She grinned. It was hers. Lock, stock and barrel as they say. She'd done it! All those years of evening classes and training, alongside keeping down a full-time teaching job and juggling single parenthood, and she'd done it! She'd followed her dream, and now they all had a proper new start.

Yes, the girls were a little annoyed at the prospect of downsizing from a three-bed house with a large garden to a cosy little flat above the shop, but it wouldn't be forever. Once she'd got the shop turning a decent profit, she'd be able to apply for a mortgage and buy a house. Maybe she could even rent out the flat for a bit of extra income. Yes, things would be good. The village was big enough to have the coffee shops and parks Lily liked to hang around in, and they were surrounded by woods boasting the

BMX track tomboy Poppy loved to explore with her friends, Harry and Ed.

Plus, with it only being twenty minutes out of town, she'd be able to run the girls back to see their friends and take Lily to her dance classes, and the bus ride into school wouldn't be so bad. Lily's friend, Georgia, lived in the village so at least she'd know someone on the bus and Poppy was Poppy, self-assured and happy-go-lucky. She'd be fine, besides, Harry and Ed got the bus from the village too.

'Excuse me, miss. Everything's unloaded, so we'll be off now.'

Crossing her arms against the slight chill, Sadie smiled and followed Doug's voice back into the shop. She would have precisely twenty-six hours to unpack as much as she could before Max dropped Lily and Poppy off after lunch tomorrow.

* * *

Sadie turned the music down and listened. Yep, that was definitely the front door to the shop. The gentle tap-tap-tapping became increasingly louder and faster as she ran down the stairs.

Tucking her hair behind her ears and pulling a stray piece of packing tape off her jeans, she pulled the door open. 'Hey, you two! Did you have a nice time at Daddy's?'

'Wow! This looks amazing! I can't believe we have our own shop!' Dropping her rucksack on the floor, Poppy twirled around, her eyes wide and her mouth open.

'Don't be a baby. It looks the same as it did when we viewed it. Actually, it looks worse. It's empty and dusty and, yuck, even the floor is muddy.' Lily held her foot up behind her and looked down at the soles of her white trainers.

'It'll be all cleaned up in a few hours. They're nice. Did Dad get them?' Sadie looked down at Lily's feet.

Rolling her eyes, Lily ignored her mum and strode through the shop towards the door leading up to the flat.

'Yep, Daddy got them for her. He got me some too, but I left them there. Lily was supposed to as well, but she wore them home.'

'Oh well, do you want to see upstairs?'

'Yes! Is it all unpacked?'

'Almost. There are just a few boxes in your rooms for you both to sort out.'

'Thanks, Mum.' Grabbing her rucksack from the floor, Poppy ran past Sadie and up the stairs.

'Take your shoes off down here...' Following her, Sadie dodged Poppy's trainers as she kicked them off on her way up the stairs. At least someone was excited about the big move.

* * *

'I'd forgotten about the little cupboard in my room! Can I use it to store all my art stuff? I'll even be able to fit my canvases in there and not have to have them scattered around the place.' Without waiting for an answer, Poppy ran into her bedroom.

'Since when did you worry about keeping your bedroom tidy?' Lily stomped from the bathroom, firmly shutting her bedroom door behind her.

Sighing, Sadie stood in the doorway to Poppy's room and watched as she pulled out paints, chalks, pastels and sketchbooks from one of the boxes piled under the window. 'I think that's a great idea, Poppy. They'll fit nicely in there.'

'When I've finished unpacking, I'm going to take loads of photos – the people at school won't believe we actually have our own shop!'

'Good idea.' That's one of the reasons Sadie had chosen The Flower Shop, so the girls didn't have to change schools. They both had good solid friendship groups, so it had been important to find somewhere close enough to their old house to be on a bus route to school.

'Should I put these in there too?' Poppy held up two tubs of clay.

'I should think so. Keep all your crafty bits together.' Smiling, Sadie sat on the floor next to her daughter. She'd go and check on Lily in a bit. It probably wouldn't hurt to give her a bit of time to cool off first.

'Where shall I put all my school bits?' Pulling her school bag out of the box, Poppy looked around the small room.

'That can go down in the hallway if you like? I'd only packed it in there because I didn't want it getting lost over the half-term holiday.'

'Okay, I'll take it down later then.' Poppy launched the bag towards the door where it landed in a heap on the cream carpet. 'Are you really going to let me take the bus tomorrow?'

'Yes, I think so. Lily will be on the same bus, and you're both going to the same school, so you'll be okay with her, won't you?'

'I'll be fine. Although Lily has already told me I can't sit next to her because Georgia catches the same bus, so she'll be sitting next to her.' Poppy began piling books onto the shelf next to her bed. 'That's okay though, I can sit with Ed and Harry or listen to some music on the way.'

'We can get to the bus stop early so you can see them before you get on the bus, if you like?'

Poppy nodded. 'Okay. Can I take my bike out over to the track after school?'

Sadie glanced towards the window. 'Remember, it gets dark early at the moment. In a few weeks, the clocks will go forward and it'll be lighter after school. Why don't you see about meeting them at the weekend? It will be fine then. One of the parents can come along too. Harry's dad normally goes to the woods with him, doesn't he?'

'Okay. Yes, he's got a BMX too. Will I be able to help you in the shop instead, then? I can help you cut the flowers and serve the customers.'

Leaning forward, Sadie hugged her. 'That would be lovely. Right, I'd better get a wriggle on and sort the shop out – our first delivery is coming in the morning.' She also needed to check in on Lily now that she'd had some time to calm down. Hopefully.

'Okay, I'll just finish here and then I'll come down and help you.'

Smiling, Sadie stood up and made her way across the landing to Lily's room. She knocked on the door before pushing it open. 'How are you getting on with your unpacking, Lily?'

'I'll do it later.' Pushing herself up to sitting, Lily put the magazine she was reading down on her bed. 'Not that I've got anywhere to put anything.'

'You have. Your room's bigger than Poppy's and she's managing to fit everything in.'

'Yes, but look, my desk is pushed right up to my bed and I don't even have space to walk to my bed properly, let alone do my dance practice!'

'The living room's nice and big though, so you can practise in there.'

'What? And have Poppy watching and laughing at me?'

'She won't laugh. You're very good – you know you are. Plus, she won't mind staying out of the living room for a bit while you practise. She's already asked to help out in the shop, so she'll likely be down with me most of the time, anyway.'

'I still don't know why we had to up and leave. We were happy back in our old home.'

Sadie perched on the edge of the bed. 'I know we were happy with the house, but with me working all the time, we never got to spend any time together. This way I can be here for you.'

'No, you won't. You'll be working in the shop.'

'Yes, but I'll be in the same building as you. I'm going to see if I can pick up a second-hand sofa we can put in the back room downstairs. That way, after school, you and Poppy can come and hang out there.'

'Exactly. You'll be working.'

'We'll all be together though. Not like when I was teaching and had to stay late every evening just to get the planning done and set up for the next day. Besides, when I close up at five, that'll be it. I'll be done. There'll be no stacks of books to be marked or reports to write or anything. I'll be free to spend time with you both. I'll be able to take you to your dance lessons and stay and watch.' Sadie smoothed the duvet cover down with the palm of her hand. Her last job had almost broken her – the ridiculous forms and progress charts they'd been expected to fill in, along with never-ending meetings and 'catch-ups' with the headteacher and academy management. This, mixed with the pressures of having 'learning walks' scheduled monthly by the academy bosses, who would wander around the school dropping in on lessons and flicking through planning folders, had been all too much.

Sadie shuddered. She wouldn't have minded so much if any of the academy management had actually taught a day in their life, or even shared their views with the staff because that may have been useful for career development, but without any feedback, it had all seemed useless and an unnecessary pressure to an already heaving workload. No, she couldn't have carried on. She'd gone into teaching to teach, to spend time with her class, but her old school had all been about the paperwork. The teaching had seemed to take a back seat.

Sadie pinched the bridge of her nose. She knew not all schools were like her last one, and she was aware she'd piled even more pressure on herself by studying floristry in the evenings, and she *did* miss teaching. Who knew? Maybe in the future she'd return to the classroom. But for now, she needed to put her little family first. She needed to be able to spend more time with her own children.

'You okay?'

'Yes, I'm fine.' Looking up, Sadie smiled at Lily. 'I was just thinking about how hectic our life was before. I know the living space is a lot smaller here than what we're used to, but I really do think this move is the best thing for us. I really do.'

Lily fiddled with the magazine, dog-earing at the corners. 'Sorry, Mum. I know you were really stressed before and I know I should be happy we've moved here but it's...'

'Different?'

Lily nodded. 'I liked being able to just wander into town and meet my mates at the coffee shop and look around the shops. It's going to be weird living in a little village.'

'There're a couple of coffee shops down the High Street. The estate agent was raving about them to me so they must be pretty good, and you've got Georgia here, haven't you? And anyway, you'll still be able to go straight into town after school and I'll be able to come and get you when I shut up shop.'

'I'll be able to just get a later bus, I guess.'

'I'll get you; I don't really want you taking buses. It's different when it's going to school and home-time, there'll be lots of other school kids, but it'll be lonely later. I'll pick you up.'

Lily shrugged.

'So, there are ways. I bet it won't actually be much different for you than when we lived in town.'

'Apart from the fact that my bedroom's minuscule.'

Sadie looked around. 'It's not so small. You were just lucky your bedroom was so big in the last house.'

'Hmmm. I'll have a walk-in wardrobe in Dad's new house.'

Looking at the floor, Sadie pushed an abandoned pen to the side with her foot. Of course, Max was moving in a couple of days. Trust him to always overshadow anything she did. They moved here, so he's moving into a massive five-bed detached house. It was always the same with holidays too, she'd tell the girls she'd booked a caravan in Wales and he'd book a villa in Madrid. She took a slow breath in. She was being daft. He'd been talking about moving for ages. It had nothing to do with the fact she'd bought The Flower Shop. It was just a coincidence. 'Think about how lucky you are then. You get a big bedroom and a walk-in wardrobe at Daddy's, and here you get this lovely cosy room, your friend living just minutes away and you're surrounded by beautiful countryside. You've got the best of both worlds.'

'I've got to ring Georgia now and arrange what time to meet tomorrow.' Picking up her mobile from her bedside table, Lily looked pointedly at the door.

'Okay, sweetheart.' Patting Lily's knee, Sadie stood up.

* * *

Sadie pulled another moving box out through the archway from the back room to the shop floor. Another three boxes of florist supplies to unpack and display then she'd be able to make a start on the back room – the room where the magic would happen. Hopefully.

'Mum.'

Turning, Sadie looked at Poppy standing by the door up to the flat, the glow-in-the-dark stars on her pyjamas bright in the dim light. 'Poppy! You made me jump! I thought you'd gone to bed?'

'I couldn't sleep. Do you want some help?'

Sadie glanced at the clock. It was 9:20. 'Yes, that'd be great, thanks. Not for long, mind. You've got to catch the school bus at eight in the morning.'

'I know. I thought I'd listen to my new album when I'm on the bus.'

'That's a good idea. Just maybe have only one earphone in though. You need to be able to hear what's going on around you, remember?'

'Don't worry, I will.'

'Good. Now, are you okay helping me unpack this box then? If you can open the pack of gift cards and put them in that holder on the counter that would be a great help.'

* * *

With the display units and flower buckets all arranged, the floor mopped, and the windows cleaned, the place was actually beginning to resemble a real florists. The only things missing were the actual flowers, but they'd be delivered early tomorrow morning.

'Mum...'

'Lily! You're awake too. What's the matter?' Putting her dusting rag down on the counter, Sadie twisted around.

'I heard something.'

'Oh, sorry that would have been me. I knocked over one of the flower buckets with the mop.'

'Is Poppy down here? She's not in her room.'

'Yes, she came down to help me unpack. She's in the back room now.'

Lily looked down at the floor and pulled the belt to her fluffy grey dressing gown tighter around her. 'Do you need any more help?'

'That would be lovely. Come here.' Holding her arms out, Sadie sank her face into Lily's curly strawberry blonde hair, the coconut-scented shampoo a welcome smell after breathing in dust for the past half hour. 'I love you.'

'Love you too, Mum.' Pulling away, Lily led the way into the back room. 'What do you want me to do?'

'Are you okay helping Poppy fill the drawers, please? Cutting tools in that one by the window and ribbons in that one over there.' Turning her attention to the large pine workbench, Sadie ran her fingers across its surface. It was both strange and amazing to think that each mark, each crevice, each cut made into its surface locked away the memories of someone's life, whether it be the nick from a bunch of roses someone had

ordered for their first date, the stain of lily pollen from a funeral arrange-
ment, or the markings made from hours of trimming flowers for someone's
wedding bouquet.

She looked across at Lily and Poppy who were, for once, working
together to get something done without arguing. Grinning, she watched as
they passed each other reels of ribbon and spoke excitedly about their first
bus trip to school. This was what everything had been about. This was
what the move was for – family.

'Do you two want a hot chocolate before bed?'

'Yes, please!'

* * *

Precariously holding three mugs and a sharing packet of chocolate buttons
she'd forgotten she'd stashed away in her handbag; Sadie opened the door
to the shop with her elbow. As she walked through towards the back room,
she could hear Lily and Poppy still chatting about their first day back at
school tomorrow.

'Here we go.' Placing the hot chocolates down on the workbench, Sadie
pulled the chocolate buttons from under her arm. 'Look what I found.'

'Ooh, yum.'

2

'That's the last one, love.' The delivery man set another large flower box on the already tall stack just inside the door to The Flower Shop. 'Sign here, please.'

Scribbling her signature, Sadie nodded at the man in front of her. 'Thank you.'

Shutting the cold out, Sadie rubbed her hands together and turned towards the stack of boxes. She'd decided to order the flowers from the suppliers the previous owners had recommended, to begin with, but had a list of horticultural auctions and wholesale markets she wanted to check out in the coming days and weeks.

After shifting the boxes into the back room where they'd keep cooler and fresher for longer, she checked the time. It was 7.05. Tilting her head, she listened for any noise from upstairs which suggested the girls had heard and reacted to their alarm clocks. Nothing. Pulling her thick gloves off, she laid them on the workbench and ran upstairs.

* * *

'Lily, it's gone seven. You must have turned your alarm off. Time to rise and shine, sweetheart.' Pulling the duvet away from Lily's face, she grinned.

'Come on, you're meeting Georgia at the bus stop soon and you don't want to be late meeting her.'

'Okay.' Sitting up in bed, Lily yawned and pulled a face.

'Up you get, we can all have an early night tonight.'

'Is Poppy in the bathroom?'

'Nope, not yet. I'm just going through to wake her up now.'

'Let me get in there first then.'

As Lily ran to be the first in the bathroom, Sadie made her way to Poppy's room. 'Wakey, wakey, sleepyhead. It's time to get up and get ready for school.'

'Five more minutes.'

'I'm afraid not. There's not enough time, you've already slept through your alarm.'

'One more minute then.' Poppy turned over to face the wall, wrapping herself in her duvet as she did so.

'Come on. You don't want to miss the bus, do you?'

'Okay, okay, I'm getting up.'

Crossing her arms, Sadie raised an eyebrow and watched as her daughter closed her eyes again. 'But you're not, are you? Up now, Poppy. I'm going back downstairs to sort the delivery out, but please get up, get dressed and get yourself some breakfast. Don't let me down on your first day.'

'Ummm.'

'I mean it.' Walking out onto the landing, Sadie paused and listened until she was sure Poppy had actually done as she'd been asked and got out of bed.

* * *

'It's cold.' Wrapping her arms around herself, Poppy jogged behind Sadie.

'I know, but the exercise will warm you up. Come on, or you'll miss it.' They should just make it before the bus leaves. Hopefully. Tomorrow they'd have to be more organised. She wouldn't have a delivery, so could get the girls' breakfast and make sure they were up earlier.

'Where is it? I thought it was only a couple of minutes away.'

'It is. It's just around the corner. Come on.' They rounded the corner and slowed their pace. The bus hadn't arrived yet. A small cluster of Hillside High students, and some from the other secondary school in town, chatted and laughed as they waited. 'Look, there's Lily and Georgia, why don't you go and chat with them?'

'No thanks. I'd rather wait on my own.'

'I'll wait with you then.'

Poppy looked at her mum, her eyes hooded beneath her dark fringe.

Holding her hands up, Sadie grinned. She remembered what it was like to be eleven, and she specifically remembered how important it was to be seen as being independent in the first year of secondary. 'I should get back and finish off prepping the flowers. Have a great day and I'll see you at The Flower Shop after school. Love you.'

Leaning towards Sadie, Poppy mumbled, 'Love you too.'

Walking away, Sadie paused just after rounding the corner to the High Street. She wasn't used to this, entrusting her children with a complete stranger who was to drive them to school. She'd just wait until the bus had been and gone, that way she'd know they'd both got on safely. She was out of sight, so wouldn't cramp their style.

* * *

Ten minutes later, with Lily and Poppy safely on their way to school, Sadie made the short walk back. Taking her time, she strolled slowly along the High Street, taking in the smell of baking bread wafting out from the bakery, and the aroma of coffee as commuters made a caffeine pit stop at the local cafés on the way to work. The clatter of shutters being pulled up, to reveal the various treasures on show in the handful of antique and vintage clothing shops, punctuated the quiet buzz of the village. She had a good feeling about their move here. The village had an eclectic range of shops and its history, and lively social events calendar, meant it was a constant attraction to visitors, both tourists and shoppers.

Yes, Serendipity Lane where The Flower Shop was located was off the main High Street, but with the castle situated at the top of the cobbled lane, The Flower Shop, the sweet patisserie, barber's shop and gift shop were almost assured a good footfall of customers.

Dipping under the barrier to the small car park shared by shop owners and staff which ran along the back of the row of small shops, Sadie picked up her pace. She didn't have long to finish prepping the flowers if she wanted to open at nine.

She heard the squeak and low rumble as the barrier lifted behind her and moved out of the way as a black 4x4 turned into the car park.

She watched as the car drove past her and pulled into the spot next to her own battered fiesta. The driver of the car must be the solicitor who occupied the office space above the barber's shop next door. She checked the time. She really should stop and introduce herself, but she still had 150 red roses and 70 chrysanthemums to unpack, prep and display, not to mention the two boxes of foliage that still remained untouched.

No, she should get on. It wouldn't look good if she opened late or wasn't sufficiently prepared, especially on her first day. Reaching into her handbag, she rummaged for her keys. That was another job she needed to get done before it drove her crazy. She needed to sort out all the junk in her handbag. It had become a dumping ground to a range of small bits and bobs on moving day, which meant it was virtually impossible to find anything she actually needed.

If she didn't find them soon, she'd more than likely get caught in the awkward dance of small talk with the solicitor. Too late, she heard the car door shut softly behind her. Finally, wrapping her fingers around the fluffy panda key ring Poppy had bought her for Christmas, she pulled her keys from her bag, plastered a smile on her face and turned around ready to introduce herself.

'Alex?' Narrowing her eyes, she balled her hand into a fist, the sharp edges of the keys digging into her palm. Was it really him?

'Woah, Sadie? Sadie Newton?' With a briefcase in one hand and a take-away coffee cup in the other, Alex Marshall stood stock-still.

'Locke. It's Sadie Locke now.' Why was he here? Please, please, don't be the solicitor next door. Please.

'Right, of course.' Alex glanced down at his black polished shoes. 'So, you've moved into The Flower Shop then? With the girls?'

Sadie nodded.

'I thought you were a teacher?' Alex shook his head. 'Sorry, it's none of my business.'

No, it wasn't. It really wasn't. Sadie swallowed. She didn't want to ask the next question. 'You're the solicitor from next door?'

'I am, yes.'

'Right.' Looking longingly at the door, Sadie pushed her shoulders back. 'I'd better get on.'

'Of course. Good to see you again.'

The keys slipped through her fingers, landing with a clatter on the tarmac.

'Here, let me get them...'

'No. I've got it.' Bending down, Sadie picked the keys back up and unlocked the door.

'Of course.'

Shutting the door firmly behind her, Sadie leaned back against it, the cool of the wood seeping through her thin cardigan. Had she just imagined it all? Was it really Alex's office above the barber's shop? Sadie closed her eyes. Of all the villages and towns surrounding Hillby, of all the florists which had been for sale. How on earth had she managed to buy the one he worked next to?

This was supposed to be her fresh start. Goodness knows she'd waited long enough and worked hard enough for it. This wasn't fair.

A hollow laugh escaped Sadie's mouth. Her whole adult life hadn't been fair. She'd been supposed to have a loving husband, a loving family. Instead, she'd been dealt the cruel card of adultery and abandonment, had to work damn hard to bring up her two girls and had to work even harder to change their stress-filled way of life. And now this. They were living and she was working next to Alex, Max's best mate. Life had a cruel habit of reminding her she couldn't escape the card she'd been dealt.

* * *

'As I said, I'm very sorry but I don't have any gerberas, but I do have these beautiful red roses. They were newly delivered today, so very fresh and will last a good long time.' Walking towards the bucket of roses, Sadie pulled out the best-looking bunch.

The customer in front of her pushed the roses away from him. 'I've told you I want gerberas. They need to be gerberas, not any old flowers you're trying to push to make a profit out of me.'

Replacing the roses, Sadie frowned. 'I'm sorry, I'm not just trying to make money out of you. Those roses are normally very popular and with good reason too.'

'It's not popular I want, it's gerberas I'm asking for.' With his face reddening, the elderly man banged the end of his walking stick on the ground. 'Patricia always had gerberas. She'd make sure she did. She knew what we locals wanted. She didn't stock flowers willy-nilly hoping to sell to the tourists, she cared for us, the community.'

Returning around the counter, Sadie placed her hands palm down on the wooden surface. 'I'm very sorry. If you'd like to place an order, I can get them by tomorrow?'

'I don't want to place an order! I need them today!'

'Sorry. I'll make sure I put them on the next delivery...'

'Argh, forget it.' The man waved her offer away with his hand, turned away and hobbled out of the door.

'You've met Old Mr Hubert then?' Alex walked into The Flower Shop and looked behind him at Mr Hubert's retreating figure, two takeaway coffee cups in his hands.

Sadie gritted her teeth. She could feel her face reddening. If it hadn't been embarrassing enough to be yelled at by her first potential customer, then it was mortifying knowing that he'd witnessed the whole fiasco. 'Is that his name?'

'Yes, he can be a cantankerous old goat, but he has a heart of gold when you get to know him.'

Sadie raised her eyebrows.

'Really, he does. He's just not very good with newcomers. He gave me a right hard time when I first moved here, but then he came into my office a month or so later and needed help with an issue with a parking ticket, which I helped him with even though it's not really in my remit. Next thing

I know he's recommended me to all his mates and I've got a good amount of business to my name.'

'Moved here? You live here as well as work here?' There was literally going to be no escape, was there?

'Yes, I live along William's Terrace at the south end of the village, do you know it? I'm neighbours with Mr and Mrs Hubert, actually.'

Sadie shook her head.

'Anyway, what I'm trying to say is, don't take his outburst personally. He's got a lot on his plate at home, what with his wife having dementia and all.'

'Dementia?'

'Yes, she's been diagnosed seven years now, apparently. He provides all her care, won't let her go into a home. It must be a lot for anyone, let alone someone as old as he is too. Let me guess, he wasn't after a small bunch of gerberas by any chance, was he?'

'Yes, he was. How did you know? I offered him some of those classic red roses, but he wouldn't accept anything else.' Sadie rolled up a loose piece of red ribbon she'd been using to make little grab-and-go posies earlier.

'That's what he always gets. You know, before, when Patricia was running this place. Every single day he'd come down first thing for his bunch of gerberas and Patricia used to even drop one by on a Sunday and Wednesday when The Flower Shop would be closed.'

'Really?'

'Yes, Mrs Hubert, I think her name is Edith though I can't quite remember, gets muddled with the dementia. Mr Hubert apparently gave her a bunch of gerberas on their first date, and since she became ill, he's apparently been buying her a bunch every day. I guess it's a routine he's in now.' Alex shrugged.

'Oh.' That would explain why he had been so upset when she hadn't stocked any then.

'Anyway, here, I bought you a coffee. My way of apologising for startling you earlier.' Alex slid one of the takeaway cups towards her. 'I got you a latte. That's what you always used to drink, wasn't it?'

Latte? He'd remembered that was her go-to drink. Sadie wrapped her hands around the cup, the heat from the coffee warming the constant chill of her hands. They'd only been to a coffee shop a handful of times together, her and Max, Alex and whoever he was with at the time. How could he have possibly remembered? She slid the cup back towards him and clasped her fingers together on top of the counter. 'I've only just had one. Thanks.'

'Right.' Alex looked down at the cup and pushed it back towards her. 'Have it anyway. You can always heat it up in the microwave later.'

'I'm fine. Thank you. Besides, I really must get on.' Sliding the cup firmly back to him again, Sadie turned and went into the back room, furiously wishing there was a door she could close.

She positioned herself in the far corner, out of sight, and waited until she'd heard the door shut softly behind him before venturing out again. This was what it was going to be like, wasn't it? Hiding away from him all of the time. She wasn't bitter towards him. She didn't blame him. But at the same time, she'd so wanted, needed, this fresh start and then to find he not only lived in the village but worked next door.

Pressing her fingertips to her temples, Sadie looked across at the workbench. She needed to finish getting the grab-and-go posies ready before the tourists began filtering past.

3

Turning off the car engine, Sadie picked up the posy of gerberas and walked the short distance towards the Victorian terraces standing grandly along the roadside. She checked the street sign – William's Terrace – she was in the right place. This was where Alex had said he lived, and he'd said he lived next door to Mr Hubert. Finding out which house would be the fun part, though.

Striding up to the house immediately in front of her, Sadie rapped her knuckles against the bright red door. No answer. She knocked again.

'Hello?' A woman in a carer's uniform opened the door and smiled.

'Hi, sorry to bother you, but is this where Mr and Mrs Hubert live?'

'No, they're two doors up, love.' The woman pointed to the right of the small row of houses.

'Great, thank you.' Grinning, Sadie followed the woman's directions until she was standing outside the house at the end of the terrace. The blue door had paint peeling in places and the net curtains desperately needed a wash and a mend. Laying the flowers on the doorstep, Sadie rang the bell and retreated to the car.

* * *

'You haven't forgotten, have you?' Tina's voice rose an octave down the phone line. 'I knew you'd forget. What with the move and settling in and everything. I just knew it.'

'No, I haven't forgotten, how could I?' Sadie ran her finger down a rose stem she'd been preparing, taking care to avoid the remaining thorns. Yes, she had forgotten. Their mutual friend Angela's wedding was next week.

'You haven't? So, you're coming then?'

'I'll be there.'

'Great. I'd better get back to work, but I'll ring you before next Saturday, okay?'

'Yes. That's fine. Bye.' Placing the phone down, Sadie slipped on her gloves again and continued cutting the rose stems. The last thing she needed right now was to celebrate someone else's wedding. Not with Alex dredging up memories of betrayal she'd thought were long gone.

'Anyone here?'

It was him. She'd recognise his northern twang anywhere. Rolling her eyes, Sadie slipped her gloves off and walked through to the shop floor. 'Alex, what do I owe this pleasure?'

Looking at her, Alex paused halfway between the door and the counter, before plastering a grin on his face and coming closer. 'Hi, I saw what you did for Mr and Mrs Hubert. I just wanted to say it was a really lovely gesture.'

He liked what she had done? What business was it of his what she did? And how did he know? 'Have you been spying on me?'

'What? No. No, I popped home for lunch. I live next door to them, I told you, remember?'

Sadie nodded. Maybe it had just been a coincidence that he'd seen her. Still, she didn't appreciate him telling her it was a nice gesture or whatever he'd said. She hadn't done it to get his approval. She hadn't left those flowers for anyone but Mr and Mrs Hubert, and even then she'd understand if Mr Hubert didn't shop with her. She'd done it because it had been the right thing to do. Shifting on her feet, she narrowed her eyes. 'I don't need your approval.'

Blinking, Alex looked genuinely taken aback. 'Of course, you don't. Sorry. I just... We've gotten off on the wrong foot, haven't we?'

Sadie stared down at the till in front of her.

'Is it something I've done? Do you feel as though I'm poking my nose into your life? I didn't mean to. I thought... I guess I thought because we know each other from before, it'd be nice to catch up.'

'Our history is precisely why it's not a good idea to catch up.'

'Our history? What do you mean? We always used to get on really well... Do you remember that weekend we all went on? You know the one to Blackpool before you and Max had kids? Max and Stella got that food poisoning and so we left them to it and went to the Pleasure Beach. Do you remember? We used to get on really well and I've got to admit when I saw you'd moved in here, I thought it'd be nice to get to know each other again.'

She *did* remember the weekend trip to Blackpool. She *did* remember the good times they'd had. 'It was Cindy.'

'Who?'

'Not Stella. The girl you took to Blackpool was Cindy.'

'Right, Cindy. Yes, it was. It was Cindy. I don't know where I got the name Stella from.'

'She was probably your next conquest.'

'Is this what this is about? You disapprove of my past love life? You didn't seem to disapprove before, you and Max used to take the mickey out of me.' Alex looked down at the floor before locking eyes with her. 'That's all in the past, though. I've not even dated since Rachel.'

Oh yes, Rachel. She remembered Max telling her what had happened. Or gloating rather. Alex had been with Rachel for four years, his longest relationship, before they'd finished. That had to have been at least two years ago now. She remembered it had been while they'd been sitting in the audience waiting for one of Poppy's Christmas plays to begin, that Max had leaned over and told her the sorry story. He'd seemed pretty happy about it. If there was anything Max loved more than infidelity, it was a good bit of drama. 'I heard about your breakup with Rachel. Sorry, but no, it's nothing about your love life. It's about mine.'

'Yours? What do you mean?'

Lowering her hands by her sides, Sadie tried to stop them shaking. He really didn't get it, did he? It was as if everything he'd done had just been his job. And it had been. She wasn't daft, but he'd known her. He'd known their girls, and he'd known the effect he was inflicting on them. 'Even if I look past the fact that you'd known about Max's affair and not told me.' She held up her hand to silence him. 'Even if I could forget that we'd been friends, and you'd seen fit to keep the fact that my husband was sleeping, heck, falling in love, with another woman behind my back, I could never forgive you for the part you played in mine and Max's divorce.'

'Your divorce?' Looking down at his feet, Alex ran his finger through his dark hair. 'I'm a divorce solicitor. It was my job.'

A hollow laugh escaped Sadie's mouth. 'Your job? You didn't need to take his case. Not when you knew it would plunge me and my girls, your godchildren, into poverty.'

'What? No, I... That's not what...'

Setting him with a steely glare, Sadie continued. Now she'd started, she couldn't stop. She knew deep down it wasn't his fault. Not really. It *had* just been his job. She knew it had been Max pursuing the divorce, controlling the situation, but Alex hadn't had to take it. He hadn't had to take the job, he could have told Max to get another solicitor. He should have. It had been unethical, him taking on the job when he'd known them both. 'And then to top things off, just when I get a bit of a break in life. When I can start to follow my dreams, which I worked damn hard training for, you... you're here.'

'But...'

Sadie pinched the bridge of her nose. 'This was supposed to be my new start.' Turning around, she ran through the back room and pulled open the door leading to the car park. Shutting it firmly behind her, she sank to the ground, hugging her knees to her chest and lowering her head. What she'd said to him hadn't been fair, she knew that, but she'd had to say it. The words had been waiting to come out ever since she'd clapped eyes on him.

A slight tap on the door behind her startled her, and she raised her head.

'I'm sorry you feel that way, Sadie. It was never my intention to take your new start away from you.' A quiet rumble penetrated the thin wooden door as he cleared his throat. 'What you said about me taking on yours and Max's divorce, there's a reason I did that. I'll leave you be now. You won't even know I'm working next door. I won't come to The Flower Shop again. I'll leave you alone.'

Looking towards her rust bucket of a car parked next to his shiny new one, Sadie blinked back the tears. She'd bottled everything up for so long now. She'd been strong for Poppy and Lily's sake. She'd carried on fighting what had seemed like a financial never-ending struggle for the past five years, but now, with Alex here, the injustice of everything had brought her right back down. Seeing him again had reminded her of how conniving Max had been in those first few months after he'd left.

It reminded her of the struggle she'd had just to keep the house, to be able to afford the mortgage repayments. How she'd had to give up her part-time job at the local primary school and find full-time work just when the girls had needed her the most. The memories of that first winter when the boiler had packed in and he'd refused to help pay anything towards it, the present-less Christmas when they'd spent the day snuggled under duvets until Max had come to pick the girls up to take them back to his and his mistress' warm house to shower them with gifts. They'd only been young, too young to understand why Santa had visited Daddy's house and not Mummy's. Yes, she'd got the house in the divorce, but she'd also got the astronomical mortgage bills and the maintenance repairs. The whole purpose of them buying the house had been to renovate it. And they had. Well, she had. Once he'd left and she'd paid off the debts that had mounted up, she'd renovated the place. But still, Max had known what he was leaving her with, he'd known she'd have been pushed to the very limit financially.

4

'Thank you, that's very kind, Mr Hubert.' Sadie sniffed the home-made biscuits Mr Hubert had brought in for her. Was it ginger or allspice she could smell? Ever since she'd left the flowers on his doorstep on Monday, he'd been in every day to buy the gerberas.

'They're cinnamon. One of my Edith's favourite recipes. She taught me the recipe a few years ago.' Mr Hubert pushed the Tupperware tub further across the counter.

Smiling, Sadie took a bite. 'They're delicious. You really didn't need to go to such an effort though.'

'After what you did for my Edith, it was my pleasure. You went above and beyond for us by dropping off those gerberas on Monday and you don't know what a difference to Edith's day you made that day, so thank you. I'm just sorry it's taken me a week to get these cookies to you, my son does our supermarket shopping on a Thursday and I'd ran out of the cinnamon so, well, I apologise for not thanking you properly earlier in the week. You see, I gave my Edith a posy of gerberas on our first date.' Mr Hubert shifted on his feet. 'Now that was a wonderful, wonderful day. It was the grand opening of The Winter Gardens across the way in Colster and...'

Nodding, Sadie caught a glimpse of Alex as he went past the window.

Had she been too harsh on him? After all, it had been Max that had paid him and instructed him what to do. How much could she really blame Alex?

Mr Hubert nodded towards the window and held his cap up in greeting to Alex, who nodded back. 'He's a good fellow. You could do worse than him.'

Opening and closing her mouth, Sadie looked across at Mr Hubert. 'What do you mean?'

'Having him as a business neighbour, you could do worse than him. He's done a lot of good around here, you know. Have you seen the pelican crossing by the school bus stop?'

Sadie nodded.

'That was him, that was. The local parents had been petitioning for, what ten years now, for a proper crossing there after too many near misses on that road.' My Hubert took his glasses off and proceeded to clean them using the bottom of his shirt. 'Ten years and along comes Alex there and, boom, a pelican crossing gets put in. He knows all the right people, you see. It's about being able to talk the talk and having the right connections, it is.'

'Oh, right? I didn't know that. I assumed he still practised family law.'

'Yes, he does, but he saw something that needed sorting. He saw what was at stake, children's lives, and he sorted it. We get a lot of the townsfolk using this road as a cut-through, but they don't slow down. They're irresponsible like that, some of them. They just want to get to work, get home, get to work, they don't give a darn about anyone else. That pelican crossing stops them now.' Pushing his glasses back up his nose, Mr Hubert shook his head. 'Yep, he's definitely an asset to this village, don't you think?'

Sadie nodded. Not only was she not getting her fresh start, she was living somewhere where everyone loved the man who had not only stood by and watched his best mate have an affair but had enabled Max to screw her over in the divorce too.

'So, are you and your family going to the castle this evening?'

'Yes, yes, we are. We're looking forward to it.' Sadie smiled. Yesterday, when Mr Hubert had come into The Flower Shop to purchase his daily posy, he'd mentioned that the family residing at the castle had a tradition of opening up to the people of the village the evening before they officially opened to tourists. When she'd mentioned it to Lily and Poppy, they'd surprisingly appeared quite excited. Hopefully, it would be a good night and the first real time they'd gone out anywhere as a family since moving in.

'Glad to hear it. Most of the village turn up, and at around seven o'clock, just before everyone heads home, they set fireworks off over the castle grounds. Such a beautiful sight.'

* * *

'Mum, have you seen my hoodie?' Poppy peered through the door to The Flower Shop and called her mum.

Looking up from the order sheet she was filling in at the counter, Sadie frowned. 'Which one? The blue one?'

'No, the pale grey one. The one with the track bike in the corner.'

'The stained one?'

'Yes.'

'Why can't you wear one of your new ones or at least one that's not got a hot chocolate stain dribbled down the front?'

'No, I want that one. You know it's my favourite and I want to wear it to the castle.'

Sadie rolled her eyes, Lily had been the same at her age, wearing the same outfit over and over again. They'd be wearing their coats, so it probably wouldn't matter, anyway. 'It's in the corner on the work surface in the kitchen, I had planned to soak it to try to get rid of the stain.' As Poppy retreated back up to the flat, the door slammed shut and Sadie looked back down at the pile of papers in front of her. 'I've just not got round to it yet.'

The bell above the front door tinkled as Lily and her friend, Georgia, walked in. 'Hey, Mum. You okay if Georgia comes round for a bit?'

'Hi, you two. We're going on the tour at the castle in...' Twisting around, Sadie glanced at the large wall clock behind the counter. 'About half an hour. How about you meet up tomorrow instead?'

'Oh, I forgot.' Lily turned to Georgia. 'Sorry, shall we meet tomorrow then?'

'Okay, cool. My parents will probably drag me along tonight too, so I might see you there.'

'Bye.' Lily shut the door behind her friend.

'So, how was school?'

Shrugging, Lily made her way towards the door up to the flat. 'It was okay, I guess. Just school. I'm going to go and get changed.'

'Okay, sweetheart.' Chewing on her bottom lip, Sadie looked around the empty shop. Custom had been picking up steadily over the past few days, and takings had been better than she'd hoped they would be in the first week of opening. She'd had a couple of orders through too. One for a funeral and one for a Christening. She suspected she had Mr Hubert to thank for some of the new customers finding their way to The Flower Shop – he'd promised he'd get the word out. Yes, things were looking pretty good. Plus, as from tomorrow, the castle would be bringing in some tourists which would dramatically increase the footfall to the florists. Yes, flowers weren't especially high up on the list of souvenirs to buy to remember a visit, but that's where the grab-and-go posies would come in. Plus, she'd been researching historical flowers to inspire the posies and she'd also been thinking about making key rings, bookmarks and other little trinkets using dried flowers.

Although the castle dated back to the 11th century, they tended to focus on an era each month, catering events to that era. So, if she could speak to someone and find out in advance what events the castle were planning, she'd be able to adapt her stock accordingly.

Sadie looked at the posters of wedding flowers she'd put up behind the counter. If she was lucky enough to land contracts for a few weddings, that would be amazing. As far as she understood, the castle had an in-house florist to cater for weddings taking part there, but the bride and groom were always free to choose and didn't have to use their services. So, if The Flower Shop could make a good impression on passing tourists, who knew where that might lead.

* * *

'Can we go and find where they're doing the fireworks now?' Poppy's eyes glinted in the lights from the hot drinks and cookies stall set up outside the castle.

'Yes, I think they're down past the walled gardens. I'm sure that's where one of the tourist guides said. Here you go.' Sadie held open the paper bag of warm cookies to Lily and Poppy before taking her own and pocketing the empty bag. Picking up her hot chocolate from the counter, she nodded at the woman serving and led the girls away from the queue.

'What did you think of the tour?' Sadie took a sip from her hot chocolate.

'It was really good. I can't believe we live right next to a castle!' Poppy bit into her cookie, crumbs flaking down the front of her coat.

'Ah, but you did hear what the guide was telling us when we went to look at the dungeons, didn't you?' A grin spread across Lily's face.

'What?'

'That it's haunted. And we only live down the lane. I'd make sure you close your curtains tonight.'

'Lily! Stop!' Sadie rolled her eyes.

Poppy looked across at her mum, her eyes wide. 'Mum, will I really be able to see the ghosts from my bedroom window?'

'It's not only about seeing them. If they see your light on, they'll come knocking! Everyone knows that they come wandering down the lane into the village when it gets dark.'

Poppy glanced around.

'Lily, really do stop now. Poppy, she's just teasing you.' Sadie used her free hand to pull Poppy in for a hug and kissed the top of her head.

'Or am I?'

'Lily! Stop now or you can't have Georgia round tomorrow!'

'Okay, okay.' Lily grinned.

'Now, let's enjoy our hot chocolates and watch the fireworks.' Wrapping her hands around her takeaway cup, Sadie stomped her feet in a bid to warm them up.

'I'm cold. Do we have to stay to watch them?' Lily rubbed her cheeks with her free hand before warming it back up on her cup.

'Yes, we do. They'll be starting soon. Here,' Sadie fished in her coat pocket and passed her a pair of gloves.

'Thanks.' Giving Sadie her cup to hold, Lily put the gloves on and took it back just as the first firework hurtled into the sky.

Sadie watched as with each bang and pop Poppy jumped. She loved fireworks, probably the most out of all of them, but however much she tried to ready herself for the noise she never could. In the end, Lily put her hand on Poppy's arm and Sadie looked on as Poppy covered Lily's hand with her own. Yes, family time was what it was all about.

'Mum is that someone we know? I recognise him.' Turning around, Poppy pointed to Alex who was standing a couple of family groups away from them.

'Yes, it's Alex, one of your dad's friends. He works next door to us in the office above the barber's shop.'

'Oh, I think I remember him from when I was younger. I've not seen him at Daddy's though. Should we go and say hello?'

Sadie stared at the fireworks ahead. 'I've already spoken to him today.'

'We haven't though.'

Trying to focus on the mesmerising cascading light in front of her, Sadie involuntarily glanced across at Alex. Standing on his own with a dark grey coat and red scarf, she really noticed how much he'd changed from those days of double-dating and drinking. He looked older, more mature. The slight white tinge to his dark hair made him look distinguished. Looking back at the fireworks, Sadie shook her head. He was still the same person who had enabled her, Lily and Poppy's lives to be upturned. With Poppy saying that though, it did suggest he'd had the decency not to visit Max when the girls were around.

'It's almost over now, please can we go? I literally can't feel my fingers and I'm pretty certain my toes have dropped off already.' Shaking Poppy's hand from her arm, Lily turned to face Sadie.

'Okay, okay. Let's go.'

5

'Have I got time to go up to the BMX track with Harry and Ed before Dad comes? I don't need to be long.' Poppy put her cycling helmet on the counter.

'No, he said he'd be here at half past ten.' Picking up the cycling helmet, Sadie placed it away from the order sheet she was filling in.

'But he's obviously running late. It's already eleven.'

'I'm sure he'll be here soon.' In about half an hour, anyway. Being an hour late was his forte.

'But what if he's not? I'm wasting my life away waiting here. I could be having fun with Harry and Ed.'

'I know, sweetheart, but by the time you get there, he'll probably have arrived, and you'd just have to come back.'

'Is that a yes then?'

Laughing, Sadie shook her head. 'How did you get a "yes" from what I just said? It's a no!'

Turning around, Poppy pulled herself up on the counter and picked up a stray frond of gypsophila.

'Is Lily ready?'

'I don't know. I think so. She's on her phone in her room.' Straightening the stem between her fingertips, Poppy tucked it behind her ear, the tiny white petals a stark contrast to her brown hair. 'How do I look?'

'Beautiful.' Sadie smiled. 'As always.'

'What have you got in your hair? You're not going to Dad's like that, are you?' Letting the door up to the flat slam shut behind her, Lily strode to the counter and dumped her rucksack next to the cycling helmet.

'Mum said I looked beautiful.' Poppy crossed her arms.

'She would do, she's your mum.'

'Come on, Lily. She is beautiful. And so are you.' Drawing Lily in for a hug, Sadie was able to sneak a quick peck to the forehead before Lily pulled away again. 'Are you all packed and ready?'

'Yes,' Lily grunted.

'Are you both looking forward to seeing your new rooms at Daddy's new house?' As always, she stumbled over the words. Was it the right thing to call it Daddy's house, or was she supposed to refer to it as their other home? They'd spent the past five years hearing it called Daddy's house, as far as she was concerned it hadn't affected them.

'We've seen the photos.' Poppy shrugged.

'Yes, but it'll be nice to see them in real life, won't it?'

'I guess so.'

'How strange is it that you've moved into both your new homes within such a short amount of time?'

'It is weird, I guess. It just means there are two lots of unpacking to do.' Poppy slumped her arms down on the counter and grinned. 'It's exciting though.'

'It sure is.'

The short, sharp noise of a car horn made them jump.

That'd be Max. He rarely went to the trouble of collecting the girls from the door. Hadn't for a long time. It was as if the split had been Sadie's fault and he didn't want to lay eyes on her, not the other way around. Oh well, she was used to it by now. It was a shame for the girls that he couldn't be more civil but...

'Bye, Mum.'

Sadie accepted the embrace from Poppy and laid her chin on her head. 'Bye, sweetheart. Have a lovely weekend.'

'Yep. You too.' Picking up her rucksack, Poppy led the way to the door to The Flower Shop.

At the door, Sadie pulled Lily in for a hug as she walked past her. 'Have a lovely weekend. Love you.'

'Love you too, Mum,' Lily mumbled as she slipped out of the hug and walked towards the waiting car.

'All right, my two little princesses?' Max stepped out the car, nodded at Sadie and went around to the boot without even a cursory 'hello'.

'Hey, Dad.' Lily gave him her rucksack and slipped into the passenger seat.

'Wow, what have you got in here? Rocks?' Taking Poppy's rucksack, Max laughed at his own joke.

'Very funny, Dad.' Poppy glanced back at her mum before she got in the car and blew a kiss. 'Bye, Mum.'

'Bye, love.' Standing at the door, Sadie blew her a kiss back before pulling her cardigan around her to ward off the morning chill still hanging in the air. What was he doing? Normally he got straight back in the car and drove off. Instead, Max was standing next to the car looking at someone or something up the street.

Oh, okay. Now it made sense. Alex was walking down the street, presumably towards his office, although with it being a Saturday Sadie had hoped she'd get the reprieve of the weekend away from him.

She watched as Max stepped forward and greeted Alex. She couldn't see Alex's face but was surprised by the stiffness in his shoulders and the way he didn't rush to greet his friend.

After a few minutes of chatting, Max got back in the car. As Alex turned towards his office, he caught Sadie's eye before looking down and away.

As was her custom, Sadie blew kisses and waved until the car had rounded the corner and was out of sight. She checked her watch. With Melissa picking her up on the way to Angela's wedding reception at five, she'd have to shut up shop early to give herself time to get ready.

* * *

Shrugging her dress on over her head, Sadie ran down the stairs and opened the front door. 'Hi, Melissa. Sorry for the wait, I was just getting ready.'

'Hey.' Melissa leaned in for a hug before turning Sadie around and zipping up her satin blue dress. 'You're cutting it a bit fine, aren't you? The taxi is getting here in twenty minutes.'

'I'll be fine. I just need to do my make-up and straighten my hair. Oh, and write the card.'

'And maybe pop on some tights or something?'

'Yes. That too. Where's Luke? I thought he was coming with us?' Sadie looked behind Melissa, expecting to see her husband, Luke, appear out of the shadows.

'He had to pop into work, some emergency with an order or something, so I said we'd pick him up on the way. So, The Flower Shop is looking lovely. How's it going?'

'Great, actually.'

'Don't sound so surprised with yourself. Everyone else knows you'll make a success of it. You just need to have a bit more faith in yourself.'

'I don't know about success. But after a relatively slow first week, this week has really picked up and today has been quite manic, to be honest. There was a craft fair or something on at the castle, and I've been having a steady stream of customers in all day. I've even sold all of the ready-made posies I'd prepared!'

'Wow, that's great!'

'Yes, it is. I'm starving, though. I didn't even get the chance to run to the toilet until three o'clock, and the most I've had since breakfast was half a crumpet Lily had left on the side.'

'Now, sit down and give me those hair straighteners.'

Doing as she was told, Sadie sat on the edge of her bed and passed the hair straighteners to Melissa. There were definitely some perks to having a hairdresser as your best mate. 'Does this dress look okay? I've not worn it since the last wedding I went to, and I can't even remember how long ago that was.' She sucked in her stomach and smoothed the dress as best she could. What with the move and setting up the shop she hadn't even had the time to think about eating healthily, yet alone trying to lose some weight.

'It looks lovely. You look lovely. I can't wait to see what wedding dress Angela has chosen. I can't even believe she's getting married!'

'I know! What's it been? Six months since they first met, and they're already getting married!' Angela had met Darryl whilst they'd both been on career breaks and travelling in Thailand. 'Talk about a whirlwind romance!'

'Exactly! They are a cute couple though.'

'Yes, they are.' The handful of times she'd met up with both Angela and Darryl since Angela had been back, any fool could see how in love they were.

'That'll be you soon.' Melissa gently pulled the straighteners through Sadie's hair.

'Oh no. No chance I'll fall into that trap again! I'm happy on my own, thank you very much. I much prefer doing what I want, when I want, and not having to worry about what a partner's up to.'

'Max was just the wrong guy. Don't tar them all with the same brush. There are some good ones out there.'

'Umm, maybe.' There was no point trying to explain to Melissa that she really didn't want to be with anyone else. Having married Luke straight out of college, Melissa was under the impression you had to be with someone to enjoy life. No chance. Even with the emotional and financial rubbish that had gone on before, during and after their divorce, Sadie knew she was much happier now than she ever had been with Max.

* * *

Forty-five minutes later, Sadie stood with Melissa on a red carpet which led from the bar in the golf course down to the large marquee waiting in line to congratulate the happy couple.

'Did you say it was a sit-down meal?' Luke whispered.

'Do you ever stop thinking about your stomach? We're here to celebrate the undying love of two people, not for a free meal ticket.' Melissa playfully knocked her handbag against his stomach.

'Of course, we are.' Luke winked at Sadie. 'So, are you sure it's a sit-down meal? People usually only invite the church guests for the meal?'

'If I haven't told you once, I've told you a thousand times, it's a sit-down meal.' Melissa shook her head lovingly at Luke. 'I told you they only had close family to the ceremony, so this is the proper works – sit-down meal, disco and buffet later for the evening guests.'

'It's evening now.'

'It's not. It's quarter past six.' Melissa laughed. 'Yes, okay, it's evening now, but only early evening.'

Luke nudged Sadie and winked at her, indicating he had every intention to continue to wind his wife up. 'Surely no one will want a buffet after a sit-down meal? It seems a waste...'

'There'll be more people coming later. Besides, I'm sure you'd happily pile your plate with buffet food straight after dessert.' Tilting her head, Melissa laughed at him before leaning over and giving him a kiss. 'Stop trying to wind me up.'

Sadie laughed as they stepped forward in the line.

Having congratulated the happy couple and been introduced to their parents, Sadie, Melissa and Luke stepped inside the marquee. Tables, beautifully decorated with winter foliage and tea lights, spread towards the back of the marquee. A dance floor and bar were situated on the far side and fairy lights were strung up, twinkling down the walls and below the ceiling. The heat from numerous heat lamps warmed the air and almost immediately Sadie could feel the goosebumps on her arms disappear. Even with her cardigan on, it had been freezing outside.

'Let's see where we're sat then.' Melissa led them to a seating plan pinned on an easel next to a small table of arrival drinks. Turning towards Sadie, she pulled a face.

Sadie nodded. 'I'm on the singles table, aren't I?' If there was something worse than being single and having to celebrate your friend's marriage, it was being stuck on the infamous singles table. She couldn't work out if it was a pitiful stab at pairing her up with another seemingly lonely soul, or if they just didn't want the truth, that not all marriages work out, staring them in the face.

'You could always buck the trend and pull up a seat at our table,' Luke suggested.

'No, it's fine. I'll be fine. I'll need one of these, though.' Shrugging off their pitying looks, Sadie grinned and picked up a glass of Cava. There went the idea of a good night with her friends. At least it couldn't get any worse.

Walking across to the table, Sadie paused and rolled her eyes. It could get worse; it had got worse. The one person she'd been trying to avoid since moving to the village – and he turns up here of all places. Taking a long gulp from her glass, Sadie strode over to the table and checked the place cards. Yep, she was next to him. 'Alex.'

'Sadie, hi. Here, let me.' Standing up, Alex pulled out her chair for her.

'Thanks.' Sitting down, she took off her cardigan and laid it over the back of her chair before looking around the table. Seven out of the eight table members had already arrived. Apart from her and Alex, the rest of the guests at the table must have been between fourteen and twenty years old. Great, not only was she on the singles table, it appeared her and Alex had been tacked onto the teenagers' table too. She smiled as she finished off her glass of Cava.

Clearing his throat, Alex leaned forward and picked up one of three bottles of wine in the centre of the table. 'It's not all bad. It just means there's more free alcohol for us two.' He tipped the bottle toward her, offering it.

Nodding, Sadie lifted the empty wine glass sat in front of her and accepted the wine. 'Thanks.'

As the teenagers surrounding them chattered excitedly about their own future wedding plans and what their future spouses would look like, Sadie resisted the urge to get up and leave. Angela and Darryl would likely not notice she'd gone, and the night would not only be less awkward for her but also for Alex, whose awkwardness she was sure she could feel emanating from his every pore.

The tinkle of glass tore her from her thoughts, and Sadie twisted around in her seat to watch as the happy couple took to their table.

'Please be upstanding for the newly married, Mr and Mrs Tipton!'

Pushing her chair back, Sadie stood up and joined in the clapping.

6

'How's yours? I think I'll need a bag of chips after this.' Alex indicated his plate.

'Umm...' Sadie had to agree, she wasn't a fan of posh food either. Not the posh food where there's hardly any on your plate, anyway.

'Look, I know things are a little awkward because of what Max did to you, but...'

'And the fact that you were his divorce solicitor. Or have you forgotten that?' Sadie pointed her fork at him before putting it to her mouth. The slimy, limp spinach puree stuck to the roof of her mouth much like the word 'divorce'.

Shifting in his chair, Alex placed his cutlery back on his plate.

'And the fact that you knew about Max's affair for goodness knows how long and yet you didn't tell me.' Sadie took a long gulp of wine before refilling her glass. 'Heck, silly me had always thought we'd gotten on well. Whenever we'd meet up for meals out or drinks, we'd talk for hours while Max and whoever you had been dating at the time drank the place dry. And for you to keep it secret... To not tell me what Max had been doing... I know you were his mate, but surely you must have had just a smidgen of morality in your being?'

Twisting around in his chair, Alex faced her. 'It was a very complex situation. I'd told Max time and time again to tell you, but then when it was obvious he wasn't going to, I told him I would but he promised me he'd finished with Tara. And he convinced me he had. I would have said something otherwise.'

Sadie took another gulp of wine and narrowed her eyes. Had he really thought Max had finished things with Tara? Or had it just been an excuse not to get involved?

'Honestly, that's what happened. It was a complete shock to me when a year later he told me he'd left you.'

Sadie scoffed, wine dribbling down her chin. 'A year later? He'd been seeing her for two years. You'd known about it for a whole year?'

'What? No, no. He'd kept it a secret from everyone. I'd only known for a month or so. Look, I'm sorry. Maybe I should have told you, but I guess I just didn't want to get involved. It had been between you and Max, not me.'

Sadie shrugged. He was right. She knew he was. Most other people would have probably done the same in his situation, but it didn't make it right. Sadie accepted the petite scoop of ice cream and slither of Bramley apple pie placed in front of her. 'I'm sorry. I know it was a long time ago. And I'm over him. I really am. Life is good. I'm much better on my own. Much happier. It's just, seeing you here, well, not here, but in the village... It was supposed to be my fresh start. It was supposed to be a chance for me to be me, instead of the poor woman whose husband had been playing around behind her back for two years.'

'It still is your fresh start. I'm not going to do anything to stop it being so.'

'No, I know, but the fact that you're here. The very firm that pulled the rug from under my feet is situated right next door to where the girls and I live.' She shook her head and took a spoonful of apple pie, the tang of the apple hitting the back of her throat.

Alex put his hands in his lap and looked down at them. 'I understand how that must have looked but...'

'You were just doing your job. I know.'

'Well, it wasn't just that, I...'

An excited scream jolted them from their conversation as two of the teenagers opposite jumped up from their seats. 'Do you see? It's Harry Harlow!'

Another one, a slightly younger girl who was sitting next to Sadie, twisted around in her seat. 'No, it's not! That's one of Angela's cousins and he hardly looks anything like Harry Harlow.' With a disgusted look, the girl turned back to her dessert.

As the excitement died down, Sadie leaned in toward Alex. 'Who's Harry Harlow?'

'Absolutely no idea. A singer or actor or someone famous, I assume.' Alex shrugged and laughed. Picking up the last wine bottle from the middle of the table, he refilled their glasses.

'Oops, have we drunk two bottles already?'

'I believe we may have done.'

Sadie leaned back in her chair as the table was cleared and caught Alex's eye. Maybe he wasn't all bad. Yes, he'd made a fair few rubbish judgement calls along the way, but Max had been the driving force behind the divorce.

'What?' Wiping his mouth with a napkin, Alex looked behind him.

'Nothing. Sorry, I was just thinking.'

'Oh yes? What were you thinking?'

'Just that I've probably been a bit harsh on you.' Sadie swivelled around in her chair to face him. '*I* moved to the village; I shouldn't be making you feel bad that you already live there. It can still be my fresh start. I mean, I don't think you pity me like all of my old neighbours do, and I'd like to think you don't think I'm completely stupid because I didn't realise what Max was up to.'

'You're not stupid. He's just a good liar. A damn good liar. And I don't pity you, I know you had a lucky escape from him.'

Sadie laughed. 'Thank you! Yes, I did. Who knows, I could still have been with him now. He could still have been living a double life.'

'Exactly!'

'Excuse me, I just need to find the ladies.' Standing up, Sadie blinked, trying to clear the alcohol fog from her vision.

'They're just outside, I believe.'

'Thanks.' Teetering toward the entrance to the marquee, Sadie jumped as Melissa linked arms. 'Where did you come from?'

'Over there. Save me! Luke has found another cycling enthusiast. It's all tyre width versus pressure.' Melissa patted Sadie's arm. 'Who am I kidding? I have absolutely no idea what they're talking about. All I know is I've got the attention span of a gnat for all things cycling.'

'I thought he was trying to get you to go along to his cycling group with him?'

'Trying is the right word. Can you imagine me out in the middle of nowhere on my bike?'

Laughing, Sadie shook her head. 'No, no, I can't.'

'Anyway, how are things going on over there? I see you're sat next to Alex? I'd forgotten he was a friend of Angela's brother.' Melissa grimaced. 'I wanted to come and rescue you, but Luke wouldn't let me make a scene.'

'It's okay. He's not all that bad.' As they stepped outside, Sadie wished she'd thought to put her cardigan back on.

'I thought you blamed him for not telling you about Max's affair?'

'Umm, it turns out Max had lied to him too. I can't blame him for my ex-husband's behaviour now, can I? I need to stop letting Max and my feelings about him control my life.' It was true. For so long now, she'd felt ashamed almost at what Max had done and for how she'd believed all of his lies. It was time to move on, time to put these feelings aside and get on with her life. She could still have her fresh start, with Alex working next door to The Flower Shop or not. It was in her mind, her control. No one else's.

'Yes! You go, girl! This is your time now. Forget about Max. This is your life.'

'Yes, it is.'

* * *

The taxi pulled up in front of The Flower Shop and Sadie picked up her handbag from the seat next to her.

'I'll jump out here too. I can walk the rest of the way.' Alex leaned forward. 'How much do I owe you, mate?'

'I'll pay half.'

'No, I've got this. I'd have had to get a taxi back here, anyway.' Pulling a couple of notes from his pocket, Alex thanked the driver and joined Sadie on the pavement. 'I'll walk you to The Flower Shop and make sure you get home safely.'

'You don't need to do that.' Sadie glanced down Serendipity Lane. The most dangerous obstacle in the way to get home were the cobbles.

'I insist. Besides...' Alex held open his suit jacket to reveal a half-full bottle of wine, '...I happened to see this on a table on the way out.'

'You stole from Angela and Darryl's wedding?' Laughing, the heel of a shoe got stuck between the cobbles and Sadie grabbed Alex's arm.

'Ahh, they won't notice. Besides it was going spare.'

'Says the solicitor...'

'You don't want any then?' Alex pulled the bottle out of reach, a slow grin spreading across his face.

'I didn't say that.' Pausing at the door, she fished in her bag for her keys. 'I suppose it would be rude not to dispose of the evidence.'

'You'd be an accomplice then...' Alex followed her through the door toward the back room.

'I don't have any glasses down here and I can't really be bothered to go upstairs. You happy with a mug?' Pulling open the cupboard doors, Sadie held up two yellow mugs.

'Perfect.' He filled up the mugs before passing one to Sadie. Instead of letting go as she wrapped her fingers around the handle, Alex pulled it in closer to him, Sadie following. Leaning down, he pressed his lips against hers.

Closing her eyes, Sadie let the heat from Alex's soft lips penetrate her own. Kissing him back, she lowered the mug to the work surface and cupped his chin with her hands.

7

'That's great. Thank you.' Shifting the last of the boxes inside, Sadie thanked the delivery driver and shut the door to The Flower Shop. As she pushed the boxes along the floor into the back room, she paused and straightened her back. Yep, she'd thought she'd heard something. The girls were having an argument. She checked the time – it was still early, only half past seven. Luckily, both of the adjoining shops had converted the upstairs into offices rather than flats, so at least the girls wouldn't wake anyone. People would begin coming to work though, and she knew the staff at the sweet patisserie next door would probably already be in baking their fresh goods – she certainly didn't want to be known as the noisy family down the lane.

Abandoning the boxes where they were, she ran up the stairs. 'Girls! Please keep it down, everyone can hear you.'

'It's not my fault we don't live in a detached house like Dad's, is it?'

'Lily, wherever we lived, I wouldn't want you two screaming at each other, especially not at this time of the morning. What on earth is going on?'

'She won't let me in the bathroom.' Lily banged on the door.

'I was in here first.' Poppy's muffled voice seeped through the wood.

'Just wait, she won't be long. It's only half seven, you've got over half an hour before you need to be at the bus stop. Why don't you come and do your hair first?'

'No, I need to do my make-up. If I had a mirror in my stupid little bedroom, I wouldn't need to do it in the bathroom.'

'We'll get you a mirror then. After school, you can have a look online, okay?'

'It doesn't help now, does it?' Turning around, Lily started going back to her bedroom before pausing and striding back to the bathroom. This time, instead of banging on the door, she turned the handle and strode straight in.

'Mum! Tell Lily to get out! I'm trying to clean my teeth.' Looking up from her position over the sink, Poppy spat out her toothpaste.

'Lily, come out and wait. You wouldn't like it if Poppy had barged in on you.'

'She did the other day.'

'Mum? Tell her, tell her to get out.'

With Lily scowling in the mirror trying to rub foundation in and Poppy standing looking at her with toothpaste around her mouth, Sadie shrugged. She knew she was fighting a losing battle, but she had to try. 'Out now, Lily, please. She'll only be another couple of minutes and then you'll have the bathroom to yourself.'

'Nope, I'm doing my make-up.'

'Okay, fine.' Huffing, Poppy pulled the hand towel from next to Lily and wiped her mouth.

'Hey! You've just got toothpaste on my school skirt! Mum, look, she's got toothpaste on my skirt.' Turning around, Lily pointed to a minuscule splodge of white on her navy skirt.

'Well, you shouldn't have barged in here while I was cleaning my teeth then, should you?'

'Mum, look...'

'Can't we get a lock put on?'

'Normal people have locks on the bathroom door. Dad has locks on all his bathroom doors and he has four. We have one dingy bathroom and we don't even have one lock.' Lily narrowed her eyes and stared at Sadie.

'Don't exaggerate, Lily. There are only three bathrooms, one's a cloakroom.'

Holding her hands up in the air, Sadie silenced them. 'I'll get a lock sorted, okay? But for this morning, please just try to get along. Poppy, have you finished?'

'I have now.' Poppy shot Lily a cold look before pushing past her and out of the door.

'Okay, you go into the kitchen then and I'll pop some toast on for you. Lily, do you want toast?'

'I've already had breakfast. I got up when my alarm went off.'

'Right, well, you finish your make-up then.' Turning on her heels, she followed Poppy into the kitchen and began the toast. She should have guessed there would be arguments about the bathroom. She'd have to try and pop out at some point and get a lock. They couldn't be too difficult to fit.

'Is that someone downstairs?' Poppy tilted her head.

A faint 'hello?' rang up the stairs. 'Yes, it is. Here, finish making your toast, will you?' Sadie passed the butter to Poppy and ran downstairs. She must have left the door unlocked after the delivery.

'Alex? Hi.' Slowly closing the door up to the flat behind her, Sadie tucked her hair behind her ears. She hadn't even brushed it yet.

'Morning! Sorry, I knocked, but there was no answer. The delivery guy caught me on the way to the office.' He held up a small box. 'He'd forgotten to give you this.'

'Oh, thank you.' Sadie took the box and grinned. It must be her new gift cards for the flowers. She'd ordered some new designs.

'You're welcome. Everything okay?' He tilted his head towards the ceiling.

Heat swept across Sadie's cheeks. He must have heard. 'Yes. They're just arguing over the bathroom.'

'Kids, hey?' Grinning, Alex leaned forward and tucked a loose strand of hair behind her ear.

Bringing her hands to her hair again, she tried to smooth it back and laughed. 'Can you tell it's not seen a brush today?'

'Still looks beautiful.'

Looking away, Sadie smiled.

Placing his hand behind her neck, Alex leant toward her.

'Mummmmm...'

As the door to the flat was pulled open, they both jumped apart.

Sadie cleared her throat. 'Thank you for bringing the parcel in.'

'No worries. Hi, Lily.' Alex waved at Lily before looking back at Sadie and heading out of the door. 'See you.'

'Bye.' Fidgeting with the parcel in her hand, Sadie watched Alex close the front door and then glanced across at Lily. 'Everything okay?'

'I still can't get this toothpaste off my skirt. What am I supposed to do? I haven't got another one and I've got to leave in five minutes. I don't want to wear my trousers, none of my friends wear trousers, they all wear skirts. I don't want to be the odd one out.'

'Come through to the back room, we'll be able to sponge that off, no problem.' Walking through to the back room, Sadie placed the parcel on the workbench and ran a cloth under the tap.

'Can we really get a lock on the bathroom door? Will you do it today?'

'I'll certainly try.'

'Good. Will it be before I get home from school? Georgia gave me a bath bomb she had left over from Christmas and I don't want Poppy to walk in on me.'

'I can't promise it will be done by then. I've got this place to run and can't really run to the shops when there are tourists coming past.' Sadie straightened her back and put the cloth in the sink. 'There you go, as good as new.'

'Thanks. I'm going to go now. I said I'd meet Georgia early and go to the corner shop with her.'

'Okay. Here, come here.' Sadie pulled Lily in for a hug. 'Have a lovely day at school. Love you.'

'Love you too,' Lily mumbled before turning to grab her bag and heading out.

* * *

'The 24th? Yes, that will be absolutely fine.' Sadie gripped the phone between her ear and shoulder and scribbled in the order book. 'No, the late notice isn't a problem, just pop in as soon as you can and we can discuss your choices... Thank you. Bye.' Putting the phone down, Sadie clapped her hands together. Her first wedding! She'd just booked her first wedding! The bride was interested in ordering bouquets for herself and three bridesmaids, plus buttonholes and table decorations.

'You look pleased. Having a good day?' The bell above the door tinkled to announce Alex's arrival.

'I'm having a great day, thanks! I've literally just put the phone down on a customer ordering flowers for her wedding! It's my first wedding!'

'Wow! That is great!' Stepping around behind the counter, Alex grinned and held out his arms.

Sinking into his warm embrace, Sadie breathed in the fresh floral smell of fabric conditioner from his shirt. She'd done the right thing in accepting the order, hadn't she? It was an awful lot for her to do, but if she could prove herself with this wedding, then more big orders would surely follow. She could cope. She was sure she could.

Taking a step back, Alex lowered a small bag to the counter. 'That really is great news. When is it?'

Sadie grimaced. 'Two weeks! The florist she was ordering from has gone bust, so she's been looking for somewhere with availability. So, admittedly she didn't book with me because she likes my work, she's never even been to the village but, still, if I can do a good job...'

'Which you will.'

'I hope so. If I can, then I can use the photos for social media and advertising. I can use it to showcase what I'm capable of doing. Unless I mess it up, of course, and then I don't know what.'

'You'll be just fine. I've seen your work.' Alex looked around the shop. 'I know what you're capable of.'

'Yes, well, it's a bit more than you liking my arrangements. A wedding is a whole different ball game. Brides-to-be are infamous for being picky.' Maybe she shouldn't have taken on such a big job, not so early in her career. Maybe she should have turned her down?

'I know what I like, and she will too. I'm certain of that.'

'Umm...' Sadie pointed to the bag on the counter. 'What have you got there?'

'I've got a lock for your bathroom door. I'm between meetings so I thought I could pop it on quickly.'

'A lock? You heard?' Bringing her hands up to her cheeks, Sadie looked at the bag. 'I'm so sorry. I know these walls are thin...'

Alex waved her apology away. 'No, don't worry, I didn't hear from the office. I just overheard when I brought the parcel in. Sorry, I must sound really rude now, I just thought I could do you a favour.'

'Oh, right?' Sadie fingered the plastic bag. She didn't want Alex thinking she couldn't cope. 'I was going to go out and get one later. Thank you for the thought, though. I'll pay for it.'

Looking from the bag and back to Sadie, Alex rubbed his hand across his stubbled chin. 'Have I overstepped the mark?'

'No, yes. Sorry. I just don't need any help. I was going to get it done.'

Alex shook his head. 'Look, I know you don't need my help. I know you're more than capable of getting a lock and fitting it yourself. I just thought it would be a nice gesture. It's not as though I can buy you a bunch of flowers to tell you how I feel.' Looking around the shop, Alex laughed nervously.

How he felt? How did he feel? Crossing her arms, Sadie rubbed her forearms, the goosebumps slowly disappearing. Where had she even left her cardigan?

Shifting his weight from foot to foot, Alex looked at her. 'If you haven't guessed already, I like you. Really like you and I wanted to show it. Sorry, I should have thought about how this would look. A bloke coming in and trying to take over your DIY, but it wasn't meant to be like that. It was meant to simply be a nice gesture. Besides, the only DIY I can do is fit a lock, and that's only after losing my key as a broke student and not being able to afford to pay a locksmith.' Alex grinned, the dimples in his cheeks showing. 'There was absolutely nothing macho about this. I'm embarrassingly useless with a drill or a paintbrush.'

Sadie laughed. 'Okay. Sorry, I didn't mean to be funny.'

'Shall I go and fit it before my next client, or did you want to do it?'

Sadie looked across at the door as a stream of tourists filed in, oohing and ahhing at the posies on display. 'I'd love you to, if you're sure you don't mind?'

'Absolutely not.' Alex grinned as he took the bag and made his way to the door up to the flat before turning back. 'Just in case you're serving when I'm done, I just wanted to ask if you'd like to come to the beach with me tomorrow?'

'The beach? Tomorrow?'

'Yes. I've got a meeting with a client down at Cliff Seas tomorrow, and thought I'd ask as The Flower Shop is closed tomorrow. The meeting should only take an hour or so, so I wondered if you'd like to come. It's a long way, so I thought we could make the day of it, go to the beach and get a spot of lunch.' Alex glanced at the customers still perusing the stock. 'I completely understand if you don't want to as it's a long way and it would mean you having to entertain yourself for a while...'

Sadie nodded. She hadn't been to the beach in months and although it wasn't exactly warm at this time of year, it would still be nice to go. 'I'd love to. Thanks for asking.'

'Great, great. And you don't mind me leaving you for a bit to go and see my client?'

'Of course not. I'm sure I can find something to keep myself busy.'

'Great. I'll pick you up just gone eight tomorrow morning then.'

'Thanks. Looking forward to it.'

Grinning, Alex backed away towards the stairs.

'Please don't judge me on the mess...' Too late, he'd already gone.

8

'Bye, enjoy school. Love you both.' Sadie waved at the door and then checked her watch. She had about ten minutes until Alex was due to pick her up. Closing the door, she double-checked the 'Closed' sign was in place and ran upstairs to grab her thick jumper.

Even though they were guaranteed a rather chilly spring day, it would still be amazing to get down to the beach. What with teaching and training to be a florist, along with saving for this place, they hadn't managed to get away last year. The girls had been abroad with their dad, so they'd still had a holiday, but she'd missed the beach.

* * *

The tap-tap on the back door startled her as she pulled her coat on over her jumper. She pulled the door open. 'Hi.'

'Morning. All ready for our trip? Here, I grabbed us both a coffee, I thought we could use it to warm up.' Leaning forward, Alex kissed her on the lips and passed her a takeaway cup.

'Great. Thanks.' After locking the door, she followed him to the car. Tracing her lips with her index finger, she smiled. She still couldn't believe the complete turnaround in feelings she had for him. He lit a spark inside her that she wasn't even sure Max ever had. Jogging to catch up with him, she slipped her arm through his as they walked the last few steps to the car.

'You okay?'

'I'm all good, thanks.'

Looking down, Alex kissed her on the forehead before opening the car door for her.

* * *

'I'm so going to win!' Holding out her hand, Sadie squinted and aimed the ball into the basketball hoop. 'Yes!'

'That was just a lucky start.' Alex laughed and aimed his basketball. Missing dismally, he picked up another.

'No such thing as a lucky start! I'm a champion at this arcade basketball game! My turn.' With her arm pulled back ready to shoot, she jerked her arm as Alex tickled her under the armpit, the ball flying off in the wrong direction. 'That's cheating.'

'I've got to do something to give me a slight advantage.' Coming towards her, he held her by the waist and pulled her towards him.

As their lips met, the flashing lights, happy seaside tunes and intermittent screeches from arcade machines, enticing gamblers, disappeared around her. As she kissed him back, she could feel her body melt into his warm embrace. Resting her forearms on his shoulders, she glanced around. The arcade was deserted, which was no surprise as it was far too early for any sort of tourist season and was during school time.

The sound of Alex's phone ringing pulled them back to reality, and they stepped apart.

'Sorry, it's the client. I'd better take this.'

Sadie nodded as he stepped away, speaking quietly into his phone. Turning back to the basketball game, she picked up the next basketball and shot it straight through the hoop to an audience of automated cheers.

'Everything okay?' Tearing off her winning tokens, she looked across at Alex as he walked back toward her and placed them on the side of the machine. Someone else would find them later.

'Yes. He wants to meet me early. Sorry, do you mind?'

'Of course not. When does he want to meet?'

Alex grimaced. 'Now.'

'Okay. That's fine. I'll go for a walk or something then.'

'Thank you.' Alex stepped toward her and kissed her. 'It shouldn't take too long so I'll give you a call when I finish.'

Sadie nodded.

* * *

With a takeaway coffee cup warming her hands, Sadie sat down on a low wall at the top of the beach. She must have walked at least a mile or two across the sand and she was surprised by how warm her latte still was. With the mid-morning sun beating down on her face, she looked out across the sand, towards the ocean. Even from the top of the beach, she could hear the waves lapping against the wooden wave breakers. Closing her eyes, she took a deep breath of the salty air and listened to the rhythmic music of the sea.

It was strange to think that just a few short months ago she'd been living in the old marital home still, juggling the emotional and physical stresses of teaching, studying floristry in the evening and the everyday stresses of home life, and now here she was – sat on a beach in the middle of the week.

Yes, she had The Flower Shop to run, but that was it. She didn't feel as torn between all the different aspects of teaching, and feeling as though she could never catch up and get to the end of the always expanding to-do list. Nope, this way she had the luxury to be able to focus on one thing at a time. Yes, there were a lot of different aspects that needed to be managed in running The Flower Shop, but she was in charge – there was no one dropping unexpected tasks in her lap or asking her to fill data into five different formats. She could cope.

Sadie took a sip of coffee, letting the liquid warm her throat. There might be problems which she didn't foresee, and she thoroughly expected things to crop up which would be stressful and would take up more time, but for now, things were going in the right direction. Now, she had more time and more emotional space for the girls. They had always been her priority, but now she didn't feel as though she had to choose between other people's children and her own. She could spend time with Lily and Poppy knowing that she could do the accounts, or other jobs, another time and not feel as though she was always chasing her tail. Yes, life was good.

And, her fledgling relationship with Alex was the icing on the cake. Lifting the cup to her lips again, she smiled. Life *was* good. It had been the right move.

* * *

Walking back along the sand, Sadie slipped her trainers off and carried them, her feet sinking slowly into the cold wet sand and the spray from the sea showering her ankles. Alex had finished his meeting and was walking up to meet her. Sadie paused and shielded her eyes with her hand. That was him now, making his way toward her.

'Hey, how did your meeting go?'

Alex shrugged and slipped out of his own shoes. 'It was bearable. Just. He's an obnoxious man with obnoxious ideas.'

Sadie rubbed his arm. 'It's over with now. Let's enjoy the rest of the day. Do you fancy a cream tea for lunch yet?'

His eyes lit up. 'Absolutely!'

'Great. Shall we go to that little café? The one with the balcony overlooking the beach? You probably walked past it on your way to meet me.'

Alex nodded and began retracing his steps.

Dipping her toes in the water, Sadie laughed.

'Are you paddling?' Pausing, Alex looked across at her and raised his eyebrow.

'I thought about it, but the water is freezing cold. Here, you see.' Sadie pulled him by the sleeve of his jacket.

'Ouch! That *is* cold!' Looking at down at the waves lapping near them, Alex grinned and looked back at her before pulling her towards him into the cold water.

'Alex!' She laughed and tried to pull away. Too late, just as she began to step out of the froth of the sea, a wave pushed the cold sea around her ankles. Bending down, she cupped the water in her hands before spraying it across Alex, the sprinkles of water turning his jacket from light grey to dark.

'That's it now!'

As Alex bent down to cup some water up, Sadie ran further up the beach, laughing until she collapsed on the sand. 'No! Don't!'

Letting the water seep through his fingers, Alex held out his hand to pull her up. Once standing, their hands clasped together, Sadie leaned forward, their lips touching.

With their arms wrapped around each other, Sadie looked out to sea. The waves were getting stronger now, the sky a little darker. The last time she'd been at the beach had been a little over a year and a half ago. She'd taken the girls to a holiday park in Norfolk and they'd found a little secluded beach away from the typical tourist hot-spots. For her, Lily and Poppy it had been the highlight of their holiday, finding the small bay and having the beach to themselves, bar one or two passing dog walkers. For the first time in a long time, Lily had let her hair down and enjoyed paddling and playing in the sea with her sister. Away from the fear of other teenagers judging her, she'd been able to have fun. They'd all had fun.

Sadie smiled. She'd book that holiday park for later in the year. They could find that bay again. All being well with The Flower Shop, anyway.

'You okay?' Alex ran his finger along her cheek.

'Yes, I am. Thanks. Just thinking about the last time I took the girls to the beach.'

'Do you remember that time we all went to Mablethorpe for the week?'

Laughing, Sadie looked across at him. 'Yes, I think Lily was nine and Poppy must have been six. You were with Rachel then, weren't you?'

Alex nodded. 'Yes. Wow, that feels like a lifetime ago now.'

'It certainly does.' Sadie stared back out at the sea. A large cruise liner was making its way across the horizon. She couldn't have wished for that holiday to have sped away any faster than it had. Things had been difficult between her and Max, as they had been for years previously, but this had been different. He'd given her his usual cold shoulder when they had been alone, but in front of Alex and Rachel, he'd been amazing. He'd helped her with the girls, he'd paid attention to her whenever she'd spoken, and he'd even kissed and hugged her. She remembered it so vividly because he had acted so differently to the way she'd grown accustomed. In their day-to-day life, it had been her who had been left to care for the girls, and the whole idea of any sort of romantic interaction out in public, or at home, had been completely off the cards. Sadie took a deep breath, letting the salty air fill her lungs before turning to Alex. 'You'd known about the affair back then, hadn't you? When we were on that holiday? You'd already spoken to him about it?'

Running his fingers through his hair, Alex swallowed. 'Yes, I'd known. I'd spoken to him about it a month or so before we went.'

Sadie nodded. 'The holiday had been booked before you found out?'

'Yes.'

'And you said you'd threatened to tell me if he didn't stop the affair, right?'

'That's right. Why?'

Sighing, Sadie shook her head. It all made sense. 'It's just I remember we hadn't seen you for ages, not got together as couples, anyway. I mean, I'd gone holiday shopping with Rachel, but that had been all and then we had the holiday. Max was acting weird. He was trying to prove to you that he'd finished with Tara, wasn't he?' Even those cuddles and public kisses had all been an act. A deceit.

Alex looked down at his feet and then across at Sadie, his forehead creased. 'I don't know.'

'That's okay. I do. It doesn't matter. Not in the great scheme of things. It just makes things make sense a little more. That's all.' Sadie picked up her trainers. It didn't change history. It didn't change what Max had done or particularly make her feelings of indifference towards him any more or less. It was just nice to know she hadn't been going crazy. 'Shall we go and get that cream tea now? I'm starving.'

9

'Is this all you're going to do on your day off from work? Sit there and stare at me cutting flowers?' Tying a yellow ribbon around a posy of lavender, Sadie grinned and looked at Tina.

Tina lowered her mug of coffee. 'Pretty much. Well, I'm going to hang around until you tell me all the juicy details, anyway.'

'I don't know what you mean?' Sadie tried to ignore the crimson rash creeping up her neck. She could feel it, but if she pretended she didn't, maybe she could trick her body into thinking she wasn't embarrassed.

'Oh, I think you do. Come on, Sadie, you spent all day at the beach with him yesterday.'

'Not all day. It was only a few hours, school time only.'

'Stop teasing me! What's going on between you two? One minute you're telling me you hate the guy and can't believe he works next door, the next you're all over him at Angela and Darryl's wedding, and now you're off playing the romantic couple at the beach!'

Straightening the stems, Sadie smiled and placed the posy in the bucket next to her. 'We weren't all over each other at the wedding. We hardly spoke two words to each other to begin with.'

'That soon changed. You know it did. Are you seeing each other now then?'

'What? No. Yes. I guess we are.' Relenting, Sadie smiled. 'Yes, I guess we're seeing each other now. Maybe. We've not had that conversation yet.'

'So, what made you change your mind about him?'

Sadie reached across and plucked some more lavender from the huge bunch she was working from. 'That's a difficult question. I guess we always used to get on really well, before Max had the affair, or at least before I found out about it I mean, which is why it hurt so much that he didn't tell me what Max was up to. That was the main reason I was so upset at finding him working and living here, I just didn't want a constant daily reminder of Max's lies and Alex's lie to me too, but at the wedding, he explained himself. He explained that, yes, he'd found out, but he'd told Max to either tell me or finish with her. Of course, Max told him that he'd finished it with Tara and Alex believed him.'

'So, it wasn't such a lie after all?'

'Alex still didn't tell me, but he didn't tell me because Max had promised him it was over and I guess Alex just assumed that would be it.' Sadie shrugged. It still sounded bad, but she understood Alex was trying to do the right thing for Max and her.

Melissa picked up a stray stem and used it to trace around the words on a leaflet advertising wedding flowers. 'Fair enough.'

'I think so.'

Replacing the stem. Melissa grinned and looked up at Sadie. 'And now you've fallen desperately in love with him...'

'Oi!' Sadie batted her across the nose with a stem of lavender and picked up the basket of finished posies. 'I must admit I do have feelings for him, yes.'

'Ha! I knew it!' Grinning, Melissa followed her across the shop floor to the window as Sadie placed the basket on display. 'For what it's worth, I think you both make a lovely couple.'

Scrunching up her nose, Sadie laughed. 'I got my first booking for a wedding the other day too.'

'Really? That's awesome! When is it?'

'That's the only slight issue. It's the Saturday after next.'

'Oh, wow...' Melissa quickly covered a frown. 'You can do it! Can't you?'

'Yes, I should be able to. The bride is coming in this afternoon to show me what she wants. From what she's said, it's all been planned and she knows exactly what she's after, so hopefully it'll just be a case of ordering the flowers and arranging it all.'

'Great. The Saturday after next? I'm about then so I'll come over and help you if you like?'

'Don't worry. You hardly ever get Saturdays off; I can't ask you to give one up to help me.'

'Don't be daft. It'll be nice to get out of the house, anyway.'

'Thanks. I'll...' Sadie looked up as a loud continuous knocking came from outside. 'What's that?'

Strolling to the window, Melissa peered out before turning back. 'It's some guy knocking on the door next door.'

'To Alex's office?' She'd seen the barber's shop had opened at eight o'clock on the dot as usual, but Alex had told her he had meetings all morning so wouldn't be in until later.

'I believe so.'

'Huh, someone's pretty desperate to see him then.' Sadie began rearranging the buckets of flowers on display. Although it was really quiet at the moment, she hoped that she'd get the usual influx of customers trickle down from the castle on their way back later.

'It looks like it. Watch out, he's coming this way.' Melissa quickly joined Sadie behind the counter as the man, tall, large and suited, strode inside.

'Do you know where Alex Marshall of Marshall Solicitors is?'

'No, I'm afraid I don't.' Not that she'd have told him anyway, not with the intimidating air around him and booming voice. Would a 'please' have cost anything?

Shaking his head, the man stared at her.

A shrill ring broke the silence, and the man strode across to the other side of the shop floor to answer his phone.

'What?' Rubbing his hand over his face, the man glanced across at Sadie and Melissa before hanging up and turning back towards the counter.

Pulling out the order book, Sadie pretended to be busy.

'Will you give him a message?'

Sadie flinched at his gruff tone and nodded. 'I can.'

'Tell him that Thomas Pritchard wants to talk to him.'

Nodding, Sadie began writing the name on a Post-it.

'Pritchard with an "r".' The man pointed to the Post-it, a jangle of gold bangles dislodging themselves from under the sleeve of his grey coat.

'Pritchard with an "r",' Sadie repeated, continuing to write the name. Not that she'd been going to spell it any other way. 'All done. I'll give him the message.'

The man nodded and held his phone to his ear before wandering around The Flower Shop again. This time he picked up a posy here, a rose stem there, seemingly inspecting them and returning them to their baskets and buckets.

As Thomas Pritchard began speaking loudly into his phone again, Melissa rolled her eyes at Sadie before rolling a Post-it note into a ball and pretending to go to flick it at him.

Grinning at her, Sadie shook her head. If he was a client of Alex's, it wasn't fair to Alex if they annoyed him, not that he didn't appear irritated already.

'...Exactly... And with her, she'll take as much as she can if I don't put a stop to it ASAP... Yes, I cancelled her bank cards.'

'What?' Melissa mouthed at Sadie.

Shrugging her shoulders, Sadie frowned. Was Alex still as cut-throat as before? Not caring who he worked for or who he hurt? Yes, he specialised in family law but surely he could also do what was morally right?

'...when he agreed to meet me at my house, I thought I could expect more from him... Yesterday, yes.'

Yesterday? Was he the client Alex had had a meeting with yesterday?

As the door to The Flower Shop opened and a group of tourists filtered in, Thomas Pritchard strode outside, the shop suddenly quiet even with six tourists pondering the posies on offer.

'Thank goodness he's gone. What a lovely man!' The sarcasm rolled off Melissa's tongue as she lounged against the counter.

'Umm. I can't believe he was the client that Alex went to see when we were at the beach yesterday.'

'How come? You knew he was going to see someone?'

Sadie took a deep breath. 'I know but, I don't know, I'd just got the impression he'd changed. I thought he'd given up taking the ruthless clients like that. Did you hear what he was saying? I'm assuming it was about his soon to be ex-wife or partner, he's obviously going to try and take everything from the poor woman.'

'He is a family solicitor. You knew that before you started seeing him. You must remember what he was like as Max's solicitor when you two broke up?'

'I do.' It wasn't as though she could forget. Max had all but taken her to the cleaners, she'd just been lucky enough to keep the house which had, unfortunately, included the hefty mortgage repayments too. She shrugged. 'I just thought he'd changed. I thought he was more caring now. Mellowed out with age, I suppose.'

'A solicitor is a solicitor. It's just his job.'

Sadie turned to serve a customer. Maybe Melissa was right. Maybe she shouldn't be thinking badly of him because of his job. Still, it didn't sit easily with her. Not one bit.

* * *

'Yes, they're a lovely choice and I can definitely get all of that sorted for your wedding.' Sadie smiled at the bride-to-be standing on the other side of the counter. She'd chosen a simple, elegant bouquet of deep red roses for herself and smaller bouquets of white roses for her three bridesmaids. On top of those, she'd ordered white rose buttonholes and corsages, and vases of deep red and white roses for the table centres.

'Thank you so much. I got myself into such a tizzy when I found out my last florist had gone out of business and my mum kept saying I'd never get another in such a short time. Didn't you, Mum?' The bride-to-be, Clare, pulled her straight blonde hair across one shoulder and looked at the woman standing next to her.

'That I did.'

'I had visions of walking down the aisle bouquet-less and having to put tea lights or something on the tables. I can't tell you how relieved I was after ringing you and, now, after you saying it will be no bother to get everything sorted in time...' Clare patted Sadie's hand.

'You're very welcome. I'm looking forward to it.' The description 'no bother' wasn't quite how Sadie would describe the situation. Having everything ready in time would be a stretch for any florist, let alone a new one working on her own and running the shop at the same time. Still, it was good money and Clare had agreed she could take photographs of her work to use in promotional materials. Well, in fact, Clare had been delighted at the prospect of having a piece of her wedding immortalised and becoming the showcase of The Flower Shop's wedding side of the business.

'Great. I'll see you next Saturday then.' Clapping her hands together, Clare squealed excitedly before leaving, her mum nodding her approval and following her out.

Scribbling notes down in her order book, Sadie was completely unaware of the presence of someone else in The Flower Shop until Alex cleared his throat and slid a takeaway coffee cup across the counter. 'Sorry I didn't hear the bell above the door go, I was miles away.'

'No, I sneaked in as two women walked out. Bride-to-be by any chance?'

'Yes, how did you guess?' As she picked up the coffee cup, she took the lid off and inhaled the bittersweet aroma of latte. 'Thanks for this.'

'My pleasure. The high-pitched tirade of excited blabbering gave it away slightly. That and the fact she was carrying half a newsagent's worth of bridal magazines in her arms.'

'Great observational skills.'

'So how did it go?'

'Good. What she's asked for is quite classic, so shouldn't be a problem to do. It'll just be the timing of everything and making sure I don't start making the bouquets too early that they begin to wilt, and not too late, so I run out of time.' Sadie took a sip of latte, the hot liquid searing the back of her throat. 'It'll be fine, I'm just panicking slightly. I have a good floral cooler out the back, it'll be fine.'

'You'll do a grand job.'

'I hope so.'

Alex looked around the shop. 'I thought Melissa was here. I've got her a latte too. I don't know what she drinks, but I guessed I couldn't go wrong with a latte.'

'Oh, she'll love that, thanks. She's just popped out to the corner shop to grab us some lunch.' Sadie rolled her eyes. 'Not that I don't have a good loaf of bread and salad upstairs in the flat.'

Relaxing his shoulders, Alex leaned forward and pecked her on the lips.

Pulling away, Sadie looked at the Post-it note next to the till. 'I forgot to say, a Thomas Pritchard popped by to see you. Apparently, he's already rang, and he didn't seem particularly happy.'

Rubbing his hand across his face, Alex took a large slug of coffee. 'Thomas Pritchard is never a happy man. Never has been and never will be. I'm so sorry you had to meet him.'

'He was hollering down his phone, telling whoever was on the end that he'd stopped his wife's bank cards and he wanted to take her to the cleaners.'

Alex narrowed his eyes and shook his head. 'I advised him not to do that.'

Straightening her back, Sadie looked at him. Had he advised that, or was he just trying to look good in front of her, trying to placate her? He knew more than most how rubbish her divorce from Max had been. He wouldn't want her believing he hadn't changed one bit. She took a deep breath. 'I'd got the impression you'd changed? That you weren't that ruthless solicitor who goes after everything for his client, not caring one iota for the poor other half.'

'I have. I don't. Not usually anyway. Thomas Pritchard is a friend of my father's. I had to take on the case. I owed it to my dad, but I can assure you I'm doing all I can to encourage him to go for a fair break. And I did for you too.'

Had she heard that right? Had he just said he'd made sure her divorce was fair, because it certainly hadn't felt like that. She'd been left with the house but no share of Max's huge pension or any of the stocks and shares he'd invested in throughout their marriage. Yes, he hadn't got hold of her pension either, but as until the moment he'd left she'd been part-time, her teacher's pension was worthless against the full-time one he'd been paying into for all the years she'd been looking after the house and kids. Plus, the house had been mortgaged to the hilt, so arguably she'd walked away with about thirty thousand in equity and that had been all. That and the huge mortgage bill she'd had to pay. 'I need to go and get some stuff done out the back, Thanks for the coffee.'

'Oh, okay. Are you all right?'

'Fine.' Turning on her heels, she disappeared through the archway, waiting out of sight until she heard the door close.

Leaning against the workbench, she sipped her latte again. Was she being unfair? After all, it had been Max she'd divorced, not him. Although Max had been the one who had instructed him, yes, but Alex would have advised him. His speciality was family law whereas Max's was criminal law, so Alex would definitely have advised him. She pinched the bridge of her nose with her free hand. She probably wouldn't be feeling like this if Alex hadn't known her before, or even if they hadn't got on so well. It was the knife in the back scenario. Alex taking on her and Max's divorce for Max had clearly shown who he'd sided with. It hadn't even all been about the money, although trying to come out of the marriage with a clear way of providing a stable home for the girls had been her priority; it had also slashed her trust in people, in her friends. If Alex could help Max pull the rug from beneath her feet so easily, who could she actually trust?

Maybe she and Alex were never meant to be. Maybe this was just too big a hurdle to get across. Who in their right mind would hook up with their ex-husband's best mate and divorce solicitor? She knew she and Alex had history too, but Max had introduced him, and during their break-up Alex had made it crystal clear where his loyalties had been. What had changed?

10

'Mum, your phone's ringing. Again. Aren't you going to get it?'

Sadie looked up from the bouquet of flowers she was preparing. With the wedding in the morning, she'd be working through the night trying to get everything cut, arranged, tied and packaged. 'No, it's probably just cold callers. Just leave it. Thanks, though.'

'Okay.' Lily shrugged and leaned against the archway. 'Can I go to the park with Georgia?'

'Now?' Sadie looked across at the clock. It was half past four already. 'It'll be getting dark soon. Why don't you ask her to come here? You can chill out upstairs and watch a film or something?'

'We want to go to the park.'

'But you'll only be there a little while. You'll have to come back in half an hour or an hour when it starts to get dark.'

'Is that a "yes" then? I'll be back before it's dark.'

Sadie shook her head. 'Well, make sure you are. I haven't got time to come looking for you. And take your mobile.'

'Will do.' Pushing herself from her slumped position, Lily slipped out of the back door before Sadie could change her mind.

'Here you go.' Poppy came through and placed a mug on the workbench in front of her mum.

'Oh, thank you.' Placing the cutting knife on the workbench, she picked up the mug and took a sip. Hot tea. Super-hot tea.

'Sorry, it's not got much milk in. That was the last of it.'

Heck, she'd meant to pick some up from the shop before making a start on Clare's bouquet. 'Never mind, I could do with a hot drink to warm me up.'

'It's freezing in here.' Poppy shoved her hands in the pouch at the front of her hoodie. 'Can I turn the heating up?'

'Not in here. You can in the flat. It needs to be cold in here, so the flowers keep fresh. Why don't you grab your coat and come and sit and talk for a bit?'

Poppy looked around the room. 'Okay.'

A few minutes later, Poppy was sat cocooned in her thick winter's coat on the stool opposite Sadie as she measured and cut the stems of the deep red roses.

'...and then this boy, Calum, shouted out in front of the WHOLE class that Phoebe had gone to see Santa at Christmas. That's not nice, is it? I mean, we don't know he's not real. No one does, not really. He could be, there could really be someone who delivers presents to some kids. Maybe not here, in England, but somewhere else. And it's not anything to do with Calum if Phoebe goes to see Santa or not. Her parents might have forced her to go. Plus, she has little sisters and a brother too, she might have had to go with them.'

'Aw, that's not fair at all of Calum. What happened? Was Phoebe okay?'

'She was all right. Harry shouted out that Calum shouldn't have been spying on Phoebe and that he was a stalker, and what was he even doing near Santa's grotto anyway if he wasn't going to see him too.'

Sadie laughed. 'So it kind of backfired on him then?'

'Yep. Harry is cool. He doesn't care who he talks to and sticks up for. Even though Calum is the popular boy in class, it doesn't stop Harry from sticking up for what he believes.'

'That's good.'

'Definitely.' Poppy rubbed her hands together. 'I might go upstairs for a bit and watch some TV.'

'Okay, sweetheart. You go and get warm.' Sadie smiled. She was a good kid. Lily was too – beyond the normal teenage angst she was still the loving and caring little girl she'd always been. Picking up the finished bouquet, Sadie turned it around in her hands, checking it from all angles before nodding and placing it in the cooler. One down, three more to go, and then she'd make a start on the buttonholes.

She slugged down the rest of her tea, cold now ironically, and went out onto the shop floor, letting the curtain fall back into place to cover the archway and keep some of the chill out of the shop. Checking the time, she sighed. It was a quarter to six now.

At the door, she pulled it open and looked down the lane. Dusk was well and truly setting in now, and the old-fashioned Victorian lampposts had already turned on lighting the small area beneath them. Where was she? For all the attitude she could give, it wasn't like Lily to miss a curfew.

Reaching into her pocket, she pulled out her phone and rang her. Pick up, pick up Lily. Come on.

Nothing.

Ducking back indoors, Sadie strode to the stairs and called up, 'Poppy!'

'Yes, Mum.' Poppy appeared at the top of the stairs.

'I'm just popping out to see if I can find Lily. She's not back yet. I'll lock the door. Just stay upstairs.'

'Okay.'

Chewing her bottom lip, Sadie looked up at Poppy. She'd be okay on her own. Just for five minutes while she ran out and found Lily. She shook her head. She was over worrying again. Other people she knew left their children younger than Poppy at home alone.

Back outside, she double checked the door was locked, pulled her cardigan tighter around herself and headed down Serendipity Lane. Soon reaching the bottom of the lane, she looked both right and left. No sign. The park was just off the main High Street; the end leading out of the village, so she turned right.

Five minutes later, and she was standing at the gate to the park. She scanned the field; the swings, roundabout, slide and climbing frame were all empty. Where on earth was she?

Fishing her phone out of her pocket, she scrolled through to find Georgia's mum's number. Just as she was about to press the call button, her own phone juddered to life, its screen flashing with Lily's number. 'Lily. Where are you? You're not at the park.'

'It's Poppy, Mum. Lily's here and she has a surprise for you!' The excitement in Poppy's voice was apparent as she sang down the phone.

'Is she okay? Where's she been?'

'Lily's fine. She said just come home and she'll tell you when you get here. You're going to be so happy!'

'Okay. I'll be back in five. Love you.'

'Love you too, Mum.'

Gripping her phone, Sadie retraced her steps towards The Flower Shop. What surprise could Lily have in store for her? It must be something good for her and Poppy to be actually getting along for once, and for Lily to have let Poppy use her phone.

As she turned to go down Serendipity Lane, she glanced down at her phone as a message pinged through and walked straight into someone coming in the opposite direction. 'Sorry.'

'Sadie. Everything okay?'

Looking up, Sadie recoiled. It was Alex. 'Sorry.'

'Don't worry. You look in a rush.'

She looked towards The Flower Shop, she could see the lights on in the shop from here, and then back at Alex and shrugged. Please don't ask why I've been ignoring your calls.

'Did you get my voicemails?'

'Voicemails?'

'Yes, I've rang a couple of times.' Alex looked down at the phone in her hand.

'Umm. Sorry, it's just been super busy. I have that wedding to prepare for and then Lily went AWOL and...' She bit down on her bottom lip.

'AWOL? Is she okay?'

'Yes, she's back now.'

'Sorry, I forgot you had that wedding tomorrow.' He looked down at his shoes and raked his fingers through his hair before looking back up at her. 'I was starting to think you were ignoring me.'

Sadie met his gaze. Should she bring it up now? Should she tell him she is uncomfortable about her feelings for him after Thomas Pritchard brought to the surface all the memories of how blindsided she'd felt during her divorce? Should she tell him how let down she felt?

'You have been, haven't you? You *have* been ignoring me?'

'No, of course not.' And there it was, the hurt in his eyes, the confusion crumpled on his forehead. 'Yes, I have.'

'What? Why? I thought what we had, the time we've enjoyed together, was going to be the start of something?'

'So did I.' Swallowing hard, Sadie took a deep breath. She had to be honest. She hated it when people weren't honest with her. Alex deserved her honesty. 'I... After Thomas Pritchard came in ranting and raving, it just reminded me about everything that happened when Max and I split. The divorce and everything.'

'The fact that I was Max's divorce solicitor, you mean?'

Sadie nodded.

'He asked me.' Alex clasped his hands in front of him. 'He asked me. He paid me. It was no favour.'

'Yes, but we had been friends. For years. We'd known each other ever since Max and I had got together, and I thought we were friends and then...'

'It was a job.'

Breathing out heavily, Sadie watched her breath take on a life of its own. The cold air condensing her warm breath, tiny water droplets dancing in the air. She had to let it out. She had to breathe life to what was churning up in her stomach. She knew it would likely mean the end to whatever had begun to happen between them, but she couldn't live a lie either, she couldn't hide how she felt. 'It wasn't just a job. Not to me. Not to Lily and Poppy. It was our lives, Max and you left me high and dry coming out of the divorce with a house which was mortgaged up to the hilt. You didn't have to do that. You put the knife in at my lowest point. I know you were mates with Max way before we even knew each other, but what you did... What you did was wrong.'

'Sadie. I...'

Turning on her heels, she ran the last few steps to The Flower Shop, fumbled with the lock and pulled the door open, making sure to shut it firmly behind her.

'Mum! You're here! How come you were so long? Quick, come upstairs. See what Lily's found.'

'I'll be there in a moment.' Keeping her back to Poppy, she squeezed her eyes tight and wiped the pads of her thumbs across her cheeks. She was being silly. Why was she letting Alex's behaviour get to her? They'd barely been seeing each other for longer than two weeks. Maybe it was for the best, maybe seeing he hadn't changed one bit – that he was still as morally challenged as he had been when he'd cleaned her out with her and Max's divorce. Maybe it was a blessing that she'd found this out now. Imagine if things had become serious between them? What if it had got to the point where the girls had been involved? Yes, it was better this way. Better to knock things on the head before anything had already started.

A loud noise tore her from her thoughts and she turned around. There it was again. Was she imagining things? The noise almost sounded like a dog. 'Poppy? Lily?'

'Come on, Mum. Quick, come and see why Lily was late!' Poppy's signalled for her mum to follow, this time her excitable voice was laced with annoyance, presumably something to do with the fact she hadn't rushed straight up there.

'Coming.' Slipping her shoes off at the bottom of the stairs, she followed Poppy up.

'Aww, here he comes to say hello.'

A shaggy black and white spaniel sped down the stairs, pausing on the step above Sadie. Shifting his weight, he balanced on his back paws and reached up towards her, his front paws landing squarely on her stomach. 'Oh, hello to you too.'

'He's sooooo cute, isn't he, Mum?'

Lowering the dog's paws carefully onto the step, Sadie tilted her head and looked at the furry creature in front of her. 'He's very skinny. And what's wrong with his eye?'

The dog pawed at his eye which had a scratch running right across the eyelid.

'Lily found him like that.'

Sadie nodded and walked into the living room, the dog following at her heels. Lily sat on the floor, arranging a blanket into a nest.

'Hey, Mum. Does this look okay for a dog bed? Do you think he'll be comfy on it until we can get him a proper one?' Lily looked up before frowning at the blanket mound in front of her.

'Dog bed?' Sadie sat down on the sofa, the dog immediately jumping up and nestling into the cushions next to her. 'Hold on. Let's start from the beginning. Where has he come from?'

'Me and Georgia found him in the park. That's why we were late because we heard a whining from the trees so had to find out what it was.'

'You're not supposed to go into the wooded area on your own, especially after dark. Anyone could have been there.'

'I know. But they weren't and we couldn't not help him, could we?'

Sadie pursed her lips together. She couldn't very well tell Lily off for rescuing the dog, but she needed her to know not to go into lonely places in the future. 'Next time, if there is a next time, ring me and I'll come and explore with you.'

'Okay. Anyway, we found him stuck in some reeds in a little pond. He literally couldn't get out, so we had to pull up the reeds and pull him out.'

'That's why you're so smelly then?' Sadie grimaced as the dog nudged his muddy nose towards her. She supposed the smell was everywhere already anyway and, relenting, she fussed him. 'You need a good bath, don't you, buddy?'

'Does that mean we can keep him then?' Lily's eyes widened.

'What? No, he's probably got an owner. It just means that he needs a bath if he's going to stay here tonight. We'll look for his owner in the morning.' She ran her fingers up and down his neck. 'He's not wearing a collar, but he might have a chip. We'll take him to the vets tomorrow and hopefully, they can trace who he belongs to.'

'But look at him! He's really skinny, and it looks like he's been in a fight. He can't go back to his owner; they obviously don't feed him!'

'He might be lost. And by the looks of it, he's been out alone for a good while, judging by the state of his fur and how skinny he is. He might have been stolen too and the thieves may have dumped him.'

'Can't we just keep him? You wanted us to move here so we could get out into the countryside, a dog would make us, wouldn't it? We'd have to take him on walks. Please, Mum?'

'Poppy, we can't just keep him.' Turning towards her, Sadie took Poppy's hands into her own. 'He might have a family who loves him very much, who misses him. We need to try to find them for him and for them. You'd want your dog back if he'd got lost or stolen, wouldn't you? You'd be missing him terribly.'

Poppy nodded. 'I guess so. Can we keep him tonight, though?'

'Yes, he can stay tonight, but after the wedding tomorrow we'll have to take him to the vets.' Sadie could feel a tight knot forming in her stomach. She was almost an hour's work behind on the wedding already.

'Okay.'

'Right, let's get him showered and settled before I go back to working on those flowers. Who's helping?' Slapping her knees, she stood up, the dog jumping up off the sofa before she'd even finished standing.

'Me!'

'I'll help too.' Lily stood up. 'Can I shower him? You'll be able to get on with your work then.'

'Yes, you can do. I'll stay with you though because we don't know how he's going to react.'

'Look at him, Mum. He's as soft as anything. Aren't you?' Lily knelt down to ruffle his fur. 'You're not going to hurt me, are you?'

'He certainly looks lovely enough, but we don't know him and we don't know what his past experiences have been.'

Lily nodded. 'I guess we don't know how he got the cuts. He might have been forced to fight or something.'

Sadie nodded. Both dog theft and dogfighting seemed to be on the rise, so anything was possible.

11

With the dog, now temporarily named as Buddy, washed and dried, the muddy sofa throw in the washing machine and dinner in the oven, including extra chicken nuggets for Buddy, Sadie made her way back down to the back room.

Scraping back her hair, she checked the time. Two hours had passed. She'd be lucky if she got any sleep at this rate. Taking a half-finished bridesmaid bouquet out of the floral cooler, she settled at the workbench, took some more rose stems and began clipping off the thorns. She could do this.

'Mum, the oven's beeping and Lily's brushing Buddy's fur so she wanted me to tell you.' Poppy pulled the hood up on her BMX hoodie.

Sadie smiled. 'Okay, I'll be up to dish up dinner in a moment. Can you just turn the timer off? It'll be fine for a few minutes.'

'Will do.'

As she watched Poppy run back upstairs to the warmth, Sadie sighed. She'd not even finished that bouquet. Oh well, at least after dinner she could really get stuck in and focus.

* * *

Breathing a sigh of relief, Sadie closed the floral cooler door and took a long swig from the flask of coffee that Lily had brought down hours earlier. She'd done a good job. All the bridesmaids' bouquets were the same and the bride's was a dash of colour amongst the white roses of the brides-maids' bouquets which made it stand out nicely. Yes, they looked perfect. She'd have definitely been happy to walk down the aisle carrying one of them on her wedding day.

With a grin spreading across her face, she turned to the order book – fifteen corsages, eighteen buttonholes, and seven table arrangements were left. But she'd done the trickiest. The bouquets were done. She checked the time. It was twenty minutes past eleven. If she could get the corsages and buttonholes done by one, then she could catch a bit of sleep before waking early and working on the table centres in the morning.

'Mum?' Lily's voice filtered through the curtain covering the archway into the back room.

'Yes, sweetheart. You okay?'

'Buddy keeps pacing. He won't settle.' Pulling back the curtain, Lily came through, Buddy at her heels. Beginning to shiver at the drop in temperature, Lily tightened the belt on her dressing gown.

'Maybe he needs to go to the toilet.' Sadie looked around before snip-ping off a length of ribbon. Kneeling down, she gently fashioned it into a collar around his neck, making sure to fasten it so it was loose enough not to feel uncomfortable and yet couldn't be yanked off. Tying a piece of twine to the ribbon, she left it long enough to act as a lead. 'Do you need to go to wee-wee, Buddy?' Sadie pulled open the door which led out into the car park and stood just inside holding the twine.

'Did he need to go?'

'Yes, he's going right now. In fact, I'm surprised we didn't have a puddle upstairs.' Sadie shut the door as Buddy trotted back inside, his tail wagging in the air, and bent down to take off the collar and lead combo. 'There you go. I bet that's better.'

Leaning back on his hind legs, Buddy stretched and laid his front paws on Sadie's knees. 'Are you looking for a fuss?'

'He's lovely, isn't he? What do you think will happen to him?'

'Hopefully, he's got a chip and the vets will be able to trace his owners.'

'But what if they can't?'

'I'm not sure. I guess he'll go to a rescue centre and be rehomed from there.'

'Can we keep him if he's not chipped? Please, Mum? He seems happy here. He likes us, and it'd be great to have a pet. You've been promising us for years that we can have one.'

'But we haven't got a garden. Besides, what would happen to him during the day when I'm working down here? It wouldn't be very fair to him to be stuck upstairs all day.' Sadie stepped closer to Lily and hugged her shoulders.

'Yes, but we own that patch out the back, don't we? Where our bins are? Can't we fence that? Like they have next door?' Lily pulled away and looked up at her mum. 'And he could stay in the shop with you during the day. We could get one of those baby gates and he could be shut in here so he can't go out into the shop?'

Lily made good suggestions, Sadie would give her that, but in reality, would it really work? They didn't know enough about Buddy yet. Yes, the barber's shop next door and the little wool shop up the lane had fenced off their bits of land out the back, but the fences were very low. She'd have to check on the deeds to see if it was possible. Sadie shook her head. Buddy's owner would no doubt be able to be traced by the vet, and none of this would even matter. 'Let's just wait and see what tomorrow brings, shall we?'

'But what if the vet can't find his owner? Can we keep him then?'

Sadie looked at Lily as she fussed over Buddy. Lily had always wanted a dog. Poppy, too. And Sadie had always had dogs growing up. They had always made her childhood house feel like a home, but she needed to be firm. She couldn't make false promises, it would break Lily's heart even more if she got her hopes up for them to only be dashed again. 'Most dogs have chips nowadays, so let's just see what happens tomorrow.'

'Okay.'

'Come here.' Holding out her arms, Sadie waited until Lily had sunk into them before kissing her on top of the head. 'Up you go and get some sleep now, sweetheart.'

'Okay. Night.'

'Love you.'

'You too. Come on, Buddy.' Tapping her side, Lily waited until Buddy had finished sniffing around the offcuts of stems which had fallen to the floor and joined her before returning upstairs.

Checking the order book, Sadie collected together the ribbon, the white roses, gypsophila and a little foliage before settling at the workbench and beginning the corsages.

* * *

As she placed the last buttonhole in the box, Sadie grinned. She'd done it. The bouquets, the corsages and the buttonholes were all done. And by two thirty-five in the morning at that. All that was left were the table centres, which she'd do first thing in the morning. Her first wedding order was almost complete!

She picked up the box, careful to keep it flat. The last thing she needed was for them all to slip across to one side and the petals crumple.

Taking the box to the floral cooler, Sadie held it with one hand as she tugged open the glass door.

'What?'

With a high-pitched bark, a flash of black and white fur raced into the back room before nudging Sadie's leg and coming to a stop at her feet.

'Buddy! What are you up to? Did something spook you? Was I too noisy?' Looking down at the dog sat at her feet in front of the floral cooler, Sadie laughed. 'You're going to have to move, I can't get the door open properly. Come on, budge over.' Gently hooking her foot under his tummy, Sadie slid him across a couple of inches.

Stretching out his paws and elongating his back, Buddy yawned.

'You *are* tired then. Come on, just move across a little further and let me put these in the floral cooler and we'll be able to get you back to bed.' Yawning herself, Sadie longed for her bed too. With Buddy now out of the way, Sadie pulled open the glass door fully. Just as she transferred the box to the shelf, Buddy jumped up at her. His paws landed on her knees as his head knocked into the bottom of the box, knocking it from her hands.

'Noooo!' Powerless, Sadie watched as eighteen perfect buttonholes fell to the floor. Dropping to her knees, she began scooping them up in her hands.

The excitement was too much for Buddy and he zoomed around the room, circling back towards Sadie and running full pelt across the tiled floor before knocking into her arms as she tried to rescue the fallen buttonholes.

'Careful, Buddy! Careful!' Too late, of the few that she'd managed to rescue, only one remained in the safety of her arms as Buddy jumped from foot to foot and barked, his paws repeatedly trampling over the carefully styled buttonholes.

Finally, sitting back on his haunches, Buddy wagged his tail across the tiles, pushing petals and leaves further across the floor.

Sitting back on the cold tiles herself, Sadie covered her eyes with the palms of her hands and pressed. Of eighteen buttonholes, one remained intact and in truth, even that one had suffered some creasing in the delicate petals and would need to be remade. So that was eighteen buttonholes that she'd need to remake before she could sink into bed.

Lowering her hands and lifting her head, she looked directly at the dog sitting expectantly in front of her. She could cry or she could get on and the only way this was going to get fixed was for her to crack on. 'Let's go and get some coffee and then get back to work, shall we, Buddy? And maybe this time, you could refrain from trampling over anything I manage to get finished?'

Buddy barked and licked her hand.

'I take that as a promise then.' Pushing herself to standing, Sadie followed Buddy up the stairs to the flat. The cheap instant stuff she'd bought for the back room wouldn't be enough to keep her awake for another couple of hours, the need for filter coffee was high.

12

Opening her eyes with a jolt, Sadie focused on the clock above the mantelpiece. Phew, it was only 6.05am. She hadn't overslept. Well, she had, but only by five minutes. She must have fallen asleep on the sofa. She vaguely remembered sitting down for a hot chocolate before planning on getting into bed. She'd obviously not got that far. As she tried to slip her legs out from under the throw, she realised she wasn't alone and sat up.

'Morning, Buddy. Can I have my legs back, please?'

Lifting his head up, Buddy opened one eye before closing it again and lowering his head back into the nook behind her knees.

Pulling the throw taut, she managed to lift the bulk of Buddy's weight enough off her so she could finally slip out. Standing up, she stretched and yawned. She must have only had about an hours' sleep, but it had certainly done the trick.

A quick wash and a change of clothes later, Sadie looked in on the girls and Buddy – all still fast asleep – grabbed a filter coffee and headed downstairs. It would only be three hours until Melissa arrived to help her take everything over to the wedding venue and she had all the table centres to create before then.

Taking a slug of coffee, she made her way into the back room. She could do this. The table centres were simple enough – vases of deep red and white roses to compliment the other wedding flowers.

* * *

Twisting the glass vase around on the table in front of her, Sadie leaned her head from one side to the other. Yes, she was happy with that. More than happy. Now she just had to replicate it another few times, and she was done.

As she pulled another vase towards her, the shrill ring from her mobile interrupted her thoughts.

'Hello?'

'Let me in.' Melissa's voice, groggy from the early morning, filtered down the line.

'Melissa! You're here already?'

'Yes, and I'm getting wet. Let me in.'

'Coming!' Pocketing her mobile, Sadie went through to the front of the shop and pulled the door open.

'How's it going?' Shaking her umbrella outside before she stepped in, Melissa passed Sadie a brown paper bag. 'I stopped by that little café on the High Street and bought us some breakfast. I figured you'd probably do your usual and forget your body still needs fuel when you're busy and I needed the grease to mop up the remnants of last night.'

'Great, thanks. Did you have a good night?'

'Don't. I can't speak about it without thinking about how sick I feel.'

Sadie laughed. 'One day, you'll learn that you can't keep up with the young apprentices you have at your place any more.'

'Don't even joke about it. I'm pretty certain half of them took a drinking course instead of studying hairdressing.'

'How come you're so early, anyway?'

'Luke woke me up with his snoring, so I thought I might as well come over. It was come and help you or have him try to get me to agree to have his parents over for lunch.'

'Fair enough.' Melissa's in-laws were nice enough, but she'd never forgiven her mother-in-law for buying her a shrug to cover up her ever so slightly risqué dress on her wedding day. She led the way into the back room, placed the paper bag on the table and pulled out a bacon butty.

'How are the flowers coming along?'

'Good. I think. I've just got the table centres to finish off now. We had a slight incident in the early hours when Buddy knocked over and ruined all the buttonholes I'd literally just finished creating.' Sadie shrugged. 'But I've redone those. Bouquets are done too and so are the corsages.'

Melissa wiped tomato ketchup from her mouth. 'Who's Buddy?'

'A dog Lily found in the park yesterday evening.'

'A dog? You've got a dog!'

'You're as bad as the girls! No, he just slept over. I'm taking him to the vets to see if they can trace his owners as soon as the flowers are delivered.'

'I can't believe you've got a dog!'

'We haven't got a dog. We were just a doggy hotel last night.' Sadie rolled her eyes. If there was one thing Melissa loved more than hair-dressing (and drinking) then it was dogs.

'So, when do I get to see the famous Buddy?'

'He's asleep at the moment, or else he was. I've not heard from him for a while.'

'I'll sneak up and see if I can find him.' Scrunching up the bag, Melissa threw it in the bin on her way out before turning around. 'Don't worry, I won't wake the girls, I remember how precious sleep is at that age.'

Shaking her head, Sadie set back to work. If there was one thing she truly missed about living in the town, it was the fact that Melissa had only been a couple of streets away. She needn't have worried though, as always, Melissa was her support and the best godmother to her girls she could have asked for.

* * *

'He's adorable! You didn't tell me he was a spaniel? Do you remember the spaniel I had when I was a teenager? Toby? Buddy reminds me so much of him. Look! He's got the same markings around the eyes.'

Sadie finished pulling the thorns from the stem she was working on and looked up. 'So he has. Toby was lovely, wasn't he? Your mum always used to let him follow us to school.'

'Yes! And then she'd meet him outside the school gates to take him for a game of fetch at the rec.' Kneeling down, Melissa ruffled Buddy's fur. 'The girls are awake, by the way. I've told them to get some breakfast and be good this morning while we get these flowers out, and then this afternoon I'll take them into town for some lunch with their Auntie Melissa while you can stay here and get some shut-eye.'

'Melissa, if I wasn't in such a rush, I'd come over and give you a massive hug.' Melissa always knew what Sadie needed without any need to ask.

'Not with the number of thorns sticking to your clothes, you won't.' Laughing, Melissa held her arms outstretched in a cross. 'How's it going? Is there anything I can do to help?'

'Umm, I don't think so. Thanks, though. You just being here and talking is a great help – it's keeping me going. I've de-thorned all the stems I'm going to use, I think, so I've just got to arrange them.' Sadie glanced at the clock. 'Where did that time go? We'll need to leave soon.'

'Mum, where are my black jeans? You know, the ones with the diamanté heart on the back pocket?' Lily stood in the archway.

'I think they're in the ironing basket. Or else on the radiator drying.'

'Come on, let's go and have a look.' Wrapping her arm around Lily's shoulders, Melissa led her back upstairs.

Three more vases to arrange, and one hour and fifteen minutes before they needed to get on the road to deliver them. Sadie rolled her shoulders back and stretched before getting back to work.

* * *

Placing the final rose stem in the vase she was working on, Sadie tried to ignore the slight tapping on The Flower Shop's door. She'd put a notice up to say they were closed until the afternoon. She'd also warned Mr Hubert and told him she'd drop his daily gerberas around sometime in the afternoon. There it was again. Whoever it was, they were persistent. That was for sure.

She really didn't have time for this. She didn't have time for going through and telling whoever it was to read the sign, but she couldn't work with that tapping either. Sighing, Sadie marched through to The Flower Shop and pulled open the door.

'Morning! I know you're busy so I thought I'd bring round some breakfast in case you hadn't had time to get any.' Alex held up a brown paper bag, the smell of bacon wafting in through the open doorway.

Momentarily closing her eyes, Sadie gripped the door handle. It was sweet of him, yes, but she'd barely had time to process the fact that he was still involved in ruthless divorce cases, let alone the time or energy to decide how it affected their new relationship. 'I've already eaten but thank you.'

'Oh, right? Well, will the girls want it?'

'Maybe. Thanks.' Taking the bag, Sadie went to close the door.

'When you've got time, maybe we could talk?'

'Alex, I...' Sadie glanced back towards the back room.

'Sorry, it's a bad time.' Holding his hands up, palms facing outward, he backed away. 'We'll catch up later? Yes?'

Sadie nodded and watched as he walked away. After closing the door, she looked in the bag, he'd bought two bacon butties. He'd wanted to have breakfast together.

She shook her head. She needed to focus. She'd think about everything else later. She needed to get the wedding flowers done now.

* * *

Shutting the car door behind her, Sadie leaned back against the headrest. 'I'm so glad that's done.'

'It looks amazing though. Clare and her husband-to-be are going to love it.' Melissa pulled out of the car park, leaving the wedding venue behind them.

'I hope so. She seemed to like the bouquets, didn't she?' The table centres had looked good on the bright white tablecloths and Clare had seemed more than happy with the bouquets, corsages and buttonholes.

'She loved them. Now, it's time for bed for you while I take the girls out.'

Sadie rubbed her eyes. 'Sleep sounds good.'

'Ahh... there's one thing to do first...'

'Buddy. How could I have forgotten? Are you okay picking him and the girls up now and we'll take him to the vets?'

'No problem at all.'

* * *

'I still don't understand why he couldn't come back home with us?' Poppy crossed her arms and stared out of the rear passenger window.

'You heard the vet. The dog warden will come and pick him up and try to locate his owners.' Sadie twisted around in her seat and patted Poppy on the knee.

'Yes, but he doesn't have a microchip. They can't find the owner anyway, so it seems daft he's got to stay there when his owner can't be found.'

'It's only for seven days. They just need to see if they can find the owner or if the owner comes forward.'

'And then he's definitely coming back to live with us.'

'If they can't trace his owners and if we get approved, yes, but nothing is definite. Someone will need to come and check our home.'

'She means it will probably be a no because we don't have a garden.'

'Lily, the vet said we might still get approved. I'll see about fencing off our back area by the car park and getting a dog gate for the back room. We might get through. We just can't get our hopes up yet, Poppy, that's all.' They had a lot to do to get the place ready for an inspection, and only a week to do it in if they stood any chance of being able to rehome Buddy. And that was if the owners didn't come forward. 'We'll try, but hopefully the dog warden will able to get in contact with his owners. That'll be the best thing for Buddy, won't it?'

'I guess so.' Poppy nodded.

'Anyway, girls, where am I taking you two for lunch?'

'How about that new pizza place in town? Georgia went with her mum and said it was really good.'

'Okay, Pizza Palace it is then. We'll swing by now and drop your mum off and then be on our way.'

'Or we could go to the burger diner instead?'

'Both are good options, shall we decide when we get there?'

13

Sadie waved as Melissa drove away. They'd be at least a couple of hours and that was if Melissa didn't go into one of her serious window-shopping modes. Yawning, Sadie rummaged in her pocket for the key. Where had she put it?

'Hi. You okay?'

Sadie looked up. Alex was standing in front of her, a takeaway coffee cup in his hand. Did he even own a kettle in that office of his? 'I can't find my keys.'

'Where did you have them last?'

'In my bag.' Sadie slumped her shoulders. How had she managed to do that? 'I gave my bag to Lily to hold at the vets. It must be in Melissa's car and she's taken them out for lunch.'

'No worries. I'm sure if you give them a call, Melissa won't mind dropping them back to you.'

Sadie indicated the road. 'My phone's in my bag too.' She looked across to The Flower Shop and slumped her shoulders. 'I'd wanted to open the shop.' Just for an hour and then she'd still have had time for a nap.

'If I'm honest, judging by the dark rings around your eyes, you deserve a rest.'

'Thanks for the compliment.'

Alex smiled and laid his hand on her forearm. 'I didn't say you didn't still look beautiful. You do. I just meant you look tired. Besides, I'm pretty sure the castle's closed for some private function so you won't be missing out on passing trade if you don't open. But I'm happy to drive you to collect your bag and keys, if you'd rather? Or else you can come to my office; I haven't got any clients today. I only came in because I have a few loose ends I want to tie up.'

She felt guilty for asking him to drive her into town, besides she didn't know where Melissa and the girls would have gone in the end. But to sit in Alex's office with the way things were between them at the moment? Sadie looked at him. She needed to clear the air. *They* needed to clear the air. 'I'll come up to your office if you're sure you don't mind?'

'Of course not. Always happy to see you, you know that. Shall I grab you a coffee?'

'I'm happy with a home-made one, thanks though.'

Alex nodded and led the way up to his office.

As she stepped into the room above the barber's shop, she was surprised at how minimalistic it was but also how homely it felt. She'd expected a very manly sparse office space, but Alex had managed to decorate it in such a way as both professionalism was conveyed but also a comforting, safe space was created too. A large black desk stood next to the window with a couple of chairs strategically positioned on the other side. Besides a small leather sofa which was pushed up against the back wall, a filing cabinet and a houseplant were all that filled the room. Certificates of qualifications hung framed behind the desk, and a large black and white beach scene covered the wall behind the sofa.

'It's lovely in here.'

'Thanks. I like it.' Alex walked across to a little alcove Sadie had missed and flicked on a kettle before dropping his takeaway cup into a recycling bin.

'You really should invest in one of those reusable travel cups.'

'That's what Rachel always used to say.' Alex poured the boiling water into two black mugs. 'She was always ahead of the times.'

'She was. It was as though she was aware of the importance of recycling and anything to do with the environment before we even knew it was something to worry about.' Throughout the time when Alex and Rachel had been in a relationship, they'd always given wooden toys as gifts to Poppy and Lily. There had never even been a piece of plastic in either the toys or on the packaging. 'Do you miss her?'

Looking up, Alex looked at Sadie. 'Umm, I've not really thought about her in that way in a long time. She broke my heart at the time certainly, but I think I'm all healed now.' Banging the palm of his hand against his chest, he laughed.

Sadie nodded. She remembered Max saying as much. Alex and Rachel had always come across as the strong couple – a 'them against the world' type of couple – and it had been a shock when Max had told her they'd split up. She hadn't seen it coming at all.

'She'd been my world for the four years we were together. We'd been so tight, so together, that our lives had almost entwined. We did everything together, live, eat, exercise, we even shared an office, which had been interesting at times, what with my divorce cases and her human rights law cases.' Alex shook his head and smiled before shrugging and bringing her coffee over. 'Here, sit down. Make yourself at home.'

Slipping out of her coat, Sadie perched on the leather sofa and took her mug. 'Thanks.'

'It's weird, isn't it? That you can be so happy in a relationship one minute and then the next it's all over.'

'Yes. What happened?' Sadie shifted along as Alex sat down. 'Sorry, I shouldn't have asked. Ignore me.'

'It's okay.' Alex took a sip of coffee. 'I don't know if I'm brutally honest. I thought we were happy. We'd been talking about having children and moving out of town and then, bam, she got the travelling bug and off she went.'

'Sorry. I didn't know that.'

'That I wanted kids?' Alex smiled. 'Ever since you and Max had Lily I became broody, I thought she had too but... Anyway, about three years ago, I decided to take the plunge and ask her to marry me. I knew she'd always been dead against marriage and had always said it was just a piece of paper and didn't mean anything outside of bureaucracy, but it had felt right, you know? I'd had a good feeling that it would be the start of something good. Of us finally settling down.'

'She said no?'

'No, I didn't even get around to asking her.' Alex laughed, a hollow laugh tinged with regret. 'I'd planned a nice romantic picnic by the river – I'd even set candles up and scattered rose petals across the picnic rug. The champagne was waiting and so was I. I remember sitting there rolling the ring box between my fingers as the minutes ticked by, these dog walkers and people out for a stroll asking me what I was doing, congratulating me even, and she didn't even show. After about an hour I got a text message from her, telling me she was on a flight to the Philippines. She'd felt trapped, apparently, so she'd gone off travelling.'

Sadie looked across at him as he rubbed his chin, the stubble making a coarse noise against the skin of his hand, and gently put her hand on his knee. 'I'm so sorry. I didn't know.'

'Why would you? Of course, by then Max and I weren't speaking and our mutual friends had always been mates I'd have a laugh with rather than pour my heart out to, so you'd have no way of knowing. I didn't really tell many people at all. Of course, they knew we'd split up, but besides my family, you're the only person who I've told about planning to propose to her.'

'You and Max weren't speaking?'

'No, not after what happened when he divorced you.' Alex looked up from his coffee cup.

'What do you mean? You were his divorce solicitor, so I know you were speaking then.' Sadie shifted in her seat and turned to look at him.

'Yes, I was then. I had to, didn't I? But when he repeatedly went against my advice, I couldn't have anything to do with him. Not after he'd put me in that position.'

Taking a sip of coffee, Sadie let the bitter taste sting the back of her throat and frowned. 'I really don't understand.'

Looking across at her, Alex met her eyes before looking away and standing up. Walking to the window, he lowered his coffee cup to the windowsill and placed the palms of his hands either side. 'You have no clue, do you?'

'No clue about what?'

'No wonder you were off with me when you realised I worked here and lived up the road. No wonder you were annoyed you weren't having the fresh start you had moved for.'

'You're not making any sense.' Standing up, Sadie joined him at the window and placed her hand on his shoulder.

Pulling away, Alex glanced at her. 'You blame me. You blame me for the divorce?'

Clearing her throat, Sadie leaned against the wall. 'Not about the divorce, no. You didn't make him cheat or make him divorce me, did you?'

'No, for the way things turned out in the divorce though. You think I did all of that?'

'Well, you were his solicitor, so, yes, I know you did that.' Looking across at him, she stifled the urge to pull him into her arms. He looked broken. She suddenly noticed the permanent creases in his forehead, the downward lines at the corners of his mouth where his famous laughter lines had always taken residence. 'It's done now, though. You were just doing your job, I see that now. Yes, I did blame you. Well, no, blame is the wrong word, but I did feel betrayed by you at the time and for a long time after, if I'm honest, but seeing you again and getting to know you now, I know that's in your past. Or else I thought it was until Mr Pritchard came storming into the shop.'

'He's just a friend of my dad's, I've told you that. Anyway, what choice do I have to take on his case? If I don't, someone else will. At least if I do, I can limit the blow to his ex in as many ways possible.'

Sadie snorted and then shook her head. Maybe he was right. Maybe he was trying to do the right thing now. He was sure right that if he didn't take the case, then someone quite probably more ruthless than him would come along and gladly pull the rug from under Mr Pritchard's poor ex. She frowned and stepped forward. 'Is that what you were trying to do with Max and me?'

'Yes, that was exactly what I was trying to do. I've known Max for so long now. Long before you learnt what he was capable of, I knew. I'd watched him on numerous occasions, both on a personal level and in the courtroom. As soon as he told me you two were getting divorced, I knew I had to be working for one of you and figured I could have the most impact if I worked for him. I was trying to limit the damage, not help him. I know you can't see that and I know that's not the way it looked at the time, or now, for that matter, but believe me, I tried. I really tried. He wanted to take you to the cleaners, completely.' Alex glanced at her. 'And I know I shouldn't say that. I know it will hurt you to hear that, but if I don't, then I know we're over. If I'm not totally honest with you now, then I know I've lost my chance with you.'

'You're wrong. It doesn't hurt. As soon as I found out he'd been seeing Tara all that time behind my back, I saw who he really was. It was you who surprised me.'

'I'm sorry. I thought I was doing the right thing. I knew you'd hate me but I figured that would be worth it if I could limit the damage to you, financially I mean. I knew I couldn't help you any other way, but I wanted to do something.' Walking back to the sofa, he sank into the cushions before leaning forward and clasping his hands between his knees. 'It kind of backfired.'

'So, the divorce settlement didn't come out the way you wanted? I know I got to keep the house and me and the girls got to live there...'

'But you also got zero from his pension and minimal from his savings... I know you've been struggling. I could see that you would be. I bet you were even struggling to pay the mortgage on that place when you were teaching full-time?'

'It wasn't easy.'

'That wasn't the plan, you know. I'd set out a provisional settlement and then he pulled me off the case. He got someone else to draw more papers up at the last minute. It wasn't me.'

Slowly picking up her mug again, Sadie gripped it between her hands, standing stock-still. 'What do you mean? He told me you were ill and that other bloke, I can't remember his name, was standing in for you.'

'Hornton, Eliott Hornton. No, he was the one who Max employed after me.'

'Okay. Okay.' Lowering herself next to Max, she looked at him as he continued to stare at the floor. 'Why didn't you tell me?'

'Honestly?' Leaning back, Alex looked at Sadie properly for the first time since their conversation had begun. 'It's taken me this long to work out why you hated me.'

'Really?'

'Yep, really. How pathetic is that?'

Sadie scrunched up her nose. 'It's not pathetic at all. You probably didn't know that Max hadn't told me that other bloke had taken over from you, did you?'

'No, I didn't. I just assumed you were off me because I had been acting against you, to begin with. I only found out through Luke how little he left you with. I'm sorry.'

Focusing on one of Alex's simply framed certificates, Sadie chewed on her bottom lip. He hadn't known. All this time, Alex hadn't realised why she'd been acting the way she had. Moving her focus across to him, she laced her hand across his, still clasped between his knees. 'I'm sorry. I didn't realise. I must have seemed really awful to you when we first met again. And at Angela and Darryl's wedding!'

'It's fine. I'm just sorry I couldn't have done more to protect you and the girls from the fallout of your divorce.'

'Hey.' Taking her hand, she placed it on his cheek and gently turned him to face her. 'The only person that has anything to apologise for is Max. Not you. Even if it had been you who had been advising Max during the divorce, it wouldn't have been your fault. I see that now. Besides, it wasn't you, so you doubly have nothing to apologise for.'

Looking her in the eye, Alex nodded slowly. 'I am sorry for the way it's worked out though and for my part in it.'

Sadie smiled. 'I'm now in a position to be doing what I've always dreamt of. I'm running my own florist, we're living in a nice little village and I've met someone I'm very happy with, thank you very much.' Leaning forward, Sadie kissed Alex, his lips warm against hers.

'I'm happy with you too.' His words tickled her lips as he spoke.

'Mum? Are you up there?'

Pulling away, Sadie pecked him on the lips briefly and stood up. 'They must have realised I'd left my keys.'

14

'Wow, this is so awesome! And we can really go that way? We're allowed?' Poppy looked back at Alex as he held the red velvet rope up for her.

'We sure can.' Looking across at Sadie, Alex grinned and indicated her to follow Lily and Poppy under the rope.

'Umm, allowed or turning a blind eye?'

'They're the same thing, aren't they?' Laughing, Alex looked back at the castle's curator, who was sat dozing in the corner of the vast ornate dining hall.

Sadie grinned. The girls were loving going on a proper adventure around the castle. Alex had said he knew a couple of the curators who worked there and would take them all to see some of the more private, more secretive locations around the castle, the places usually off-limits to the general public. Lily was enjoying the taste of rebellion, but poor Poppy, who had always had strong morals, was a little more cautious. Sadie was sure the poor girl thought the armed police would tap them on the shoulder at any moment.

'This way.' Taking the lead, Alex led them past the long, beautifully laid out table towards the far corner. A large door loomed in front of them, which he swiftly avoided and instead tapped a corner of the wood panelling, which to the girls' amazement swung open to reveal a narrow corridor.

'We can go in there?' Poppy's eyes widened.

'Yep. Here.' Swinging the rucksack from his back, Alex rummaged around and pulled out four torches and passed them around. 'You'll need these. This is a secret passageway built on the instructions of one of the Lords a couple of hundred years ago.'

'That's awesome! Why don't they tell you about it when you visit the castle?' Taking a torch, Lily turned it on, lighting the narrow passage behind the panelling.

'They do. Normally people aren't allowed to come down here though.'

'So how come we are?'

'Because you're with me.' Alex winked. 'Honestly, it's fine. They don't mind a few people at a time, but imagine if the crowds of tourists all wanted to come to these little places all at once. It wouldn't be safe either for the people or for the castle.'

'I guess. It's definitely okay then? We're not breaking the law?'

'No, we're not. It's all good. Why don't you girls go on ahead and we'll follow?'

'Okay. Come on, Poppy.' Lily didn't need any more encouragement and surged ahead through the narrow passageway.

Looking back, Alex held out his hand to Sadie.

Taking Alex's hand, Sadie allowed herself to be led down the passageway. Although they hadn't officially come out and told Lily and Poppy that they were now dating, Alex had been spending more and more time at The Flower Shop since their big talk at the weekend. He'd popped by for a quick chat on Monday and had ended up staying for dinner. Then the next day, Lily had needed some help with her homework when he'd popped into The Flower Shop with a coffee for Sadie, so he'd happily helped her research the Kings and Queens of England while she'd closed up and counted the till out with Poppy. It had been nice. The four of them had stood around at the counter, history books, coins and receipts sprawled across the wooden surface. Really nice.

Sadie gripped tighter, her fingers laced together within Alex's strong grasp. Looking ahead, Sadie could see the girls were too busy chatting excitedly and forging down the passageway to notice her and Alex were holding hands. Not that they'd mind. She actually thought they'd be happy for her, happy that she had found love again, especially as they got on so well with him, but it was far too early in their relationship for them to be anything but friends in Lily and Poppy's eyes. No, she needed to be completely sure, or as certain as she could be, that he'd be sticking around for a good while before they found out about them.

'You okay?' Looking back, Alex whispered.

'Yes, I'm good, thanks. Thank you for this. The girls are loving it.'

'You're very welcome.' Grinning, Alex turned to face forward again just as Poppy's shriek penetrated the silence.

'What's the matter, Poppy? Are you okay?' Pushing ahead, Sadie ran towards Lily and Poppy, Alex following closely behind.

'It's just a spider,' Lily answered, the rolling of her eyes evident in her voice.

'Is that what it is? A spider?'

'Yes, sorry. I saw something hanging down in front of me and I thought it was a ghost, but it was just a spider.'

'Or was it the ghost of a spider?'

'Lily! Don't tease her.'

'We must be close to the end of the passageway now. When you get to the end, if you turn left, there's a flight of stairs up and then you'll see where we come out. Just go carefully because they're very steep and very narrow.' Alex shone his torch ahead of them.

'Where does it go if we go right?' Lily swung her torch back.

'It'll just take you to a door back to the dining hall.'

'Where does the other way take us?'

'You'll have to wait and see. Trust me, you'll love it.'

'You're not taking us to the dungeons, are you?' Poppy's voice shook a little.

'He said the stairs take us up, not down. Dungeons are down.' Lily's voice was tinged with exasperation.

'We can always go to the dungeons next, if you like?'

'Yes! Can we?'

'No, I don't want to.'

'Don't be a scaredy-cat, Poppy. The dungeons will be ultra-cool.'

'One vote for and one against. Looks like your mum's got the deciding vote,' Alex laughed.

'Let's see what the time is when we've been to this part first, shall we?'

'Now that sounds like a very sensible idea.'

* * *

'I think my legs are going to fall off.' Poppy turned and looked behind her.

'I think mine are too, Poppy. Keep going though, we must be almost there?' Sadie looked down at Alex.

'Not much further now.'

'Oh, I can see something. Does it lead us outside?' With a dose of adrenalin at nearing the top, Poppy quickened her pace and soon they were at the top of the narrow stone staircase. Ahead of them stood a narrow door, the moonlight had been coming from an arrow slit positioned to the left of the door. 'The door's locked.'

'It's a good job I have the key then.' Pulling a large rusty key from his back pocket, Alex weaved his way to the front. 'Okay, now go careful when you step out. It'll take us out on top of the tower so we're very high up. There is a parapet, a wall running around it, but it's quite low so be careful, use your torches because it's dark now, and stay away from the edge.' Unlocking the door, he held it open.

Moonlight swathed the dark staircase with light, and Sadie followed Lily and Poppy out into the night.

'It feels as though we're up in the sky! Look at the stars!' Leaning her head back, Poppy slowly turned around, staring at the sky above them.

'It's beautiful. Ooh, I've got that stargazing app on my mobile. I bet we can use that to work out what constellations we can see.' Lily pulled her phone from the pocket of her coat and swiped through, opened the app and held the phone above her, aligning the stars in the sky to the ones on her screen.

'That's a really good idea, Lily, sweetheart. What does it say?' Sadie made her way towards Lily and peered at the phone screen.

'I think that's the Orion up there. Is that right?'

'Yes, I think you're right. Well done. It's beautiful, isn't it?'

'It sure is and, look, I bet that's another constellation up there where those three stars are grouped together, don't you think?'

'I think you might be right.'

'Can I see?'

Stepping back, Sadie watched as Lily showed Poppy the stars and taught her the constellations. 'Wow, this really is a hit. Poppy and Lily talking and sharing something?' She turned towards Alex and grinned. 'Thank you for this. It's really special.'

'You're very welcome. I love it up here. I've even been known to bring some case notes up in the summer to work on if I've got a particularly difficult case. There's something about being on top of the world that helps me clear my head and focus.'

'I can see why. I bet you can see for miles in the daylight.'

'You sure can. I'll bring you all up again during the day one weekend. I do think it's beautiful at night too though.'

'Definitely.' Tilting her head back, Sadie took in the almost full moon and the stars sparkling like glitter upon black velvet. It reminded her how tiny they were, how minuscule against everything else. It was a good feeling. A feeling of being part of something bigger.

'Who fancies some hot chocolate?' Alex pulled out a stack of plastic beakers and a flask from his rucksack.

'Wow, you really have thought of everything.'

15

'...and then we had hot chocolate up there on the top of the tower. It was epic!' Poppy grasped the phone and tilted her head, nodding at whatever the person on the other end was saying. 'Okay, bye.'

'Everything okay, Poppy, sweetheart?' Flattening the cardboard box she'd just emptied, Sadie walked past her daughter behind the counter.

'Yes, it was Dad. He's going to pick us up a bit later tomorrow. About half five, I think he said, so we need to have dinner here. Is that okay?'

'Of course, it's okay. This is your home!' However much Max messed them around, Sadie wanted Lily and Poppy to know that this was their home. That was the main reason she never refused Max's pleas for changes to access. She didn't want the girls to feel they were being pushed from pillar to post, she wanted them to know this was their home at all times. Yes, they had another home with him, Tara and the twins, but they needed to know they could come and go from The Flower Shop whenever they wanted or needed. Much to Melissa's disgust, who felt Sadie was just letting Max to walk all over her. Sadie shrugged, she didn't really care what it looked like to other people, she was just trying to do the right thing for her girls. 'You'd best hurry up and brush your hair if you're going to catch the school bus on time.'

'I know. I will.' Poppy put down her mobile on the counter and looked across at her mum. 'Can you do it? I really want plaits. You know the pigtails like Matilda? Susie at school has started wearing them and they look really nice.'

'Yes, of course. Have you got the hairbrush?'

'Yep.' Poppy passed Sadie the brush and turned her back on her. 'Can I go to the track with Ed and Harry next weekend? They're planning on going for the day. Well, they're going this weekend too, but I'll be at Dad's, so can I definitely go next weekend?'

'Is Harry's dad going to be there?' Sadie began brushing Poppy's long brown hair, starting at the ends to try to detangle it. 'You didn't comb it through after your shower last night, did you?'

'Umm, I might have forgotten. Yes, I think so at least. He normally does.'

'Okay, if Harry's dad is definitely going to be there, you can. Although we'll have to check the weather first.'

'Awesome. Thanks.' Poppy squirmed and pulled her head away. 'Ouch! That hurt.'

Wrapping her arms around Poppy's shoulders, Sadie kissed the top of her head. 'Sorry, I didn't mean to catch you. Although if you remembered to comb it through with that wide-tooth comb I bought you, it wouldn't get so knotty.'

'I know. I'll try to remember next time.'

'That's my girl. Did Daddy say what you're doing this weekend?'

'It's Toby and Tammy's birthday tomorrow and he said something about a party.'

'Of course, it is. I'll pop out at lunchtime and pick up a present for them from you two.'

'No, it's cool. Dad said he's already got something from us for them.'

'Right.' Sadie shrugged as she began plaiting Poppy's now tangle-free hair. It was normally her job to pick something up from Lily and Poppy, but if he'd done it anyway, there wouldn't be much point. Maybe she could just grab a card and a little something each for them from her. 'A party sounds good. Where is it?'

'I think it's at theirs. They're hiring a bouncy castle although he said it's not just a kid's party, their friends are going too and there will be some kids mine and Lily's age.'

'Wow, sounds like it'll be really fun then.'

'Yes, I think so.'

Wrapping the second hairband around the end of the second plait, Sadie patted Poppy's shoulders. 'There you go, all done.'

'Thanks. Do they look okay?' Pulling one of the plaits across her shoulder, Poppy inspected it.

'You look beautiful, as always. Now go and pop your shoes on and I'll grab my coat.'

'You don't need to walk me to the bus stop, you know. I *am* old enough.'

Sadie smiled. 'I know, but I like to see that you've got there. It gives me a little walk too, gets me out in the fresh air for a few minutes. Don't worry, I'll leave you at the corner.'

'Okay. You wouldn't need to if Lily let me walk with her and Georgia.' Pulling her school shoes on, Poppy shrugged into her coat and picked up her bag.

'I know, but like I said I like the walk, and it's nice to have Poppy and Mummy time.'

'I guess.'

'Oi!' Laughing, Sadie pulled open the door, and they stepped into the brisk cold spring air.

* * *

'Sadie?' Alex's voice floated through to the back room.

Tying the ribbon on the bouquet, Sadie picked it up and followed Alex's voice through to the shop floor. 'Hi, sorry I was just finishing up this. What do you think? It's a birthday bouquet for the barber's wife next door.'

'Wow, that looks awesome. Who knew you were so talented?'

'Hey!' Opening her mouth in mock horror, Sadie laughed.

'No, it really is beautiful. Rather like its creator.' Alex leaned over the counter.

Leaning forward, Sadie grinned as their lips touched, his cold from being outside and hers a little cool too from being in the back room. 'You're cold. And that was a really cheesy line you know.'

Straightening up, Alex fixed his tie. 'You don't think I can pull off cheese? Even in my suit?'

'Especially not in your suit!' Laughing, Sadie eyed the paper bags laid on the counter. 'Have you been to the café by any chance?'

'I sure have. I've got you a brie and cranberry toasted panini, that's the one you like, isn't it? And I've got myself the same because it smelt so good as Beryl was making yours.'

'Yum. Thank you. I could get used to this!'

'You're more than welcome.' Passing Sadie over a coffee takeaway cup, Alex rummaged in the bags and pulled out the two paninis. 'How are things here?'

'Good. Really good. You're lucky you've come in a lull. It's been really busy today.'

'I think the castle has some craft fair or something going on?'

'Yes, a medieval craft fair, apparently. Sounds fun. I might take the girls up after school if the shop gets any quieter, if you want to tag along? Max isn't picking them up until a bit later, so we should have time for a quick look.'

'Sounds like a good plan. I've got a meeting with Mr Pritchard in half an hour, hence the tie with the suit today.' Alex rolled his eyes. 'But it shouldn't go on for too long. Hopefully. Although I am planning on telling him a few home truths so it might finish even earlier than I expect.'

'Home truths?'

'Yes, I know he's my dad's mate and everything, but I've tried so hard to hint and steer him in the right direction to leave his soon to be ex-wife more than a pittance, which in my view she deserves simply for putting up with him this long, but he's not been taking any of it on board and still wants to take her to the cleaners.'

'He really isn't a very nice person.'

'That's putting it mildly. I want to stay representing him just to attempt to limit the fallout, but at this rate, he's going to sack me anyway.'

'You can only try your best. I reckon she's probably better off without him even if she ends up living in a shed.'

'You're right. I know you're right, but I still feel bad.' Putting down his panini, Alex ran the palm of his hand across his stubble. 'I just wish I could do more for her.'

'I know you do, but you're trying. Any other solicitor wouldn't be even attempting to make the divorce fair, they'd just be doing exactly what Thomas Pritchard asked them to without any questions asked.' Sadie walked around the counter and pulled him towards her.

'I guess so.' Wrapping his arms around her, he placed his lips on her forehead. 'Any plans for the weekend?'

'Working tomorrow and I think Melissa is popping by, but nothing apart from that. Do you fancy doing something?'

'Absolutely. Maybe we could escape to the beach again on Sunday or something?'

'That sounds perfect.'

'That's what I thought. I know it'll likely be cold again, but it'll still be nice to get away. Or else we could spend the day binge-watching films and eating copious amounts of chocolate and takeaways?'

'Umm, they both sound good options. Shall we go with the flow and just see what the weather's like?'

'Perfect.' Reaching down, he cupped Sadie's chin, gently leaning her face towards his and kissed her.

* * *

Pulling open the door to The Flower Shop, Sadie embraced the rush of warm air escaping into the lane. 'Quick, in you go before you let all the heat out.'

'I love this, Mum.' Lily unfolded the fabric in her hands to reveal the castle's shield printed on the other side. 'It'll look really good on my wall above my bed, won't it?'

'It will.' Sadie shut the door behind them before pulling her gloves off and rubbing her hands together. 'I think that was a really good buy.'

'Do you like mine too?' Poppy pulled two beeswax candles from a small striped paper bag she was holding.

'Yes, they'll smell ever so nice when they're lit.'

'Can I light one now?'

'Umm, yes, why not? Daddy is coming in a few minutes, but there will still be time to see what it smells like. There are some matches in the cupboard above the kettle in the back room. You can always take one to Daddy's house?' Too late, Poppy had already disappeared to find the matches.

'Tara wouldn't let us have anything like that at hers. I mean at hers and Dad's.'

'How come?'

Lily shrugged. 'She just doesn't like things, you know homely things, she likes it all proper.'

'Proper?'

'Yes, no, you know what I mean.'

'Uncluttered?'

'Yes, but not just uncluttered, she doesn't like anything homely. Even the twins have to put their toys away straight away and keep them in the playroom.'

'She's got them more trained than I had you two then!' Sadie laughed.

'Not in a good way, though. I remember I used to love being able to leave my toys out mid-game so I could carry on playing the next day. Do you remember that time you let me and Poppy leave that den up in the living room in the old house when we went to Dad's for the weekend?'

'Yes, I remember. I had to squash onto one cushion on the sofa to watch TV so I didn't mess it up.' Sadie laughed. 'Actually, I think Melissa had come round that weekend for a takeaway and a catch-up and we'd had to sit on the floor.'

Lily grinned. 'See, it was homely. And it is here now. Not cluttered, just homely, but Tara likes things just-so and there's no way she'd ever let Poppy use a candle.'

'Got them!' Poppy came back through brandishing the small box of matches. 'Shall I light it in here?'

'Yes, pop it on the counter, it'll make the shop smell nice.' Drawing Lily in for a hug, Sadie kissed the top of her head before going across and helping Poppy light the candle.

With Sadie's guidance, Poppy lit it and took a deep breath. 'It smells lovely, doesn't it? All honey-like.'

'Yum, yes it does. I think you both found some really good things at that craft fair.'

'I like craft fairs, can we go to another one?'

'Of course.'

'Can Alex come again too? He always treats us.' Poppy grinned and wiped at a stray piece of ketchup on the collar of her coat from the burgers he'd insisted on buying.

'I'm sure he will, but next time we'll make sure *we* treat him to dinner. How about that?'

'Yes, okay.'

A tap on the glass made them jump. 'That must be Daddy now.' Although it was unusual that he hadn't just beeped the car horn or rang or texted Lily. It wasn't like him to collect them at the door any more, which could only mean two things – he was in a particularly good mood or he had something to talk to her about.

'Hi, Dad.' Lily pulled the door open and stood back as Max stepped inside.

'Hello, girls. Hello, Sadie.' Max glanced around the shop. 'Do you mind if we have a quick word?'

'Okay. Why don't you two run upstairs and grab your bags?' Sadie watched as Lily and Poppy made their way up through the door up to the flat before turning to face him. 'Has something happened?'

'I just wanted a quick word about Alex.'

'Alex?' What did Alex have to do with Max? 'I didn't even think you two were close friends any more?'

'No, we're not.' Max looked down at the floor and shifted on his feet.

'Right.' What was he trying to say?

Looking back up, Max met Sadie's eye. 'Poppy mentioned that you'd all been hanging around with Alex. I just don't think it's wise you getting involved with him and the girls spending so much time with him.'

Sadie crossed her arms. Why on earth would it bother him? He used to be best mates with Alex. The girls had spent plenty of time around him when she and Max had been together. Of course, that was it, wasn't it? He didn't want her, or more importantly, Lily or Poppy, finding out about how much Max had screwed her over in the divorce. He didn't want their image of him to be anything less than perfect. 'I know what this is about.'

'I just don't think it's wise to bring someone else into the girls' lives, not when they've had so much change recently. Between moving to the village and you running a shop, it's a lot for anyone to adjust to, let alone kids. And now, you and Alex...' Max waved his hand, indicating Sadie. 'When he walks away, it'll just be more upheaval for them.'

Clasping her hands together, Sadie blinked back the tears which had begun to sting the back of her eyes. 'I think you'll find it has been you who has caused the most upheaval in the girls' lives.'

'There's no need to get personal. That was a long time ago. Why bring that up now?'

Taking a deep breath, Sadie tried to slow her breathing. She didn't need an argument. She didn't want to allow him to belittle her and she really couldn't just stand there and accept what he was accusing her of. 'Both Lily and Poppy are settled here now, they're enjoying the village life and both have friends close by. Running this place is allowing me to spend a lot more time with them. Not that I have to justify my life decisions to you any more, at all, but we have a much better work-life balance than we ever used to. If you'll remember when you left, I was forced to go back to work full-time in order to pay the extremely high mortgage rates on the house, which was extremely difficult as you are probably aware, and now...'

Max held up his hand, palm forward. 'You're right, you don't need to justify yourself to me, I'm merely trying to look out for our girls.'

Gritting her teeth, Sadie shook her head. He was happy turning a blind eye when life was tough on both her and the children, but now things were looking up and actually better than they ever had been, he was trying to stick his oar in? 'Max, I can't and I won't have this conversation any longer. I can do what I want and see who I wish. You have no hold over me. If it's the fact that you don't want me to find out what games you played to screw me over in the divorce, well, I'm sorry, I already know. If it's the fact that you don't want Lily or Poppy to find out and look at you differently because, let's face it, your actions affected them the most, then rest assured, I'm not going to tell them. I love those girls and I don't want to hurt them.'

Whistling through his teeth, Max looked away and then back to Sadie again. 'Thank you.'

'Don't thank me. The reason I won't tell them has nothing to do with you, it's for them. Everything I do is for them. And if I want to spend time with a guy who I know is a decent person and makes me and the girls smile, then I will.'

'Right. Okay. Thanks.' Max mumbled and checked his watch. 'I appreciate you not telling the girls, it was a long time ago and I'm not that person any more.'

Sadie flared her nostrils. He wasn't that person any more? Who was he kidding? Not that it mattered.

'Not tell me and Poppy what?' The door opened and Lily dumped her rucksack at Sadie's feet before dropping to the floor and tying the laces on her bright white trainers.

'Nothing, sweetheart.'

'No, what? There was something. I heard.' Lily glanced up at her mum.

'It's just something your dad has planned for tomorrow. A surprise at the twins' birthday party.'

'Oh, right? Like a clown or something? As if me or Poppy are going to be interested in that! It's baby stuff.' Lily shrugged her shoulders and shifted to tying the other lace. 'Actually, Poppy probably would like it.'

'Thank you.' Max mouthed across Lily's slumped body.

Sadie narrowed her eyes and shook her head. Again, keeping quiet hadn't been for his benefit. What was the point? He was always going to be egotistically self-centred, however much she explained her actions.

'What have you got for me? What's the surprise?' Poppy bounded through the door from the flat.

'Nothing. Just a stupid clown at the party, that's all.' Lily stood up and grabbed her rucksack again.

'A clown? Wow, that's cool.'

'There is no clown. It's not a clown. We're having a bouncy castle.' Max held out his hands to take Lily and Poppy's rucksacks.

'Oh, awesome.' Poppy wrapped her arms around Sadie. 'Love you, Mum.'

'Love you too, sweetheart. Have a lovely time, won't you?'

'Yep, I will. And I'll try not to eat too much birthday cake and throw up like last year.'

'Now, that would be good.' Kissing her on top of her head, Sadie released Poppy and turned towards Lily. 'You okay?'

'Yep.'

'Good. You have a lovely time too, won't you? Enjoy the party. There won't be anyone from school, so you can try to let your hair down and enjoy yourself. Show the little ones what cool moves you have on the bouncy castle, okay?'

'Umm.'

'Okay, love you, Lily.'

'Love you too, Mum.' Squeezing Sadie's shoulders, Lily stepped back.

'Not so quick.' Pulling her towards her again, Sadie kissed the top of her head before Lily escaped again. 'Have a good time, both of you. Love you both.' Following them to the front door, Sadie stood and watched as they all piled into Max's car and set off down the road. Picking up her coat from where she'd dumped it on the counter earlier, she stepped into the cold air and pulled her phone out. If ever she needed a nice gin and tonic in front of the roaring fire at the local pub, it was now. 'Hi, Alex, what are you up to?'

16

'Thank you. Have a lovely day.' Sadie smiled as a family of castle tourists left the shop, pinning their lavender posies onto their coats.

'I've said it before and I'll say it again, that's some mean marketing you've done there linking to the castle's theme of the time.' Melissa pushed Sadie's coffee mug across towards her before resting her elbows on the counter and her chin on her hands.

'Why, thank you.' Sadie grinned. 'Are you actually comfortable like that?'

'Not really. You need to get a bar stool or something so I can perch in a bit more comfort.'

'That's actually not a bad idea. I'll have a look on the local selling pages.'

'Awesome. I'll take a look too.' Melissa pulled her mobile from her back pocket and set it down on the counter. 'Sooo?'

'So?'

'So, how are things with you and Alex going?' Tilting her head, Melissa looked at Sadie and laughed. 'I knew it! You've got that soppy smile on your face at the mere mention of his name! Things are going well, I assume?'

Sadie held the palms of her hands against her cheeks. 'I don't know what you mean! Yes, things are going well.'

'And...'

'And what?'

'Details! I want some details.'

Sadie shrugged. 'There's not much to tell, just that I'm really happy. He makes me happy. He's the first person since me and Max split up that I've actually thought I might be able to make a future with. I don't know if it's because I already know him, so I haven't got that niggling worry about whether he's safe or has a history of being an armed robber or anything, but it feels good. The girls love spending time with him and he always goes the extra mile too. Like he took us behind the scenes in the castle and had brought hot chocolate for us all.'

'Aww, that's really sweet.'

'It is. He is.' Sadie picked up her coffee mug, wrapping her hands around the warm ceramic. 'I'm not getting my hopes up though, I know it's super early days and we're probably only getting on so well because we used to be good friends, so it all might just turn out to be a friendship rather than anything else.'

'Girl! Stop that! You always put a dampener on everything.'

'I'm just being realistic. I don't want to get my hopes up and get my heart broken, that's all.'

'And that's the problem with you and relationships. You never jump, you need to trust and jump in. Let's be honest, you're smitten already so if things don't work out you're likely to get your heart broken anyway. So it's no different if you trust him and jump in. The only difference is that it's more likely to work if you let him in.'

'I guess so.'

'You know so. Yes, a lot of the guys you've dated since breaking up with Max have been complete weirdos, but a couple haven't. Think about Matthew, for example, he was nice, really sweet, but you didn't let him in and he got fed up of waiting.'

'I'm not just going to introduce the girls to anyone and everyone though, am I?'

'No, but he was a teacher, so he was used to kids and you'd dated him for seven months and he still hadn't even been round to your house even when the girls were at Max's.'

'I know, but... I don't know.'

'The good thing with Alex is...' Melissa picked up her mug and pointed it at Sadie before taking a sip. 'He knows you, he knows the girls. He's immersed in your family already and going by what you said he told you about the divorce, he's got your best interests at heart. He wants you to be happy.'

'Umm.'

'Jump, Sadie. Just jump and see where it takes you.'

'I don't know.'

'I do.' Melissa glanced behind her as the bell above the door tinkled, announcing someone's arrival. 'And this is the perfect time.'

'Hi, Alex.' Stepping slightly to the right, Sadie tried to hide a little behind a large display of lilies to camouflage the heat cascading across her face.

'Hi, how're things going? Have you recovered from last night?'

'Last night?' Melissa raised her eyebrows.

'We went to the pub. And I'm fine. I didn't have that much to drink.'

Melissa straightened her back. 'Why don't you two go and grab lunch? I'll look after the shop.'

'It's barely eleven!'

'Well, go for a coffee or a walk or something. I want to play at being a florist.' Walking behind the counter, Melissa picked up Sadie's coat and threw it at her.

'Okay. Are you sure?'

'Go.' Melissa pulled a spare apron over her head and waved them away.

'Is she always so bossy?' Alex laughed as they turned the corner of Serendipity Lane onto the High Street.

'You know she is. You've known her long enough.'

'That's true.' Turning around, Alex took her hand in his, their fingers slotting together perfectly. 'Do you fancy grabbing a coffee and then going for a walk around the castle grounds?'

'Sounds like a great idea.' The tune of her ringtone rang from her pocket and Sadie slipped her hand from Alex's and answered it. 'Hello... right... okay... thanks, bye.'

'Everything okay?'

'Yes, I think so. It was the dog warden. No one's come forward to claim Buddy so he'll either go to a rescue centre and be rehomed or, because we expressed an interest in him, he can come live with us. We'll need to be approved by the rescue centre first and Buddy's details will still be on the Lost Dog's register so his owners still might come forward...'

'What are you going to do?'

Sadie patted her phone against the palm of her other hand. 'I don't think I have much choice. I'm going to have to see if we can be approved to rehome him. Can you imagine what Lily and Poppy would say if I didn't at least try?'

'Do you want to then?'

'Yes, I think so. I've always wanted a dog or a cat or something. It was always Max who wouldn't allow it, and then after we'd split I spent so long either at work or working from home that there was no way we could get one. Now life's a bit less fast-paced I think it would be nice. Yes, I think it's the right time.'

'There are so many places for nice walks around here too.'

'Exactly. Of course, whether we'll actually pass the rehoming assessment, I'm not so sure.'

'Did they give you a date when they'd come round and check everything?'

'The dog warden said the rehoming centre is pretty maxed out, so they'd probably be willing to try and fit the assessment in pretty soon so Buddy doesn't have to stay at the centre very long. He's given me a number to ring.'

'Why don't you give them a call? At least then you'll know how long you've got to figure everything out.'

'Yes, I guess so.' Sadie glanced down at her phone before grimacing and taking a step away to ring them. Alex was right, it would be better to get an appointment booked.

* * *

'Well?'

'They have a slot for late afternoon.' Sadie chewed at her bottom lip.

'What day?'

'Today!'

'Today? Wow, they don't hang about, do they?' Alex rubbed his hand across his chin.

'No, they don't. She said they haven't really got the room to take him in, although, obviously, they would find the space if they needed to, but she offered today. And I said yes.'

'Right, okay. Don't worry, it'll be okay. I haven't got any clients this afternoon so I can help, and Melissa's here too. What is there to sort out?'

'I'm not sure, really. I need to get a dog gate for the arch leading into the back room so that he can stay downstairs with me when the girls are at school, and I'll need to grab a dog bed or something and food and bowls and all of that.'

'Won't it be worth waiting until you've been given the go-ahead first?'

'Maybe. Yes, probably. Oh, and I need to sort something with that outside area, so he has access to some outdoor space during the day.' Sadie ran her fingers through her hair, tugging at the knots that had seemingly appeared from nowhere. 'I need to check that I can fence off my little bit first. I'm going to have to postpone it. I'll need to get in touch with the council and ask them, and they won't be in until Monday, and that will be if I can reach the right person straight away, and if they don't need to do any research to find out. I've been too rash, haven't I? I'll have to ring them back.'

Turning to Sadie, Alex took her hands in his. 'Hold on. We can do this. You, Melissa and me, we can work together. Patrick from the barber's shop only got his outside patch done last year, and I looked through the deeds for him as a favour. There was nothing to stop him from fencing it off, so yours will be the same. The couple running the patisserie are planning on doing theirs too before the summer and the wool shop have already done theirs. All we'll need is a few fence posts and some fencing wire, and I can have them up before the assessor comes. I can always put in proper fence panels another time if you want.'

'Really? I can't ask you to do that.'

'You're not asking me, I'm offering. If you want me to, that is.'

'Well, yes, that would be amazing, if you're really sure you don't mind?'

'I don't. Right, come on then, let's grab my car and pop to the DIY place, we can grab everything we need from there.'

* * *

'Hey, Buddy out of my pizza, mate!' Luke swooshed Buddy's nose away from the open pizza box as he sat on the floor of Sadie's living room and took a swig from his beer bottle. 'Although to be fair, I probably couldn't tell him off with a face like that even if he ate the whole thing.'

'Is he cute? Do you think it's time we got another one?' Melissa leaned forward on the sofa and wrapped her arms around Luke's shoulders.

'No chance. We have enough furry beings in our lives already.' Laughing, Luke ruffled Buddy's ears.

Pouting, Melissa sank back against the sofa cushions. 'What do you think the girls will say?'

'I don't know. I can't wait for them to come home tomorrow. They don't have a clue.' Sadie grinned.

'It'll be a great surprise. They'll love it.' Melissa reached over and picked up another slice of pepperoni pizza.

'Yes, they will. Thanks again for helping, you guys.' As she leaned in against Alex, who was sitting to her left, she smiled. Luke had come across on his break from the salon and between him and Alex they'd got the fence up in record time. Yes, it didn't look particularly great and would never withstand a hurricane, but it would do a good enough job for now. That was exactly how the assessor, a lovely lady named Margo, had described it too. She'd said it would allow Buddy the outdoor space between walks, and once told that it had only been put in earlier, she'd said it showed that Buddy would be well cared for, loved and was wanted. Within the space of a couple of hours, the place had been assessed and Buddy had been dropped off.

'Right, what film are we going to watch?' Luke pointed the remote control at the TV and looked back at them.

17

'Buddy, get down. Look, go and play with your toys.' Gently lifting his big paws off the dog gate, Sadie ruffled Buddy's fur as he lowered his paws to the floor. 'That's it. Well done, Buds.'

'So Poppy and Lily were happy to see him here then when they got back from Max's?' Melissa doodled on a discarded receipt.

'Yes, they were made up! It's been difficult getting Poppy to go to school for the past few days because she's just wanted to be at home with him. I think I'll be a size twelve by summer though, going by the amount of walks we've been taking him on! That's the only way I've been able to get her into school without her getting upset about leaving him – a walk in the morning before the bus and a walk once I've shut up The Flower Shop. Plus, I walk him at lunchtimes too.'

'Wow, you will be then! Poppy usually loves school, doesn't she?'

'Normally, and she still comes home buzzing. I think it's just the fact she's worried about him getting out and us losing him.'

'Oh, bless her, she thinks he escaped from his old home then and that's why Lily found him?'

'Yes. I've tried to tell her that normally when dogs are lost the owners get in contact with the dog warden and register them as missing, so if they get found the dog warden can find them on the system, but I think she's just got in her head that he was lost and he's going to get lost again.' Sadie placed the posy she'd just arranged aside and picked up some more lavender. 'Anyway, you seem to be spending more and more time here and less time at home. Not that I'm complaining, it's lovely having you come over on your days off, but is there something you're avoiding?'

'Well...' Melissa placed the pen next to the doodle covered receipt and stretched her arms above her head. 'My neighbour is being a pain again. If he knows we're in, he's knocking on the door every two minutes complaining about something or other; the dogs barking, the fencing bowing if there's the slightest bit of wind even though it's his fence and his responsibility to fix, the list goes on.'

'I bet you can't wait for your house sale to go through?'

'No, I really can't. Really, can't wait.'

'Any news yet?'

'Nope, nothing. There's someone along the chain having some issues with the house they're buying, I believe, so it looks like we'll likely be stuck with Mr Annoying Neighbour for a few months yet.'

'Just think though, you'll be in your new house by the summer. That'll be lovely.'

Melissa slumped her arms across the counter. 'Oh, I hope so. That would be absolute bliss.'

'Can you just keep an eye here while I grab some more flowers from the back room, please?'

'Yes, of course.'

Unlocking and slipping through the dog gate, Sadie was immediately welcomed by Buddy, who jumped up and laid his paws against her knees. 'Hey, you. Why don't you play with some of your new toys?' Bending down, she retrieved a stuffed elephant and a rope of plastic sausages from underneath the workbench. 'Here you go.'

What was it she'd come in for? That was it, some more of the lilies, there'd been a bit of a rush of customers earlier, and for some reason, the mix of yellow and white lilies had gone down a treat.

'Sadie, quick, come out here.' Melissa peered through to the back room.

Gathering up the lilies, Sadie hurried through the gate to join Melissa behind the counter.

'You recognise her?'

'Who?'

'The woman leaning her bike on the lamppost opposite.' Melissa used the pen to point as a woman wearing jeans and a flowery cardie took off her cycling helmet, a cascade of red hair falling across her shoulders.

'No, I don't think so.'

'Hold on, wait until those people have gone past and look again. Forget red hair, imagine blonde…'

'Wow!'

'And there you have it.'

'It's Rachel, isn't it? Alex's ex? The one who ran off on the night he was planning to propose and broke his heart?'

Lowering the pen, Melissa looked across at Sadie. 'Really? I never knew that. He never said anything about proposing.'

Sadie shrugged. She probably shouldn't have told Melissa that. 'He didn't tell many people.'

'Huh?'

'Where's she gone now?' Walking towards the front of the shop, Sadie peered out of the window.

'Probably next door to see Alex.'

'You think she knows he works in the village?'

'I certainly don't think she's rocked up here and set her bike opposite where he works by coincidence, do you?'

'No, no, of course not.' Sadie swallowed hard. What did Rachel want? Why hadn't Alex mentioned that he was still in contact with his ex? She shook her head. It was none of her business who he chose to speak to. Besides, they had only just started seeing each other. Maybe Alex just hadn't thought it was important to tell her.

'Customer.' Melissa indicated towards the door.

'Sorry. Morning, come on in. It's a bit chilly out there, isn't it?' Plastering a smile on her face, Sadie pulled the door open as a woman with a buggy came through.

Nodding politely, the woman thanked Sadie and pushed the buggy towards the buckets of lilies.

'I'm just about to put some more lilies out. They've been rather popular today.' What was it with lilies today?

'Oh great. It's a friend's party today, and myself and a few others have promised to fill her house with her favourite flowers – lilies.' The woman looked down sheepishly. 'I know it sounds silly, but she's had a really rubbish year. Her husband left her on Christmas Day, so we're all getting together and trying to cheer her up. You know, trying to make the first birthday being single one to remember. I know it sounds silly...'

'Not at all. Melissa, here, strong-armed me to a theme park on my first birthday after my ex-husband left. I must admit I wasn't thrilled with the idea,' Sadie glanced across at Melissa and grinned. 'But it was just what I needed. Something different to mark the day. I think what you and your friends are doing is a great idea. Something fun and beautiful to remember.'

'I hope so. We're having a proper old-fashioned tea party too.' The woman smiled.

'That sounds lovely.' Sadie took the ten stems of lilies from the customer and wrapped them carefully. 'A real mixture. Such graceful flowers.'

'Yes.' The woman paid and took the lilies, resting them on the hood of her buggy. 'Thank you.'

'Hold on, I'll grab the door for you.' Jumping up from the stool Sadie had found on a sales site, Melissa lunged for the door.

'Thank you.'

'You're welcome.' Melissa pulled the door open and waited until the woman had begun walking down the lane before she peered outside. 'I wonder where Rachel's gone?'

'I don't know. I'm sure Alex said he was out at a meeting this morning. I may have got it wrong though.'

'Oh, there she is.' Stepping outside, Melissa waved her arms in the air. 'Rachel! Over here, Rachel.'

Sadie looked down at the counter and delicately scooped up some loose leaves, depositing them in the bin under the counter. Maybe Rachel wouldn't notice Melissa. Maybe she'd just go on to wherever she was going.

'No way!' Rachel's familiar excited shriek floated across the lane and inside. 'Melissa! It can't be. Is it really you? What on earth are you doing here?'

'Rachel! I could ask you the same thing!'

Taking the few short strides from her bike to Melissa, Rachel wrapped her arms around her. 'I would never have pictured you in a lovely, quiet little place like this. You were always the partygoer of the group!'

'Haha, it's not mine. You remember Sadie, right?' Melissa waved Sadie over.

Tapping the countertop with her fingers, Sadie took a deep breath before joining Melissa at the door. 'Rachel, hi. Fancy seeing you here.'

'So, this is your place then?' Rachel stood back and took a good look at The Flower Shop. 'It's beautiful.'

'Thanks.' Sadie pulled her cardigan closed around her.

Melissa glanced at Sadie before cupping her hand around Rachel's elbow. 'Come in and warm up. It's freezing out here.'

Leading the way back inside, Sadie held the door open.

'Anyone for a cuppa?' Making her way through to the back room, Melissa fussed Buddy before switching the kettle on and standing in the archway. 'Coffees all round?'

'Do you have any herbal tea?' Rachel made her way around the counter, leaned over the dog gate and stroked Buddy. 'Oh, he's absolutely gorgeous.'

'That's Buddy, we've only had him a few days. Lily found him at the park last week and no one's come forward for him, so we were allowed to rehome him.'

'Lily? Of course, how is she? She's the youngest of your two girls, isn't she? Is it still two?'

'Lily's the oldest, Poppy is the youngest. Still the two.'

'Poppy, yes. How are they?'

'Great. Thanks.'

'And Max, how's he doing? I used to love our get-togethers. He was always so much fun.'

'He's fine as far as I'm aware. He's still with Tara.'

'Tara?' Rachel brought her hands to her face. 'Oh, I'm so sorry. How could it have slipped my mind? You must think I'm a complete klutz asking you about Max. How have you been coping?'

Sadie trailed her fingers along the edge of the counter. How had she been coping? I bet no one had ever asked Rachel that question. Did she really need to be asked how she was coping? Why not how has life been for you? Or how are you? Just because she had children and had become a single parent when Max walked out, it didn't mean that she'd had to 'cope'. Surely a single parent could thrive too? Could just live? 'I've been good, thanks. Great, even. I bought this place a couple of months ago.'

'Wow, good for you. Have you met someone else yet?'

Good for her? Good for her? Was Rachel being serious? She'd split up with her long-term partner shortly after Sadie's marriage had broken down. Should Sadie use Rachel's phrase on her? Looking across at Buddy, Sadie pretended to be distracted by the rope of sausages Buddy had brought across to them.

'Here you go. A coffee and a chamomile tea, I hope that's okay, Rachel?'

'Lovely, thanks.' Turning around, Rachel perched on the stool.

Glancing at Sadie, Melissa nodded. She had this. 'How about you, Rachel? Is there a special man in your life? And what's brought you back to sunny ole England? Last I heard you were protesting against the rain-forests being cut down in the Amazon?'

'I was there for a while, yes, but I've been doing a lot of thinking and I think my backpacking days are numbered, if not over entirely. I've made mistakes in my life, made decisions which I possibly shouldn't have, and the time's come for me to make things right and make up for lost time.' She took a sip of her chamomile tea.

'So, what's on the cards for you now then?' Melissa glanced across at Sadie and gave a little 'are you okay?' smile.

Sadie nodded quickly before stepping away to serve a customer.

'Thanks, have a lovely day at the castle.' Grinning as the customer left, Sadie re-joined Melissa and Rachel at the end of the counter.

Looking up, Melissa passed Sadie's coffee mug to her. 'Rachel was just saying she's thinking about getting into teaching.'

'Oh, right, are you?'

'Just thinking at the moment. I need to decide between teaching, counselling and becoming an art therapist. It's on the cards.'

Sadie nodded and took a sip of lukewarm coffee. It seemed everything was on the cards for Rachel at that moment. Was Alex on the cards too? 'It sounds like you've got a lot to think about.'

'Yes, a lot.' Rachel lowered her mug. 'I've got some open days at a few universities in the coming weeks, so I hope I'll get some inspiration and make my decision then.'

'That sounds like a solid plan. What are you doing in the meantime?' Melissa drained her coffee.

'Well, I'm hoping as Alex's work neighbour you'll be able to help me actually, Sadie.'

'In what way?'

'I really need to talk to him.'

That was it, then. She wanted Alex back.

'So, do you know where I can find him?'

'Umm, he'll be back by lunchtime.'

'Okay, great. Thanks. I think I might take a wander around. Is there a decent coffee shop around here?'

'Yes, there's a couple down the High Street.'

'Great. Catch you later then.' Swinging her legs around, Rachel jumped from the stool, waved and left The Flower Shop.

'So, what did you think of that then?' With the stool now empty, Melissa hopped on.

'I'm not sure...'

A chirpy ringtone sounded from Melissa's handbag. Pulling her phone out, Melissa grimaced. 'Sorry I'd best get this, it's Holly from the salon.'

Sadie nodded and busied herself straightening the flower buckets.

* * *

'Sadie, I'm really sorry, but I'm going to have to rush off. Chelsea, our new stylist, has just thrown up and her day's jam-packed with clients. I'm going to have to take over.' Gathering up her coat and handbag, Melissa rested her hand on Sadie's arm. 'It'll be okay, you know. Alex is one of the good guys. You're meeting him for lunch, talk to him then.'

'No worries. Hope everything's okay.' With the shop now empty, Sadie leaned her elbows on the counter and rested her chin in her hands. Yes, she was supposed to be meeting him for lunch, but really was that the best thing to do?

18

A high-pitched whining shook Sadie from her thoughts, and she looked behind her. Buddy was sitting on his haunches next to the gate, his front paws leaning on the top.

'Do you know what I think? I think we both need a walk. I think we both need to escape into the countryside for a few minutes and clear our heads. What do you say, Buddy?'

Buddy's tail wagged as he stuck his tongue out.

'I'll take that as a yes then.'

* * *

Twenty minutes later, Sadie was sat on a tree stump at the edge of a field. She rolled her mobile over and over in her hands as Buddy enjoyed the freedom of an extendable lead and sniffed the grass in front of her.

Rachel was back. Alex had already said how badly she'd broken his heart, but Melissa was right, Alex was one of the good guys. Sadie knew he wouldn't cheat on her; she knew he wouldn't even think about Rachel for a second if they were still seeing each other. But he had loved Rachel. He'd been planning on proposing before she'd ran off around the world. He'd loved her a lot and how could Sadie stand in the way of that?

'What do you think of it all, Buds?'

Buddy nudged Sadie's pocket with his nose.

'You know I've got treats in there, don't you?' Taking a couple of bone-shaped biscuits from her pocket, she let Buddy eat them from her hand. If she stood in the way of Alex and Rachel, then she'd never know if Alex truly wanted her or had just missed an opportunity with Rachel. If she stood back and gave Rachel the chance of getting back with him, then at least Sadie would know one way or the other. If he *did* rekindle his love for Rachel, then Sadie would know, and if he didn't and chose to get back with Sadie, then she'd know his feelings were sincere.

There was nothing else for it. She had to let him go. She had to let him choose his own path. Even if it didn't lead back to her.

Sadie typed a short message telling him she wouldn't be able to meet him for lunch and that she thought it best if they remained as friends. With her finger hovering over the 'send' button, Sadie pinched the bridge of her nose. She was being cruel. She should speak to him.

Taking a deep breath, she pressed 'call'.

'Sadie, hi. How's your morning going?'

'It's been okay, thanks. How about yours?'

'Busy. It's been busy. I've been thinking do you fancy checking out that new gastro pub on the outskirts of the village?'

'I...' Sadie swallowed. 'That's why I'm ringing. I'm not going to be able to make lunch. Sorry.'

'Oh. Okay, never mind. Shall I grab a take-out and pop round to the shop?'

'I... umm...' Looking down the ground, Sadie focused on a stem of grass Buddy had trampled on, watching as it slowly and determinedly sprung back to life. She had to say this. She had to do this. She had to set him free if she was ever going to know one way or the other if he still had feelings for Rachel. She knew he did. Well, she was sure he did, and it wasn't fair on him if she didn't let him go, didn't give him the opportunity to get back with Rachel. 'I don't think it's working.'

'What? The lunch dates? That's fine. I understand you've got the shop to run, I'm more than happy with lunch in the shop, you know that.'

'No, not the lunch dates. All of it.'

The line went quiet.

'Alex?'

After clearing his throat, Alex spoke quietly, his voice barely audible. 'Why?'

Sadie swallowed. Why did she feel like the horrible one? This was for his own good. He'd see that when he realised Rachel was back. He'd be thankful to her. 'I just...'

'Have I done something wrong? Is it the Mr Pritchard case?'

'No, no, it's not. It's nothing you've done wrong. I just don't think it's such good timing. I'm sorry.'

'Right.' Alex cleared his throat again. 'Right.'

'Sorry. I'd... umm... better go.' Ending the call, Sadie held her phone in her hands and stared at the field. A rabbit darted across between tufts of grass. It was early for that. For rabbits. Weren't they usually more active during the night? At dusk and dawn, yes, but at 11.15 in the morning? Shouldn't they be sleeping now?

Buddy barked, pulling on the extendable lead. He'd spotted the rabbit.

'It's not for you.' Wiping her eyes, she leaned her head back and looked at the sky. The clouds were dark and more were forming quickly. It was going to rain, and soon. She checked her watch. She should get back to The Flower Shop. She needed to open up again. There might be time to entice some tourists who had come to walk around the castle grounds and spotted the impending rain – she'd probably get a few customers popping in on their way back to their cars.

Did it matter? Did any of it? She'd really thought her luck was changing. What with the shop and then meeting Alex again, the way she felt about him...

A raindrop landed on her forehead. With her face upturned to the sky, she let the raindrop mix with her tears and trickle down her cheeks. This was her decision, and she had to live with it.

* * *

'So girls, who wants to help your Auntie Melissa with the chips?' Pushing the door open with her foot, Melissa waltzed into The Flower Shop, a huge brown paper bag in her arms.

'Chips? You got us chips?' Poppy looked up from the science homework she was completing as she sat at the counter.

'I sure have. Where's Lily?'

'She's upstairs.'

'Great. Here, take these. Will you two be okay dishing them out while I speak to your mum for a bit?'

'Yes, course.' Pushing her science book to the side, Lily stood up from the stool and held her arms out for the bag.

'Where is your mum?' Looking around, Melissa frowned. She couldn't see Sadie or hear her in the back room.

'She's just out in the garden bit with Buddy. She'll be back in a moment.'

'Okay, great. We'll see you up in a couple of minutes then. Please tell me you have mayo?'

'We sure do.' Grinning, Poppy disappeared through the door up to the flat.

'Sadie?'

Pinching some colour in her cheeks, Sadie pushed herself off the work surface she'd been leaning on in the back room. Poppy had been right, she had been outside with Buddy, but she'd come back in five minutes ago, just needing a bit of space to think. Melissa wouldn't give up though. She'd have to show herself. 'Back here, Melissa.'

'Hey. No, stay here, boy.' Opening the gate, Melissa tried and failed to keep Buddy inside.

'It's okay. He can go up to the girls now.'

'Okay.' Melissa walked across and let Buddy upstairs before joining Sadie in the back room again.

'How come you're here? Don't they still need you at the salon?'

Melissa shrugged. 'They'll cope.'

Sadie nodded. She shouldn't have answered Melissa's text. She shouldn't have told her what she'd said to Alex.

'Come here.' Holding out her arms, Melissa indicated to Sadie.

Sinking into Melissa's embrace, Sadie leaned her head against her shoulder before pulling herself away again.

'Why? Why did you do it?'

'You know why. If I hadn't, I'd never know if Alex really wanted to be with me or if he wanted to be with Rachel.'

'That's the silliest thing I've heard. Alex was with you. He wasn't with Rachel. Rachel's an old flame to him. That's all.'

'The way he spoke of her though, the way his eyes drooped, and he looked so sad when he was telling me about when he was going to propose. He still has feelings for her and, if I'd stayed with him, I'd always be doubting the way he felt about me.'

Melissa shook her head. 'If Alex had wanted to get back with Rachel, he would have. He would have finished things with you. He didn't, so he obviously wanted things to carry on between you both.'

'I spoke to him before Rachel went back to see him, though. I spoke to him before lunchtime, before he probably even knew she was back.'

'You don't know that. She might have caught up with him before lunchtime.'

'No, he was in meetings.' Sadie raked her fingers through her hair. She should have brushed it when she'd got in after the rain. It would be a nightmare to get all the knots out now. 'As you said, he's one of the good guys. He wouldn't have just dumped me because Rachel had shown up, he would have viewed himself as off the market. This way I'm giving him the chance to get back with her. To do what he really wants. I can't stand in the way of that. I don't want to. I don't want a future knowing that I was always going to be second best to the love of his life.'

'I just think you've thrown something really good away.'

'Maybe. But I had to do it.'

Shaking her head, Melissa sighed. 'I got chips.'

'Thanks.'

'Come on then. Let's go and have something to eat before it gets cold.' Melissa held out her arm.

'Yep.' Sadie linked arms with Melissa.

19

Tying the ribbon, Sadie stood back. The bouquet of sunflowers looked great, even if she thought so herself. No one could possibly be sad around sunflowers, not with their huge faces and deep yellow petals. Carrying them through to the shop floor, her face fell. He was there. Alex was there. He was hanging back behind the customer waiting for the sunflowers, but he was still there.

'They're lovely. Thank you. Jenny is going to love these.' The man in front of her grinned and took the flowers.

'You can choose one of these cards if you like?' With her lips straining to keep smiling, she indicated the stand of small cards.

'No, it's okay. Thanks. I've already got a card.'

'Okay, great. Well, I hope Jenny has a lovely birthday.'

'I hope she does too. I'm hoping it'll be one of the best.' The man leaned forward and patted his pocket. 'I'm proposing! So wish me luck.'

'Good luck, although I'm sure you won't need it.' She watched as he left, the bell above the door tinkling as a gust of cool wind seeped through from the outside. It was strange, Jenny, whoever she was, was being proposed to, and yet here she was about to tell Alex again that it was over.

'Sadie.' Stepping forward, Alex passed a takeaway coffee cup towards her. 'I'm sorry... I just really needed to see you. I need to know what's happened? What's changed between us? I thought we were having a really good time.'

Taking the cup, Sadie gripped it in her hands, the heat from the coffee radiating through the thin cardboard and burning her skin. 'We were. We have been, I just...'

'Is it because of Rachel?'

'She caught up with you then?'

'Yes, she came to find me at lunchtime yesterday. She told me you'd told her I'd be back in the office by then?'

'I did.'

'Well? Is it because of her you've broken up with me?'

'I just...' What was she supposed to say? Did she tell the truth, or did she make something up?

'If it's because she's back, it doesn't change anything, you know. I want to be with you. Me and Rachel were over a long time ago. There's nothing between us any more. What happened, the way I felt about her, it's all in the past.'

'I just think you need some time. You need to see what you want. What you really want. I don't want to be stuck in the middle or be the reason you don't try things with her.'

'I don't want to get back with her. I want to be with you.'

Sadie blinked; she could feel Alex's eyes penetrating hers. She had no doubt that he was telling the truth, but it didn't mean anything. He might think he didn't want to get back with Rachel, but unless he was free from Sadie, he wouldn't know for sure. Looking away, she focused on the steam coming up through the lid of the cup. 'I'm sorry, Alex. I just can't. It's not just Rachel, it's...'

'What else is it? What have I done wrong? I can fix it. I can walk away from the Mr Pritchard case. I can change.'

'I don't want you to change.' She looked back up at him. 'You don't need to change. And it's not the Mr Pritchard case. I know you're only keeping with it to try and protect his ex-wife's interests as you tried to do for me.'

'Then what is it?'

Glancing back down to her coffee, Sadie shifted on her feet. He didn't understand what she was trying to do, he didn't understand it was for his own good. Looking back up, she tried to keep her gaze steady. 'I think there's just too much history between us. I'm sorry.'

'I thought you said you understood what had happened during your divorce? I thought you knew it wasn't my doing?' His voice cracked.

'I do. I understand, and I don't blame you. Not at all. It's not that. I just...' Sadie shrugged. 'I'm just not ready for this.'

Buddy barked as someone knocked on the back door.

'Sorry. That'll be a delivery. I'd better go.'

'Of course.' Nodding. Alex picked up his drink and left.

'Thanks. Bye.' Shutting the back door, Sadie lifted the box onto the workbench and sunk into a chair. She'd done the right thing, she knew she had, so why did she feel so rubbish? Why did she feel as though she'd made everything worse? What if Melissa was right, and she'd just thrown everything away with Alex for no reason?

She shook her head. What will be, will be. That's what her mum had always said. If she and Alex were meant to be together, they would be, however corny it sounded. She *had* made the right decision, she'd let Alex go so he could make up his own mind, free from her.

Pushing herself to standing, Sadie opened the box in front of her. Brilliant, it was the new selection of ribbons she'd ordered. She fingered the white ribbon with the quote, 'Live your best life' before shaking her head and making her way back through to the shop floor.

20

'It's freezing! I could literally still be in bed now.' Lily pulled her woolly hat down lower and glared at her mum.

'You can go back to bed when we get home if you really need to. A nice walk around the castle grounds and a bit of fresh air will do you good.' Sadie pressed the release button on the extendable lead and let Buddy run down the path ahead of them.

'It won't. It's just freezing my lungs.'

Sadie chuckled. 'Stop being overdramatic, Lily. It's not that cold. In fact, it's the warmest day of the year so far. Look over there by the tree.'

'What am I looking at? Grass?'

'No, look properly.' Sadie pointed to the small green shoots which had bravely pushed themselves up from the ground.

'Ooh, are they daffodils, Mum?' Poppy clapped her gloved hands and ran across to them.

'Yes, they are. The first ones of spring by the looks of it.'

'How come she's suddenly so interested in flowers?' Lily rolled her eyes.

Sadie watched as Poppy delicately touched the leaves. Lily was right. Ever since moving to The Flower Shop and being surrounded by flowers every day, Poppy was becoming more and more interested in them. She smiled. It was good to see Poppy enjoying the things she did. Of course, Lily still thought they were 'lame' but there was time yet, maybe even she'd begin to enjoy them. 'I think it's nice that she likes them.'

'Are you disappointed in me because I'm not bothered about flowers?'

Sadie looked across at Lily. 'Of course not. We all like different things, don't we? Besides, there's still time for you to realise how beautiful they are.'

'Urgh.'

Sadie laughed. She'd known she'd get that reaction. 'You've got your dance competition coming up this weekend, haven't you? How are you feeling about it?'

'Great. I'm really looking forward to it.' Lily smiled, her whole face lighting up with enthusiasm.

'I can't wait either.' Placing her arm across Lily's shoulders, she squeezed. 'My super talented dancer.'

'I'm not.' Lily pulled away. 'You should see Georgia. Now, she's talented.'

'Umm, I'm sure she is, but so are you. You just need to believe in yourself more and start seeing yourself as the world sees you.'

'That's what Ms Thetford keeps telling me. But I'm rubbish compared to the rest of them.'

'Hey, you're not. You're brilliant.' However many times Sadie or Lily's dance teacher, Ms Thetford, told her what a great dancer she was, Lily still couldn't see it. 'And I'm not just saying that because I'm your mum. You really are very talented.'

'Umm, anyway, can we go back now?'

'Not yet. Let's walk around to the walled garden at least.' Sadie looked across at Poppy. 'Come on, Poppy, let's go and see what's waking up in the walled garden.'

'Yay! Coming!'

Taking a deep breath, Sadie let the morning air fill her lungs. There was something about the air at this time of the day, the earlier the better. There was hope. Hope for the day ahead and hope for the future. She looked across at the castle towering above her. They were lucky to be able to walk in the vast grounds of a place like this. So many of the castles nowadays closed their grounds to the public or charged an extortionate rate to wander through them. To have all of this on their doorstep was great.

Ten minutes later, Poppy knelt by the herb bed reading the name tags to Sadie while Lily walked Buddy around the gravel pathways.

'Sadie! Don't tell me these are your two girls! Lily! Poppy! Look at you both! How much you've grown.'

Sadie closed her eyes. She knew exactly who that voice belonged to. Opening her eyes again, she smiled and stood up to face Rachel. 'Hey, Rachel. Lovely to see you again. Yes, this is Lily and Poppy. A little older than when you last saw them.'

'They sure are! Wow, you two are turning into such beautiful young ladies.' Touching Poppy's arm, Rachel grinned.

'Hi. Are you Auntie Rachel?' Lily led Buddy over to them.

'Yes, I am. Aw, you remember me?'

'A little.' Lily nodded.

'Hey, Alex. Look who I've found!' Turning around, Rachel called.

Oh great. Alex was here too. With Rachel. Sadie chewed down on her bottom lip as Alex walked through the open wrought-iron gates into the walled garden. He paused, before joining them.

'Hi, girls. Sadie.' Nodding, he smiled.

'Alex, hi.'

'Hey, Alex, I thought you were going to come over last night? I was going to ask you about my maths homework. I've asked Mum, but she doesn't have a clue and I thought I'd ask you.' Lily looked down at the lead in her hand.

'Oh sorry, Lily. I said I would, didn't I?' Shuffling, Alex's feet shifted on the gravel. 'I can still help you, if that's okay with your mum?'

'Why wouldn't it be?' Frowning, Lily looked between Sadie and Alex.

'Yes, why wouldn't it be? Have I missed something?' Rachel glanced across at Sadie and furrowed her brow.

Alex hadn't told her about them. She'd obviously made the right decision in finishing things with Alex then. He obviously did still have feelings for Rachel.

'No reason.' Alex hit his forehead. 'I'd forget my head if it wasn't glued on.'

'Can you help me or not then? It doesn't matter if you can't, I can find Mr Spencer at break.'

'Of course, I can help you.' Alex looked across at Sadie and raised his eyebrows, asking if it was okay.

Sadie nodded slightly.

'Great. Thanks. It's algebra. Yuck. I still don't know why we even need to know about algebra. I mean, if someone wants to go on and become a... I don't know... do a job where they need algebra, then why don't they go to uni to learn about it. We don't all need to be subjected to something we're never going to use. It's just stressful and a waste of time.' Lily kicked at the gravel.

'Don't worry. I'm sure we can figure it out between us.'

'Thanks.'

'Who wants ice cream?' Rachel pulled out a purse from a rainbow-coloured cloth bag hung over her shoulder.

'Me, please!' Poppy's eyes widened. 'Mum wouldn't let us. She said it was too cold.'

'Oh, I don't have to if they're not allowed?' Looking across at Sadie, Rachel shrugged.

'No, it's fine. Thank you.'

'Great, come on then, girls. The first one there gets an extra flake.'

Sadie watched as Rachel, Lily and Poppy ran out of the walled garden in the direction of the small castle café.

Alex cleared his throat. 'How have you been?'

She nodded. 'I'm okay, thanks. How about you?'

Looking back down to the floor, Alex shrugged. 'I miss you.'

'I miss you too.' She needed to be strong. It had only been a couple of days ago that she'd finished things with him, and yet here he was going for an early morning stroll with Rachel. She'd definitely made the right decision. He needed time to figure out what he wanted, who he wanted, if he hadn't already.

'I...'

A loud squeal from behind the wall stopped Alex, and they both watched as Poppy ran around the corner, shortly followed by Lily, Buddy and Rachel.

'Quick, Mum. Hide me! Rachel's going to throw her ice cream at me!' Grabbing her mum's shoulders, Poppy ducked behind her.

'I'm sure, she's not.'

'I wouldn't be surprised.' Alex lifted his eyebrows and grinned at Poppy.

Sadie swallowed. Alex's grin hadn't reached his eyes and yet he was still trying to be normal for the girls' sake. 'We'd better get a wriggle on. Buddy will need his breakfast. Lily, Poppy, what do you say to Rachel?'

'Thanks for the ice cream.' Their voices rang out in unison as Sadie led the way back through the gates.

* * *

'Can I make us a cooked breakfast when we get home?' Lily crumpled up the napkin from her ice cream and pushed it into her coat pocket.

'Yes, that would be lovely. I'm starving.' Sadie gave Lily a quick hug as they walked down the lane back towards The Flower Shop.

'And, I've been thinking, I'd quite like to try and be veggie, so when you get the shopping next can you get me some vegetarian stuff please?'

'Ha, that's only because Rachel told you she was vegetarian!' Poppy pointed at her sister before throwing the last piece of cone in her mouth and passing Sadie her napkin.

'Thanks for that.' Taking the ice cream covered napkin, Sadie put it in her pocket and turned to Lily. 'If that's what you want then, yes, I can. We can have a look online later if you like and choose some recipes?'

'Okay, thanks. And by the way, it's not because Rachel is vegetarian.' Lily glared at her sister. 'I've been thinking of giving up meat for a while now.'

'I think it's a good idea. We don't eat a lot of meat anyway so it shouldn't be too hard. I'll join you. How about you, Poppy? Fancy trying some new stuff?'

'Yes, okay.' Poppy took Buddy's lead from Lily and picked up her pace before glancing over her shoulder. 'I still think you're copying Rachel.'

'I'm not! Mum, tell her.'

21

'Mum, I can't get back to sleep.'

Blinking against the light Poppy had turned on, Sadie shielded her eyes. 'Have you had a bad dream, sweetheart?'

'No, I heard a bang and I can't get back to sleep. The rain is too noisy.'

Pushing her duvet back, Sadie sat up and looked towards the window. The curtains were closed, but the patter of raindrops hitting the glass was unmistakable. That was some downpour, for sure. 'Do you want to come in with me?'

'Umm, I don't think I'd be able to get to sleep, anyway. It's still noisy in here and I'm sure I heard thunder too.' Poppy shrugged and pulled the sleeves of her pyjama top down over her hands.

'Let's see what the time is.' Reaching across to the bedside table, Sadie picked up her alarm clock. The glowing orange numbers read, 05:45. 'It's almost six o'clock. Shall we go into the living room and pop the TV on? You can lay down on the sofa and you might drift off again with the distraction of the TV.'

'Okay.'

Swinging her legs out from under the duvet, Sadie winced. It was cold. She led Poppy into the living room and switched the TV on. 'Here, lay down, sweetheart.'

Yawning, Poppy nodded and sank into the cushions.é

Pulling the throw off from the back of the sofa, Sadie laid it across Poppy just as Buddy jumped up and nestled on her legs. 'Looks like you have your own personal leg warmer.'

'Yes. Hey, Buddy.'

As she switched through the channels, Sadie listened as a tap-tap noise sounded from underneath them. It was louder than the rain pelting against the windows and not as fast, rhythmic but fairly slow. 'Is that the noise that kept you awake?'

'Yes. There was a louder bang and then that noise there.'

'Okay, I might just wander down and check on the shop. Try and get back to sleep or at least rest.' Tapping the remote, she settled on a re-run of Friends before bending and kissing Poppy on the forehead. 'I won't be a moment. I'll shut this door to keep Buddy in, if he comes down with me he'll think it's time for his morning walk and I'm not awake enough for that.'

'Okay.'

Closing the door quietly behind her, Sadie checked in on Lily and made her way downstairs.

* * *

The noise was louder down here. Maybe something had been knocked over outside? A sign or something being battered by the wind.

She pushed the door to the shop floor open and reached for the light switch. Nothing. That was strange, the lights and TV were working fine upstairs. She tried again. Nope. The bulb must have gone.

Sadie switched the torch app on her phone on and looked around. Swinging her phone towards the front of the shop, the light illuminated the shelves and flower buckets all standing as they should. Walking towards the door, she pulled up the blind and peered outside – the light from the lamppost opposite highlighted a torrent of water cascading down the lane, the cobbles had all but disappeared under a couple of inches of water. Thank goodness there was a step up to The Flower Shop. Without it, who knew what would have happened. It didn't look as though any signs or anything had worked loose though, so where that noise was coming from she had no idea.

She sighed. There must have been a burst drain further up the lane or something. Custom would be slow if not non-existent all day, depending on when the rain stopped and how long it took for the water to find other drains to disappear down into.

As she made her way back to the door upstairs, she paused and listened. The noise was louder here. It must have been coming from the back of the shop. Walking around the counter, she stepped down the shallow step into the back room.

Grimacing as freezing cold water seeped through her sock, she shone the light around the back room. An inch deep of water covered the tiles, cascading in from the open back door. That's what the rhythmic thudding noise was then – the back door swinging shut to open, open to shut.

What had happened? How had the door opened and where was the water coming from? The water streaming down the lane must be from a blocked drain, but surely that wouldn't affect the car park too? Unless there was more than one blocked drain?

There was only one thing for it, she needed to close that door to stop any more water coming inside. Taking a deep breath, she plunged her dry foot into the murky water, gritting her teeth so she didn't scream out against the cold. Picking her way across the tiles, trying to avoid the bits of floral foam which floated across the surface of the water, she made it to the back door.

Focusing the torch beam on the door, Sadie saw that it must have been forced open, the lock was still attached to the doorframe but the surrounding wood had splintered leaving the door free to swing open.

She swallowed and swung the torchlight behind her. Had there been a break-in? Was there someone inside? What if they'd gone upstairs? Every evening the till was emptied. What if they'd gone in search of the safe? The girls. They'd find the girls up there.

Turning, she waded her way around the workbench towards the shop floor again. She had to get to Lily and Poppy. A creaking noise, different to the rhythmic tapping, stopped her in her tracks and she looked back towards the back door.

It had stopped now, but there had definitely been a noise – and a loud one at that. A creaking, scraping noise. Whoever had done this wasn't inside, whoever had done this was on the other side of that door.

Looking around, her eyes searched something out, anything which would protect her from whoever was out there. She picked up the closest thing to her, a metal ruler, and shook her head. It would have to do.

Brandishing the ruler, she waded her way back through the water towards the back door. Taking a deep breath, she pulled the door open and screamed, backing away as a large branch fell in-wards. Quickly stepping back, she knocked her back into the workbench and ducked as the branch swung towards her. As it fell, it knocked against her head and scraped her face before it lodged itself against the workbench beside her.

Sadie reached her hand to her face, winced and pulled it away. Her fingers were covered in blood, more of which she could feel dribbling down her cheek. She shook her head. She didn't have time for any of that. She needed to somehow get that branch back outside and get the door closed if she was going to stop more rainwater coming in. Pushing herself away from where she had fallen, she stepped around the branch which had lodged itself against the workbench and followed it to its end. It was long, at least two metres long. The wind must have blown it down. Not that it had been particularly windy, or not from what she'd heard, anyway. All that she'd been able to hear was the rain pelting down.

Stepping out of the back door, the moonlight illuminated the damage. Two fence posts had been broken, which had crumpled the fencing wire between them, but the others were still standing. Apart from that, every-thing else looked okay. The bins hadn't been blown over and from what she could see, there wasn't any damage anywhere else. Water covered the ground though, a clear sheen across the tarmac. Gripping her phone under her armpit, she reached down and grabbed the end of the branch and began pulling. It was well and truly stuck. Standing up, she stretched before bending again. Wrapping her fingers around the branch, she stepped back and pulled as hard as she could. Slowly, inch by inch, it gave way. She heard a crash, muffled by water. It must have dislodged and fallen to the floor from the workbench.

It was easier now to pull it out of the way. As she backed out, pulling the branch with her, she picked her way around the broken fence, careful not to stand on anything sharp with her socked feet.

Finally, with the branch fully outside, she hurried back inside, pushing the door shut against the water behind her. With one hand against the door, she looked around for something to lodge the door shut. The chair. The chair would work. Leaving her position, she went and dragged the chair towards her, leaning it against the door.

'Mum! Mum! Where are you?' Lily's voice, high-pitched and laced with panic, come through the darkness.

'I'm in here. Don't come through.'

Lily appeared in the archway, her torchlight illuminating the back room. 'What's happened? Mum, you're bleeding!'

'It's okay. I'm okay. A branch has come down and been blown into the back door. It must have splintered around the lock and the branch must have wedged it open, letting the water in.' Sadie looked at Lily, her face had paled and her forehead had creased with worry. 'It's all right. It'll all be all right. Luckily, we've got that step up into the shop, and this is all tiled so it won't take much to clean it all up.'

'Where's the water coming from though? It's like a stream out the front.'

'I think there must be a blocked drain further up the lane. As soon as the rain stops the water will drain away down the bottom of the lane, so it'll be okay.' She'd have to ring the water board or whoever dealt with drains, though. She didn't fancy this becoming a regular occurrence.

'What about your face? Why are you bleeding?'

Lifting her hand back up to her temple, she winced. Now she'd dealt with the branch and got the door shut, she could actually feel the pain. 'It's just where part of the branch scraped against me. It's nothing. Just a cut.'

'Are you sure?'

'I am. I'm fine.' She looked down at her herself. Her hands were streaked with blood from her head mixed with bits of bark which had rubbed off from the branch. Her once pale blue pyjama bottoms were now a muddied brown, the bottom of the legs were so wet they were stuck to her shins. The skin on her ankles had turned a bright red from the cold of the water, and her once fluffy white bed socks were now brown and matted against her skin. She grinned. 'I look a bit of a state though.'

A nervous laugh escaped Lily's lips. 'You do. Shall I get my boots and help you?'

'What's the time?' Reaching down to her phone, which she'd placed on the workbench, Sadie shook her head. 'It's almost half seven. I'll clean this up when you two have left for school. Could you grab me a wet soapy flannel and a towel though, please? I don't fancy traipsing this lot through the shop and up to the flat.'

Nodding, Lily turned and ran back upstairs.

Leaning her hands on the workbench, Sadie looked around and surveyed the mess. The chair seemed to be working, and the door was holding, which had stopped everything but a small dribble of water seeping through. Although the floor was covered in water, nothing else was ruined, apart from some floral foam. Everything else was kept in the cupboards above and below the work surface which lined two of the walls. It wouldn't take long to get everything cleaned up. Not once the rain had stopped. She was just grateful for that step. If the water had got onto the shop floor, more would have been destroyed.

'Here you go.' Lily returned holding a dripping flannel and a dry towel.

'Thanks, sweetheart.' Wading across towards her, Sadie took the flannel, leaned against the wall and proceeded to roll off her sodden socks and wash her feet.

'Why aren't the lights working down here?'

'I'm not sure.' Sadie's heart sank. If all the electrics were out downstairs, that would mean the floral cooler had stopped working too, which would ruin the bouquets she'd made up for today's orders. Closing her eyes momentarily, she pushed the thought to the back of her mind. If she didn't open it, the floral cooler should still be keeping them cool, but she'd need to get someone out to fix the electrics as soon as possible. 'Something must have knocked into the wires or something, or else maybe the water got into one of the plugs and it all short-circuited.'

'Will it be able to be fixed?'

'Yes, I'll get someone out.' Chucking the now filthy flannel and towel on the floor, Sadie looked across at Lily. 'Honestly, everything will be fine. I'd give you a hug, but I don't think you'd appreciate me doing that.'

Lily looked across at her mum's hands, still covered in a mixture of mud and blood, and laughed. 'No thanks.'

'Okay, let's get up those stairs, I'm going to get changed and we need to wake your sister.'

'She's awake, but I told her to stay upstairs with Buddy.'

'Thank you, sweetheart.' Sadie smiled and waved Lily ahead of her.

Turning back, Lily pointed towards the front door. Sunlight had begun to flood through the window. 'The rain's stopped.'

'That's a relief. I bet it will all drain away quite quickly now then.'

22

Sadie waved as Lily and Poppy turned the corner onto the High Street from Serendipity Lane. Lily had offered for Poppy to walk with her and Georgia to the bus stop so that Sadie could get on with the clearing up. She smiled, at least something good had come out of all the mess.

She'd been right. It hadn't taken long for the water to disperse once it had stopped raining. The lane was now only covered by a sheen of wet after the majority of it had drained away at the bottom of the lane.

There was still a lot to do, though. She needed to contact an electrician and clean out the back room. She also needed to get the door sorted, although how she wasn't sure. She needed a new one, but would she even be able to buy one and organise someone to fit one before the evening?

Closing the door behind her, she checked the note explaining to customers that she was only open to people to pick up orders and went around the counter. Standing in the archway, she surveyed the damage in the harsh light of day; the floral foam had all but disintegrated, the small fragments of green mixing with the muddy water on the floor.

Pulling her boots on, Sadie stepped down into the water, this time grateful for dry feet, and waded through to the back door. Removing the chair, she pushed the door open. Where did she start? Did she ring around electricians and try to find a door fitter, or should she clear up first and then try to work it all out?

Reaching out, she gripped the doorframe as her eyesight danced with black dots. She felt her head where the branch had caught her and winced. She shook her head, blinking until her eyesight returned to normal. There wasn't time for this. She needed to get everything cleaned up so she could open properly tomorrow, or she'd lose too much money.

Stepping outside, she reached down for the branch, wrapped her hands around it and began to pull it away, she'd need to be able to get in and out to the bins when she cleaned the floor and she didn't fancy having to step over the huge branch every time she did so.

'Sadie! Wait, we'll help you.'

Closing her eyes, Sadie slumped her shoulders. This was all she needed, Rachel and Alex coming to her rescue.

'Hey, what's happened?'

Too late. Lowering the branch, Sadie straightened and looked at Rachel. 'The door got pushed open when this branch fell.'

'Pushed open? It's broken.'

Sadie nodded. Yep, state the obvious. A beep behind her signalled Alex had locked his car. He'd no doubt be over in a moment, too.

'Ouch, Sadie, are you okay?' Dropping his briefcase, Alex walked across and touched Sadie's elbow. 'Looks like that branch is off one of those trees at the back there. I've been on to the council no end of times to treat them or cut them down, I'm sure they've got some sort of disease. Whenever it gets remotely windy you always get some branches falling down. I've not seen one come down this big though.'

'I'm fine.' Looking away, she tried to avoid his concerned gaze.

'You're not. You've been bleeding.'

'Honestly, I'm fine. I just got knocked with the branch when I tried to move it earlier.'

'Wow, that must have hurt. Let me have a look. I was a volunteer at a hospital in one of the refugee camps I helped out at.' Tucking her finger beneath Sadie's chin, Rachel turned her to look at her.

'No, honestly, I'm fine. I've got too much to do. I'll clean myself up later. Thanks, though.' Sadie stepped away, tripping over a broken piece of fence post as she did. Before she knew it, Alex had her by the hand and pulled her upright again. 'Thanks.'

'Okay, but I really think you should get that looked at. It's a nasty gash.'

'Please, I'm fine.' There were bigger things to worry about rather than a little cut to the head.

'On one condition then,' Rachel looked across at Alex and grinned. 'You let us help you clean up and then you let me look at your gash properly.'

'No, really. I'll be okay. I can get this sorted.'

'Sadie, let us help. We know you can do it yourself, but it will be quicker with the three of us.' Rachel walked past her into the back room.

'Are you sure you're all right? You're not going dizzy or anything, are you?'

'I'm fine.' Their eyes met and just for a split second Sadie could see true concern in his. Looking away, she grinned and nodded. 'Really, I'm good. It hardly hurt.'

Nodding slowly, Alex picked up his briefcase again. 'Let me come and see if I can fix your door for you?'

What was the point in telling him to go when Rachel was busy-bodying herself around, anyway? Why not have both of the lovebirds? 'Okay, but I'm not sure anything can be done for it, to be honest.'

'I think you might be right. That must have been some force from the branch to splinter the wood like that.'

'I think it was past its best days, anyway. It was on my list of things to do, to replace the door, I just thought it'd last a tad bit longer.' Sadie shrugged. It was what it was.

'I think I might know someone who will be able to help. I represented a locksmith last year. A real decent chap he was, he told me I could pull in a favour.'

'Will he be able to get a new door, though? And by tonight?' The village was quiet, but she didn't fancy having to sleep without a back door.

'I should think so. You might not get as much choice of door styles as you otherwise would, though.'

'I don't mind about that. I'd just rather have something up.'

'Sadie, do you know your electrics aren't working? Your lights won't turn on.' Rachel appeared in the doorway. With her long skirt rolled up around the waistband she looked as though she was going to cross the Thames rather than wade through barely an inch of water.

'I know. I'm not sure why. I was going to let it dry out a bit and see if they come back on.'

Rachel whistled through her teeth. 'I wouldn't be trusting anything that's been mixing electricity and water. I think you need a professional electrician to come and take a look.' Rachel grinned, a glint in her eye. 'And I know exactly who I can call for you.'

'Thanks.' There was no point in arguing with her. Sadie had learnt that much by now.

With both Alex and Rachel now on their phones, Sadie grabbed the broom and began swishing the remaining water out of the back room.

* * *

'Hello? Is anyone about?' A voice filtered through from the shop floor.

'I'll go.' Squeezing her rag out into the bucket, Rachel raced into the shop.

They'd managed to get the majority of the water outside by sweeping it out and now they each had a rag, which they were wiping any remnants with, and squeezing the water into a bucket. Standing up, Sadie leaned down to pick the bucket up. 'I'll just empty this.'

'Here, let me.' Jumping to his feet, Alex took the bucket from her, their fingers brushing as he did.

'Thanks.' Standing there, their skin touching and tingling, Sadie looked into his eyes. Had she done the right thing by ending it with him? She looked away. Of course, she had. Something was obviously going on between him and Rachel. The number of times she'd seen them both together over the past few days, and the fact that she was travelling in his car this early, confirmed her suspicions. She wouldn't be surprised if she'd been staying over at his. She let go. 'Sorry.'

Pausing, Alex smiled before taking the bucket and throwing its contents outside.

'Thanks.'

'You're welcome.' Looking at her, he placed the bucket back down between them and began soaking up the excess water again.

Sadie smiled and looked away. He was so close she could feel the warmth from his arms. Holding on to the edge of the workbench, she pulled herself to standing. After being knelt down for what felt like forever, she needed to stretch her back out again. Tiny lights danced across her vision and she leaned against the side of the workbench, gripping its edge with her fingers.

Before she knew what was happening, Alex was up on his feet, holding her beneath the arms as her body became heavy and her vision blacked completely.

'I've got you.'

Blinking as she leaned her weight against him, she waited for her vision to slowly return. 'Sorry, I just got up a little too quick.'

'You need to get that bump checked out. I'm taking you down to the doctors' surgery. No arguments.' With his arms still supporting her, he turned and called through to Rachel, telling her where they were going.

'I really am fine. I've got so much to do here. I haven't got time to sit around waiting at the surgery. At the worst, they'll tell me I have a concussion. There really is no point.' There wasn't. Yes, she'd had a knock to the head, but it wasn't as if she was alone. Alex and Rachel were with her. There literally was no point.

'Probably, but I'll still feel happier once you've been checked over.' Wrapping his arm around her back, he pivoted and led her out of the door towards his car.

As he rummaged in his pocket for the car fob, she looked at the back of the row of shops. It looked as though it was just The Flower Shop which had borne the brunt of last night's storm. Everything else looked fine and normal.

'Here, in you get.' Pulling the passenger door open, he helped Sadie in.

'Thanks.' There was no point arguing with him. And she knew he was making a sensible decision. If it had been anyone else, it would have been her who insisted on taking them to get checked over. 'And thank you for everything you're doing. Thank you for helping.'

'Anytime. We might not be seeing each other any more, but I still care for you.' Looking forward, he drove out of the car park. 'A lot.'

* * *

'Oops!' As the car went around the roundabout, Sadie momentarily lost her grip on the pouch of takeaway coffee cups. One toppled as she righted them, pouring out a slug of brown liquid.

Glancing across at her, Alex laughed. 'To be fair, you can't really notice it. Not with the state of your top, anyway.'

Grinning, Sadie tapped him playfully. 'Oi! Your shirt isn't much better, you know.'

Looking down at his once pale blue newly ironed shirt, his face took on a look of mock horror. 'And that's what I get for offering you my cleaning services!'

'Apart from you've not actually done much cleaning. You've been ferrying me to the surgery.'

'Ah yes, but I was right to, wasn't I? Even Dr Hilton said that.' Nodding, he gave her a wink.

'No. Okay, yes, but I was right too. I told you I was fine, and Dr Hilton gave me the all clear.' Licking the spilt coffee from her forefinger, Sadie grabbed the paper bag of sandwiches as they threatened to slip from her knees.

'The all clear? He did no such thing! You're going to be a terrible patient, aren't you?' Slapping his forehead, he smiled. 'In case you weren't listening, he said you had a concussion and that you shouldn't be left alone for twenty-four hours.'

'Mild concussion. He said I had a mild concussion. There's a difference. And I won't be on my own. Once the back room is all cleared up, I'll open the shop and I'll have customers coming in and out all day. Later, the girls will be back from school.'

'Oh no, there's no chance you're being left alone even for one minute. I'll stay over tonight. You can explain to the girls what's happened and I'll sleep on the couch.'

Rolling her eyes, Sadie smiled. Yes, it was infuriating, but it did show he cared. Really cared about her. She shook her head. What was she think-ing? 'That's one step too far. I'll be asleep, anyway. I really won't need a babysitter all night.'

'Okay, we'll see how you are later, but I'm staying until late. Now, hold on to those coffees we have another roundabout ahead.'

'Hey, that was just a moment's lack of concentration. I can usually be trusted with this job.'

'Just hold on to them for dear life. We both need our caffeine today. I don't know how Rachel can live on that herbal tea. How can anybody cope without a daily caffeine fix?'

'Or an hourly caffeine fix, as in your case!' Sadie grinned. She liked this playful side to him. She'd never had that with Max, he'd always been so serious. Although, she had seen a different side of him with Tara, so maybe it was Sadie who had brought out the serious side to him. She shrugged, it didn't matter. Not now.

23

'Rachel, we have herbal tea and food!' Holding what remained of the back door open for Sadie, Alex followed her in.

Sadie paused. Maybe the idea of opening up later today had been a little optimistic. There was still so much that needed to be done.

Walking around her, Alex placed the takeaway cups on the workbench and pulled out the chair, indicating for Sadie to sit down.

'I'm not an invalid, you know,' she laughed.

'I know but you do have a concussion.' Taking the paper bag of sandwiches from her hand, he placed it next to the cups and cupped his hands beneath her elbows, guiding her into the seat. 'And I'm here to take care of you.'

She could feel his breath against her cheek as he lowered her into the seat and the electricity between them from his touch.

'Awesome! I'm starving!'

Turning, Sadie looked across at Rachel standing in the archway and looked down, hoping she couldn't see the warmth flushing across her cheeks.

Rachel came across the wet floor and delved into the bag, pulling out the three sandwiches. Handing one to Sadie, she winked.

'Thanks.' What had that been about? Had Rachel thought she and

Alex had been flirting? Was that her way of telling Sadie that she'd noticed and warning her to back off?

The bell above the shop door tinkled and Rachel ran through. Why had she wanted to get out of there so quickly?

As if reading her mind, Alex shrugged.

Tilting her head, Sadie listened. She could hear a man's voice; it wasn't a voice she recognised so he couldn't have been a regular customer. Maybe she should go through and see if Rachel needed help. Standing up, Sadie turned towards the archway just as Rachel bounced back in, a huge grin on her face.

'This is Alan, and he's the electrician. Yes, it's Alan the Electrician.' Waving her hands in a ta-da fashion, Rachel laughed as a clean-shaven man wearing dark jeans and a pale grey jumper, and carrying a huge blue bag, followed her through.

'Hello, everyone.' Even as he was addressing Sadie and Alex, his gaze didn't leave Rachel.

'Morning.' Standing up, Alex held out his hand, forcing Alan's eyes to focus on him for a few seconds. 'Thank you for coming round with such short notice.'

'No worries. No worries at all.' Looking back towards Rachel, he grinned. 'Right, where's the fuse box?'

'Sadie?'

'It's upstairs on the landing. Shall I show you?'

'It's fine. I can show him. Come on, Alan.'

'Okay, thanks. Remember Buddy's up there,' Sadie called after them.

'Umm?' Looking across at Sadie, he raised his eyebrows.

'Umm, indeed.' Was he one of Rachel's exes? There was definitely something between them, that was for sure. She searched Alex's face for a sign of jealously or annoyance – there wasn't any. He looked to be more interested in his sandwich than the echoes of laughter they could hear coming from upstairs. It wasn't very fair on him though, was it?

* * *

'Aw, my favourite!' Poppy pulled open the pizza box and took a slice of cheese and tomato pizza. 'Thanks, Mum.'

'Yes, thanks for this. Are you sure you don't want us to chip in?' Rachel looked across at Sadie as she tucked in.

'No, no, it's the least I can do after what you two have done for me today.' Filling up her plate, Sadie leaned against the kitchen work surface.

'Are you sure you don't want to sit down?' Alex stood up from his chair at the table.

'No, I'm good thanks.' Sadie grinned. It had taken all day, but between them, the back room had been completely cleaned out, the back door replaced and Alan the Electrician had done his thing too. Alex had even been on the phone to the council about getting the trees seen to, and Rachel had walked Buddy so she could open up for the last hour of trading time. She was lucky. Very lucky to have their support even if it did feel slightly odd.

24

'Yes, I'll make sure it's ready just before four o'clock then. Thank you for your order. Bye.' Placing the phone down, Sadie scribbled the order for a birthday bouquet made up of deep red roses and then looked up. 'Rachel, hi.'

'Morning! I don't think your bell's working.' She turned and pointed to the door.

'It sometimes gets itself tangled up. What can I do for you?'

'I just popped in for a catch-up and to see how you're doing after the flooding the other day.'

'I'm good thanks. Do you fancy a coffee?'

'A herbal tea if you've got one would be great, please.'

'Of course.' One day she'd be capable of remembering people's drinks orders. Walking through to the back room, she looked back to check the front door to The Flower Shop was closed and released Buddy, who had been pawing the gate ever since he'd heard Rachel walk through the door. 'I'm releasing the hound.'

'Aw, Buddy! Great to see you, my furry little man.'

As she made the drinks, Sadie listened to Rachel making a fuss over Buddy and smiled.

'Here you go. It's chamomile again, I hope that's okay?'

'That's perfect. Thanks.' Taking her mug, Rachel slipped onto the stool. 'I've been meaning to catch you on your own. Whenever I pop in, I either seem to be with Alex or he pops in straight after.'

Sadie nodded. Yes, they did always seem to be together. 'What can I do for you?'

'It's more what I can do for you.' Placing her mug down, Rachel nodded.

'Oh, right? In what way?'

'When the three of us were sorting out your back room, I happened to catch a few glances between you and Alex...'

Picking up her coffee, Sadie took a sip and swallowed hard. Rachel had noticed glances? She was here to warn her off. 'I...'

'Please don't deny it. I took a course to be a relationship counsellor when I was travelling. I know the signs. I know when people harbour feelings for each other, and you and Alex...' Rachel pointed to Sadie and then up to the far corner of the ceiling in the general direction of Alex's office. 'There are a lot of unsaid feelings going on there.'

'There's not. There really isn't.'

'Don't worry. He told me about your brief relationship and he told me it was you who shut it down.'

'Good.' She hadn't realised that Alex had told Rachel about them, she'd just assumed he wouldn't. Why wouldn't he have? It would make more sense for him to have been upfront and honest with Rachel than not.

'And I might have been able to put my suspicions down to the fact that the relationship between you both had one, been so short, and two, had ended so recently. I may have written my suspicions off as some little excess feelings between you both as a result of your relationship.'

'Okay.' Sadie nodded.

'But, when you two came in with the lunch, after he'd taken you to see the doctor, I was there when he insisted you sat down, when he cupped your elbows with his hands and lowered you into the chair. And that's when I realised that the connection you both have towards each other isn't a case of residual feelings from your relationship, it's real. It's how you both feel now.' Rachel stubbed her forefinger onto the counter.

Sadie looked down and fussed over Buddy. She could feel the fierce heat of embarrassment flushing across her face. What was she supposed to say? Yes, she did still have feelings for him and, yes; she felt a connection between them too? She couldn't. Not when Rachel had just got back into Alex's life. She couldn't and wouldn't do that. Not to Rachel and not to Alex.

'And there's only one question I have...'

Sadie gulped. Here it was.

'Why on earth aren't you both still dating each other?'

Scratching the side of her neck, Sadie looked at Rachel. 'Sorry?'

'There's something between you, that's obvious, and from what he's told me, he definitely still has feelings for you, so why on earth aren't you dating still? Why did you finish with him?'

'Oh, but I thought...' Swallowing, Sadie looked at Rachel.

'What? You thought that me and Alex...? Seriously?' Leaning back on the stool, Rachel laughed. 'Is that why you broke up with Alex? He told me it happened just before I met up with him again. You didn't break up because I came back, did you? Did you think that was the reason I was back? For Alex.'

This time, Sadie didn't try to hide the redness colouring her cheeks. 'I... I thought that... When you came back... I didn't want to get in the way of you both getting back together.' There, she'd said it.

'Girl! What me and Alex had back then was deep, it was meaningful, and it was real, but it was a long time ago and we've both changed. We've changed as people and we've changed as in what we want or look for in a partner. I didn't come back for Alex. Well, I did come to the village to see him, but not in that way. Not in a romantic way. At all. I came back to ask him to be my best man.'

'Your best man?'

'Yes, I know it's a tad unconventional for the bride to have a best man, and even more unconventional for him to be an ex, but it feels right. It feels perfect. There's not going to be anything conventional about mine and Lance's wedding anyway, so I thought, why not? Alex has been there for me in soooo many ways. He's been in my thoughts, powering me on through any stumbles I've had in my journey, and he'll be the best person for the job.'

'Oh, okay.'

'He's like my brother and I'm his sister, or as good as. There's nothing even vaguely romantic between us any more, but he's still a really special person to me. He still means such a lot and I love him.' Rachel held up her hand, the palm facing forward. 'Like a brother, I mean. I love him as my brother.'

'Sorry, I just assumed...' Sadie shrugged. What had she assumed? That after two years or so, Alex and Rachel still harboured feelings for each other and would want to jump straight back into a relationship together? Yes, that's exactly what she'd assumed. It all sounded so silly, so illogical now, but when she'd seen Rachel and how excited she'd been at the prospect of seeing Alex again, she'd just put two and two together and it sounded like she might as well have come up with seven hundred and forty-eight rather than four or even five.

'And so I'm asking you, why aren't you two together?'

'What about Alan the Electrician? What was that about if you're with this Lance guy?'

'What about him?'

'Well, I got the impression you were flirting with him?'

'Alan? No, he's just fun, that's all. Literally fun to talk to. He's married with five kids. We were laughing about the capers they get up to, that's all.'

Sadie shook her head. 'I feel really stupid now.'

'Why don't you pop over tonight? I'll make myself scarce and you and Alex can have a chat?'

'So, you are staying at Alex's then?'

'Yes, my hotel let me down last minute. They double-booked. You've not got the girls this evening, have you? They're going to Max's tonight, aren't they? So come over. I'll arrange to meet some mates and stay out as late as possible. You can tell Alex how you feel about him.'

'I don't know. I've probably blown it. Plus, if he still felt anything for me, he'd have said by now.'

'No, he wouldn't. You dumped him, remember? You were the one to break it off. He thinks you don't want him. It needs to be you who steps up and tells him how you feel.'

'Okay.' She could feel the knot forming in her stomach already. What if it was too late, and he had moved on? What if she'd ruined the whole thing? Or worse still, what if he'd thought Rachel *was* coming back for him? Sadie would still be second best.

'And, before you say anything, Alex knew about Lance months ago and he's known about the wedding for at least three months now.' Rachel shifted on the stool. 'And to further prove to you that we're not harbouring any long lost romantic feelings for each other, I asked him to get back with me before I met Lance and he turned me down.'

Sadie nodded. She'd really thought that he still loved Rachel. The way he'd spoken about her that day when they'd had the heart-to-heart... he must have spoken so fondly of her because he still cared about her, not because he was in love with her still. She picked up her coffee and leaned forward. She needed to change the subject before she threw up with the nerves. 'So, tell me about Lance.'

25

Sadie checked the time. It was half past four already. Where had today gone? Ever since Rachel had come to the shop and told her Alex still had feelings for her, the hours had seemed to flash by. She knew why; she knew exactly why. The knot in her stomach had grown with each passing hour. She knew she had to do what Rachel had advised. She knew she had to go round to Alex's and talk to him, try to put things straight, but with so much riding on one conversation she didn't know if she could. Not without throwing up in any case. It was silly, though, wasn't it? To feel so nervous. Rachel had all but said Alex wanted to get back with her, so why was she getting herself into such a state?

'Mum, Dad's just text. He's not picking us up this evening now.' Poppy looked up from the end of the counter where she was perched doing her homework.

'Oh, okay. No worries. Is he picking you up tomorrow?' Max probably wanted to pick them up after Lily's dance competition – it would mean less travelling for him.

'Nope, he says, can he swap weekends?'

'Yes, of course. Can you go and tell Lily that you're both staying here so she doesn't waste any time packing, please?'

'Yep, will do.'

Before Poppy had the chance to even stand up, Lily pushed open the door from the flat and strode up to the counter, her face pale and her eyes watery. 'Dad's not having us this weekend. He's obviously not going to come for my competition, which means he literally doesn't care about anything I do or how I feel or anything.'

'Has he said he's not coming then?'

'No, but if he's too busy to have us this weekend, then he'll be too busy to waste time coming to see me dance.'

'Hey, he wouldn't be wasting time coming to watch you dance. It'll be lovely, and I know he was looking forward to it so I'm sure he'll be there.'

'I doubt it. I'm not one of the golden twins, am I?' Lily slammed her mobile down on the counter in front of her mum.

Walking towards her, Sadie put her arms around Lily. 'You know Daddy loves you. He'll be there. I know he will.'

'Doubt it.' Shrugging away from the hug, Lily grabbed her mobile and disappeared back upstairs, the slam from her bedroom door audible from downstairs.

Sadie chewed on her bottom lip and looked across at Poppy. 'Poppy, can you do me a favour and go and feed Buddy please?'

'I thought his dinnertime was after ours?'

'It normally is, but he's been acting hungry all day so he might as well have it a bit early.'

'Okay.' Jumping off the stool again, Poppy ran upstairs.

Pulling her mobile from her pocket, Sadie walked across to the front door, checked the empty lane for any potential customers and spun the sign to 'closed'. Scrolling through, she found Max's name, took a deep breath and pressed 'call'.

Three rings later, and he picked up. 'Hello. Sadie.'

'Hi... I was ringing to...'

'Look, if this is about swapping weekends, I'm sorry it's such short notice. Tara arranged something with her friendship group a while back and there must have been a bit of a mix up because, when she'd booked it, she was sure it was a weekend when I didn't have the girls.'

Tara had a friendship thing? What did that have to do with Max? Unless he was thinking it would be too much hassle looking after all of his children on his own. Sadie rolled her eyes. 'That wasn't why I was ringing. Lily is worried that it means you won't be coming to her dance competition.'

'Dance competition? Is that this weekend?'

Picking up a blank order form, Sadie scrunched it into a small ball. 'Yes, it's tomorrow morning at ten.'

'Oh, I don't know if...'

'She's pretty upset. She thinks that you've forgotten about it or you don't want to come and see her dance.' Which, by the sounds of it, was true. Flattening the order form out again, she used her fingernail to pierce a hole through the thin paper.

Max cleared his throat. 'That's just silly. Of course, I want to come and see her dance. Hold on.'

Smoothing the edges of the order form out on the top of the counter, Sadie gripped her mobile between her ear and shoulder and began doodling, outlining The Flower Shop's name with a dark rectangle of ink. She could hear muffled voices over the line.

'Are you still there?'

'Yes.'

'We'll be there. We'll be at the dance competition.'

'Okay, great.' The words 'thank you' were on the tip of her tongue and she was too aware that they were what Max wanted to hear from her, but she wouldn't, she wouldn't thank him for putting his daughter first for once, for carrying out a promise that a parent shouldn't need to be badgered into keeping.

'I'll ring Lily and speak to her and tell her we're coming.'

'Great. See you tomorrow then.' Placing the phone down, Sadie crumpled up the order form and threw it in the bin. She might as well lock up for good now. It was only fifteen minutes before closing anyway, and no one had even wandered by. Yes, she'd sort out the takings and the float and spend some time with the girls. Lily would no doubt want an early night, so if they started a film now there would be plenty of time to finish it before she went to bed. First, though, she'd grab a coffee.

As she waited for the kettle to boil, the bell above the door to The Flower Shop tinkled. Hadn't she locked it? She must have just turned the sign around when she'd rung Max. Walking back out onto the shop floor, she saw Rachel.

'Rachel, hi. Everything okay?'

'Yep. I was just passing, so thought I'd pop in and check if you're still planning on going to see Alex tonight?'

Sadie shrugged. 'I can't. Max isn't having the girls now.'

Tilting her head, Rachel raised her eyebrows. 'It's a good job I popped in then. Alex will be back by now. He had a meeting this afternoon, which was supposed to finish at four. I'll look after the girls while you pop over.'

'I can't. Lily's upset because she thought Max wasn't coming to her dance competition tomorrow.'

The door to the flat opened and Lily came in, holding her phone out in front of her and grinning. 'Mum, Dad's just rung. He *is* coming tomorrow. He didn't forget. He was planning on coming all along.'

'That's great then. I knew he wouldn't want to miss it.'

'No, he said he wouldn't miss it for the world.' Lily looked across at Rachel. 'Hi, Auntie Rachel.'

'Hey, Lily, how about I paint your nails ready for tomorrow?'

'Really?'

'Yes. If that's okay with your mum, obviously?' Rachel looked across at Sadie and winked.

'That's fine.'

'Great. Up you go then, Lily, and I'll come up in a moment. Get all your nail varnish and bits out ready.'

'Awesome.' Lily ran back up the stairs to the flat.

'This'll keep us busy for a good hour. Off you go.' Rachel pointed to the door.

'I just need to...'

'Go.' Laughing, Rachel pointed at the door again. 'Everything else can wait.'

Sadie nodded. She didn't really have a choice, did she?

* * *

Walking up to Alex's terrace, Sadie smoothed her hair down and tucked a loose strand behind her ear. Did she really want to do this? She wanted to get back with him, yes, but was she ready to plead her case? She rolled her shoulders back in an attempt to loosen her muscles. Rachel had said he wanted to get back with her, she literally had nothing to lose. He liked her; she liked him. She just needed to apologise and then hopefully they'd be able to get back to how they had been. It might take a while, she knew that, but it'd be worth it.

As she approached his front door, she swallowed hard. She could do this. And the sooner she did, the sooner they'd be back together again. Before she had time to talk herself out of it, she knocked on the door.

No answer.

Maybe he wasn't in. The meeting must have overrun. She'd come back another time. Taking a step back, she turned.

'Sadie?' Alex stepped out of his car, which was parked outside his house, and held his hand up to wave.

'Alex. Hi.' Had he seen her smoothing her hair down? Had he watched her walk up the small hill? How hadn't she noticed his car there or the fact he was sitting in it?

'Everything all right?'

'Yes, everything's fine, thanks. How are you? Rachel said you had a meeting? Did it go okay?' Great, so now he'd know that she and Rachel had been talking about him.

'Yes, it was fine. It took longer than I thought, but it was okay.' Alex shut the car door behind him. 'Were you coming to see me?'

'Umm, yes, I was just wondering if you had a couple of minutes to have a chat? Don't worry if you haven't though.'

'Of course.' After taking his briefcase from the back seat, he pulled out his keys and opened the door, indicating Sadie to go through first.

'Thanks.'

'Did you want a coffee or something to drink?'

Did she? She didn't think she could drink anything, not with her stomach feeling the way it did at the moment, but then again, it'd be a good distraction. 'A coffee would be great, please.'

Dropping his briefcase to the floor and slipping off his shoes, Alex went through to the kitchen. 'How's the new back door holding up?'

'It's great. Thanks. Thanks again for helping with all of that. I couldn't have done it without you and Rachel.' She followed him through and watched as he switched the kettle on and spooned in coffee granules.

'Is instant okay? Sorry, I've run out of filter coffee. I meant to pop to the shop on the way home but completely forgot.'

'Instant is great. Thanks.'

'I don't mind it. It's not the same as proper coffee, but it does the job.' After pouring the water in, Alex added a splash of milk to one mug and passed it to Sadie.

'Thanks.' As she took the mug from him, their fingers touched and they looked at each other. It would be fine. He would accept her apology. She knew that. She just needed to work up the courage and talk to him.

'So, what can I help you with?'

Looking down at her mug, she took a deep breath. 'I wanted to talk about us.'

'Us?'

'Yes. I know I hurt your feelings when I broke things off with you and I wanted to explain and apologise.'

'Okay.' Alex shifted on his feet and loosened his tie.

'I... umm.' What was she supposed to say? She'd just have to come out and tell him the truth, wouldn't she? She gripped the mug between her hands, the scorching heat a welcome distraction. 'If I'm completely honest, and I feel there's no point in me not being honest, so I'll just come out and say it, I finished things with you because I wanted to give you and Rachel a chance. I thought you still had feelings for her, and I didn't want to come between anything that might have happened when she came back.' There, she'd said it. There was no going back now.

'I love Rachel as my sister. There's no romantic connection between us any more. There hasn't been for a long time. A very long time.'

'I know. That's what Rachel said. She also told me she'd come back to ask you to be her best man.' She looked him in the eye. 'I'm sorry. I read the situation completely wrong. I was too hasty and I guess I just didn't want to always feel like second best. I didn't want to not give you the opportunity to get back with her if you wanted to. I needed to give you the chance to make a move on her. Does that make sense?'

'Honestly? No. It doesn't make any sense at all.' Alex shifted on his feet. 'So, let me get this right, you finished things with me because you wanted me to get back with Rachel?'

'Yes, no. No, I didn't want you to get back with her, I just needed to give you the chance to if you wanted to. I thought you still had feelings for her and when she came into The Flower Shop asking after you, I guess I just jumped to the conclusion that she wanted you back.' Sadie chewed on her bottom lip. 'And after the way you'd spoken about her that time, I assumed that's what you wanted too.'

'You thought I was only seeing you because I couldn't date Rachel? And as soon as she walked back into my life you assumed I'd finish things with you and go running after her, so you got in there first?'

That was exactly what she had meant. It just hadn't sounded like that in her head. 'I guess. I thought you still had feelings for her and I didn't want to be the reason you didn't get back with her.'

Running his fingers through his hair, Alex looked down at his feet.

'I'm sorry. I really messed up.'

'You're only here because Rachel told you nothing was going on between us, aren't you?'

She turned the mug around in her hands, a little dribble of coffee spilling over the edge. Catching it with her finger, she wiped it against the ridge of the mug. 'I probably would have left it and given you time to figure out what you wanted, yes.'

'I didn't need time to figure out what I wanted. I wanted you.'

'Sorry.'

Alex picked up his mug. 'You didn't trust me. You didn't trust me to know what I wanted.'

He was right. Of course he was. She hadn't thought of it like that. She shouldn't have bolted; she should have had more trust in him. 'I made a mistake. A rash decision.'

Lowering his mug onto the work surface again, he turned to look out of the window before turning back to her. 'Thank you for apologising and telling me what was going on.'

That was it? Rachel had said he wanted to get back with her. Wasn't he going to make a move? Tell her that he forgave her? That he understood why she'd reacted the way she did? She cleared her throat, put her mug down and pointed to the front door. 'I'd better get back.'

'Okay.'

Nodding, Sadie watched as Alex stood still before turning and letting herself out.

26

The cold enveloped her as she stepped out into the street and pulled Alex's door behind her. What had actually just happened? She'd done what Rachel had advised. She'd spoken to him. She'd told him why she'd finished with him.

Turning down an alley which would take her on a shortcut back to The Flower Shop, Sadie paused and wiped her eyes. He just didn't feel the same about her as she did about him. That was clear now. He didn't care. All that rubbish that Rachel had said about noticing a connection and Alex having told her he still had feelings for her was rubbish. Rachel must have read him completely wrong. And she'd just made a complete fool of herself for nothing. For literally nothing. She'd poured her heart out for no reason. No reason at all.

As she picked up the pace, she came out of the alley. It hadn't led her the way she'd expected it to. She didn't recognise this street. Looking around, she saw another alleyway opposite. She'd try that.

Pausing at the end of the alleyway, Sadie sighed. It had taken her to the park. She couldn't even walk home the right way. She couldn't do anything right any more. She'd messed it all up.

She strode towards the bench next to the deserted swing set and sank onto the cold wood. Leaning forward, she rested her elbows on her knees and put her chin in her hands. She'd felt something for Alex. She really had. And now she'd messed it up. He didn't want to be with her any more, and how could she blame him? Would she have forgiven him if he'd thought he'd known her better than herself? If he hadn't trusted her not to run off with an ex?

That was it though. It was over. Well and truly over. Alex had made it clear there wasn't any turning back. He'd made it clear he didn't want anything to do with her after the way she'd behaved.

She sighed. There was no point in staying here, sat in the cold. She needed to get back. She needed to get home to the girls. It just meant seeing Rachel again and having to explain to her what had happened at Alex's.

'Hi, girls. Hi, Rachel. Thanks for looking after them.' Pausing in the doorway to the living room, Sadie looked around. The coffee table was covered in bottles of nail varnish, nail varnish remover, cocktail sticks and bits of tissue.

'You're very welcome.' Rachel grinned and raised her eyebrows.

With the slightest of movements, Sadie shook her head.

Frowning, Rachel stood up. 'I'd better get a wriggle on. Come on, Sadie, you can show me out.'

'Mum, look at my nails! Rachel drew snowflakes on them.' Holding out her bright blue nails, Poppy pointed to the tiny silver flakes delicately painted on top of the blue.

Coughing, Rachel laughed. 'They're supposed to be stars, remember, Poppy?'

'Oh yeah.' Poppy held her fingers up to her face, inspecting them. 'They do look like snowflakes too though.'

'They're lovely and I think they make brilliant snowflakes *or* stars. What did you have done, Lily?'

'Auntie Rachel did a grown-up French manicure for me so that it looks professional for tomorrow.' Lily showed her mum her fingernails and grinned.

'Wow, they're very neat. It's a good job you were here, Rachel, I'd have done wobbly lines and totally messed up.'

'Auntie Rachel says all the top professional dancers have French manicures.'

'I bet they do. They're lovely.'

'Right, come on, Sadie. Bye, girls and good luck with your competition tomorrow, Lily. Not that you're going to need it.' Pulling Lily in for a hug, Rachel kissed her head before turning to Poppy.

As they left the living room. Rachel cupped Sadie's elbow, drawing her towards her. 'So, tell me. What happened?'

Looking behind them to double-check the girls hadn't followed them, Sadie swallowed. 'He doesn't want me.'

'What do you mean?'

'Just that, he doesn't want a relationship with me.'

'Hold on,' Rachel paused. 'We are talking about Alex here, aren't we?'

Sadie nodded.

'Did you explain what had happened? Why you finished it and that you wanted to get back together?' Rachel led the way down the stairs.

'Yes, I explained why I'd finished things. I told him that I'd made a mistake, but he doesn't want to get back together. I can understand. I mean, I hadn't trusted him. If I'd trusted him, then...' Sadie shook her head as she pushed the door into The Flower Shop open. 'I just thought I was doing the right thing.'

Closing the door behind her, Rachel turned to face Sadie. 'That'll be his pride talking. I'll talk to him.'

'No. No, don't talk to him. I've spoken to him and he's made his decision. I certainly don't want to get back with him if the only reason is that you've talked him round. Please, don't talk to him. Please don't even mention that we spoke about what he said. Please?'

Rachel slumped her shoulders and held her hands out, palms facing forward. 'Okay, okay. I won't say anything.'

'Promise?'

'You have my word.'

Sadie nodded. She may not have seen her in years, but she knew she could trust Rachel's word. She wouldn't speak to Alex about them. 'Thank you. And thank you for watching the girls for me.'

'You're very welcome. It was good to catch up with them properly again.' Pulling open the front door, Rachel shrugged her coat on and stepped out into the lane. 'Go and watch a film with those gorgeous girls of yours or something.'

'I will. Thanks again.' She stood and watched as Rachel walked down the cobbled lane before closing the door. Turning the lock, she pinched the bridge of her nose and closed her eyes. Had all of that really happened? Had Alex really rebuffed her? Why hadn't she trusted him? Why had she felt she was in a better-placed position to make his mind up for him than he was? She'd made a really big mistake. She should have respected his decision.

'Mum? Are you coming back up?'

'Hey, Lily. Yes, I'm coming up now. What film do you want to watch?'

'We could watch that one about the two girls at High School? The one where they go to the prom? The one we were looking at the other day?'

'Good idea. That looked good.' Sadie followed her daughter up the stairs. 'You go on into the living room and put it on, I'll make us up some nachos.'

'Awesome! Remember, Poppy doesn't like the sour cream though.'

'Will do. No sour cream for Poppy.' Rubbing Lily's back, she waited until she'd gone into the living room before going into her bedroom. Sitting on the edge of her bed, Sadie grabbed her pillow and gripped onto it tightly. Clenching her teeth into the soft fabric, she let the tears flow. As they rolled down her cheeks and onto the pale blue fabric, she tried to reason with herself. Her and Alex's relationship had only lasted a few weeks. Many wouldn't even class it as a proper relationship, but it had been. It had been deep, and she'd fallen fast. She hadn't felt so strongly for anyone before. Possibly not even Max. With Alex it had been something different, it hadn't been the fast young flush of lust she'd had with Max, it had meant more, much more and in a shorter space of time.

'Mum?'

'Coming.' Lifting her face from the pillow she called back through to the living room. She and Alex had been close, had been good friends when she'd been married to Max and he'd been with Rachel. Just friends, but they'd got on so well back then and she'd assumed he'd forgive her for this. It wasn't as though she hadn't forgiven him for things recently.

Yes, she'd learnt that actually, he hadn't been plotting against her as she'd assumed during her and Max's divorce, but he'd still known about Tara a year if not longer before she had. She'd forgiven him for keeping that secret. She'd understood that he'd been trying to look out for her, trying not to hurt her. Why couldn't he forgive her? She'd only been doing the same. She'd only been looking out for him. She'd had his best interests at heart.

'Mum? The film's starting.'

'On my way.' Throwing the pillow back on the bed, Sadie stood up and wiped her eyes. Looking in the mirror, she dried her cheeks with the sleeves of her jumper before rubbing her hands against her skin to bring out some colour.

Nachos. She needed to get the nachos.

27

'Have you seen my hair scrunchie?' Running into the kitchen, Lily disappeared before Sadie even had time to process the question, let alone answer it. 'Poppy! Have you got my sparkly black hair scrunchie? I need it. Tell me where you've put it.'

Letting the dishcloth sink to the bottom of the washing-up bowl, Sadie followed Lily into Poppy's room.

'I haven't even seen it. Why would I want to wear that?' Looking up from her sketchbook, Poppy pulled a face before picking up another pen.

'Mum, Poppy's had my scrunchie. I need it. I need *that* one. Everyone else will be wearing theirs and we're all supposed to dress the same.'

'Don't panic. I'll find it. Where did you have it last?'

'Don't panic? Mum, I need to be at the theatre in an hour and I've still got to do my hair. I'm going to be late!' Turning around, Lily strode out of the bedroom.

'Lily, love. Come here.' Following her out onto the landing, Sadie held her arms wide.

'I haven't got time for that.'

'Come here.' Sadie nodded and wrapped her arms around her daughter as Lily sank against her body. 'It'll be fine. We've got time. Just take a few deep breaths. I'll find the hair scrunchie while you make sure you've packed the rest of your outfit, okay?'

'Okay.' Pushing away, Lily turned.

'And Lily?'

'What?'

'I love you and you'll be brilliant. I know you will.'

Lily blew a curl away from her eyes before rushing through to her bedroom. 'Love you too.'

Sadie smiled. Even a mumbled 'love you too' made everything worthwhile.

* * *

'So, do you know where you're sitting?' Lifting her holdall up higher on her shoulder, Lily's eyes darted from Sadie and Poppy to Ms Thetford, who was standing by the door down to the back of the stage.

'Yes, we'll find our seats. Don't worry about us and remember, whatever place your group comes in the competition, I'm proud of you. Super proud.' Sadie blinked as her eyes filled with tears.

'Mum! Don't cry. You'll embarrass me.'

'At least you don't have to sit next to her,' Poppy piped up and grinned.

'Oi! That's enough, Poppy!' Sadie laughed. 'Go on, Lily, off you go and sparkle.'

'Yeah, go and break a leg.'

Standing still, Sadie watched until Lily had been greeted and taken into the care of Ms Thetford before turning to Poppy and holding up the tickets. 'Any idea where our seats are then?'

'Nope.'

'Right. Well, it looks as though we're down there somewhere.' Sadie led the way down the carpeted aisle. People chattered excitedly in the rows of chairs either side of them, a hubbub of suspense and friendly competition.

'Is that Dad, Tara, and the twins over there?'

'Where?' Sadie squinted in the dim half-light.

'A couple of rows from the front.'

Sadie looked to where Poppy was pointing and closed her eyes momentarily. 'Oh yes, I see them. And I think these seats are ours. Why don't you go over and say hi while I get to our seats?'

'Yes, okay.' Poppy ran the short distance towards her dad.

'Sorry. Excuse me.' Careful not to knock their coats into anyone, Sadie sidled down the row towards their allocated seats. Great, they were literally two rows behind Max, Tara and the twins. Exactly behind. She rolled her eyes. The seats had apparently been allocated randomly, but surely this had been some joke by some person needing a laugh?

Sadie sank into her chair and laid the coats over her lap. She watched as Tara stood up and hugged Poppy, bringing her slight frame in close to her. Poppy, obviously feeling a little awkward by this public display of affection, looked sheepishly across to her mum. Jerking her head away, Sadie pretended to be interested in the family sat next to her. The last thing she wanted was for Poppy to feel awkward for hugging her stepmum. The past was the past and as much as she blamed Tara for the breakup of her family; she was also thankful to her for taking Max away. And above everything else, she was grateful to Tara for looking after Lily and Poppy when they visited. She knew Tara at least attempted to treat them and the twins the same; it was Max who seemed to have his favourites.

'Mum, I'm back.'

'Hey, Poppy, are they all okay? Are the twins looking forward to watching Lily dance?' Sadie held out her hand as Poppy squeezed past the people sat next to them.

'Yes, I think so. Tara said hello.'

'Oh, lovely. I'll say hello after the competition. There'll be more time to chat then.' She smiled at Poppy.

'Okay. When's it starting?'

Sadie checked the time on her mobile before turning it off. It was a shame they weren't allowed to take photos, but she guessed it would be fairly distracting for the dancers with a hundred different flashes going off as they tried to perform. 'Any time now.'

'Cool.'

Right on cue, the lights dimmed and a man in a dinner jacket and a woman in a bright blue cocktail dress strode onto the stage to introduce the competition.

As dancing school after dancing school was welcomed on stage to perform their competition piece, Sadie tried to concentrate on the dancers on stage instead of looking at Max and Tara. With them directly in front of her, it was a mean feat and one which she didn't always win.

They were sitting together with a child either side of them, Max's arm was laid across Tara's shoulders the entire time apart from small snippets of moments when the audience clapped. He'd never been that affectionate to her when they'd been married. In fact, in the last few years of marriage, she didn't think they'd had any physical contact at all. Sadie rolled her eyes. Obviously, it had been because he'd started seeing Tara behind her back, but at the time she'd just felt unworthy of attention, unworthy of love.

She chewed her bottom lip. Maybe the way Max had treated her had changed the way she thought of herself. Obviously, it had for a long time but she'd always thought she had got over his actions long ago, but maybe, just maybe that unworthy feeling had somehow embedded into her very being and that was why she'd pushed Alex away. Maybe she just hadn't felt worthy enough of his love. She shook her head. She was getting all philosophical for no reason. She was who she was, and she'd made the decision to end things with Alex. She hadn't had to. She'd decided to. It wasn't anyone's fault but her own.

'Look, it's Ms Thetford. Does that mean Lily's group is up next?' Poppy tugged on her mum's sleeve.

'Yes, they must be.' Sadie grinned and watched as Lily and her classmates danced elegantly onto the stage.

Mesmerised by the way Lily and her group performed, Sadie found herself lost in the music and the movements of the dancers. When the dance finished, she clapped until her palms were sore. Lily had done it. Lily and her group had shone.

* * *

As the final group disappeared from the stage, the curtain was drawn and the lights blared down on the audience.

'How long will they take to decide who's won?' Poppy stretched her arms out in front of her.

'The break's usually about twenty minutes and then they'll announce the winners.'

'That's not long.'

'No, but the judges will have written their scores down after each dance, so it'll just be a case of tallying them up and discussing any differences of opinion.'

'Oh, okay. Can we go and get a drink or cake or something?'

'We sure can.' Standing up, Sadie picked up her handbag and left the coats on the seat, indicating Poppy to lead the way.

Joining the long queue for the refreshments station, Sadie felt a tap on her shoulder. Turning around, she tried to keep her smile from fading. 'Tara. Hello.'

'Hello, darling. Lovely to see you here. What did you think of sweet little Lily's performance?'

Sadie wrinkled up her nose at the stench of Tara's perfume and took a silent, deep breath in. Had she really implied that she was surprised to see her there? Was it not a given that Sadie would be at her own daughter's dance competition? 'Great to see you here too. Lily and her group were fantastic.' Obviously.

'Of course, of course, she was. They all were. It was a very high standard of entries this year, don't you think?'

'It was.' She still maintained that Lily's had been the best, and she wasn't being biased. They just had been. All the dance groups had done phenomenally well, but Lily's group had stood out.

'So how have you been? And how's that sweet little flower shop of yours? Do you think you'll be able to turn a profit? I imagine it's quite quiet in a tiny village like that.'

'Tara, can you get the twins an ice cream each, love?' Holding a child with each hand, Max joined the queue.

For once Sadie was actually grateful to see him. 'Max, hi. Lily did us proud, didn't she?'

Turning quickly around, Max eventually noticed her. 'Sadie, I didn't see you there. Yes, she did.'

'Next please?' A young lad wearing a stripy cap called out.

Stepping forward, Sadie gave her order, relieved to be able to escape from the nightmare of small talk.

* * *

As they joined a small crowd of parents and siblings around the door they'd been told Lily's dance group would be coming out of, Sadie weaved through the people towards the middle of the group. Any chance of not having to stand and make polite conversation with Max and Tara, she was going to take it.

'Mum, can I go up the BMX track when we get home?'

'Shall we see what the weather's like? I think it's supposed to rain later.'

Poppy pointed to a tall window behind them. 'It's not raining now, though. Can I at least go out for a bit?'

'Are Ed, Harry and his dad going?'

'Yes.'

'Okay then. Just for a while though, you know how boggy the woods and track get when it rains.'

'Great. Thanks.' Grinning, Poppy took her mobile from her coat pocket and began texting Harry and Ed.

'Here they come now!' Standing on her tiptoes, Sadie tried to peer over the heads of the people in front of her as applause erupted from the small crowd. There she was. Waving her hand in the air, Sadie finally caught Lily's attention, and she made her way towards them.

'Lily! Well done, sweetheart. You were absolutely amazing! More than amazing, I think we're going to have to invent a new word. Well done!'

'Thanks, Mum.' Lily grinned and held out her medal – a golden number one hung from a red ribbon around her neck.

Sadie pulled her into a hug and kissed the top of her head. 'You did so well, my sweetheart.'

As the crowd dispersed, the twins ran across the carpet and jumped up at Lily, their hands reaching out for the medal.

'Well done, Lily.' Max gave her a small hug before stepping back and letting Tara in.

Holding her at arm's length, Tara kissed Lily on each cheek. 'You, my darling, were fantastic. The very best.'

'Thanks.' Glancing across at Sadie, Lily stepped back.

'Tara, we'd better get going.' Looking pointedly at his watch, Max tapped Tara on the forearm.

'Yes, we must rush but, amazing, Lily, you were truly amazing. A true little star. Bye-bye, Poppy, darling. Bye-bye, Sadie.'

'Yes, well done again, Lily.' Holding out his hands, Max waited until each twin was accounted for and followed Tara towards the exit.

'Right, who wants to stop by that dessert café on the way home to celebrate?' Holding out her arms, Sadie waited until Lily and Poppy had linked with her and began moving towards the street.

'Really? We can have dessert for lunch? No sandwiches or anything? Just ice cream?' Poppy looked wide-eyed up at her mum.

'Ice cream, waffles, pancakes, whatever you want. No sandwiches.'

'Yes, please! I'll tell Harry and Ed I'll be a bit late.'

'Okay.' Sadie looked at Lily. 'What do you think? Dessert to celebrate?'

'That sounds good. I could eat a whole cake right now.'

'I bet you're hungry after all that dancing and I don't suppose you ate any of that toast I made you for breakfast, did you?'

'I was too nervous.'

'I know, sweetheart, but you were fantastic. I'm so so proud of you.'

'Don't start crying again, Mum.' Lily laughed and rolled her eyes, hiding her face in mock embarrassment.

28

'Can we go now?' Poppy strapped her cycling helmet up.

Looking down at the lavender posies she was making, Sadie shrugged. They could wait. 'Yes. I'll just grab my coat and call up to Lily and Georgia.'

'Okay, cool. I'll go and get my bike.'

'Remember your knee and elbow pads.'

'Yep, I will.'

On her way to the bottom of the stairs, Sadie locked the shop door and turned the sign to indicate they were closed. Business was particularly quiet today, so she doubted she'd miss much custom. She hadn't even planned on opening up after Lily's dance competition, she'd thought they could celebrate together, but Lily had wanted Georgia round and Poppy was desperate to go up to the BMX track, so it seemed a waste if she didn't open.

Standing at the bottom of the stairs, she shrugged into her coat. 'Lily, Georgia. I'm just walking Poppy down to the woods, I won't be long.'

'Okay.' Lily appeared at the top of the stairs. 'Mum, can we go out to the park when you get back? And can you take Buddy with you? He's trying to eat our snacks.'

'Yes, of course. Buddy!' Bracing herself, Sadie waited as Buddy half-fell, half-jumped down the stairs in his haste not to miss out on walkies. 'Come on, Buds, let's pop your lead on.'

With Buddy at her heels, he pulled her through to the back room to find Poppy waiting with her bike.

'Ready?'

'We're ready.' Sadie waited until Poppy had wheeled her bike out from its spot in the back room and followed, remembering to grab a couple of dog poop bags on her way out. 'Now, remember if it starts to rain, go to the tarmac track, okay? I know it's not as difficult, but it'll still be fun and you'll still be spending time with Ed and Harry.'

'I will. It might not rain.' Poppy looked up at the clouds, scrunched up her nose and turned to her mum. 'Or not much anyway.'

'Hopefully, it'll just be a quick shower, but if it gets bad, you'll have to reschedule for another day.'

'I know. Don't worry.'

* * *

'And then if you could include some freesias in the bouquet, that would be lovely. Lilac ones if you have some, please?'

'That shouldn't be a problem.' Sadie smiled at the lady opposite her and jotted the order down in her notebook.

'And you'll be able to include a card as well?'

'Yes, of course. Did you want to choose one?' She pointed to the small metal rack in front of the till. 'Here's a pen if you want to write your message out now.'

'Mum, it's chucking it down out there.' Coming through from the back room, Lily lowered her hood, her face flushed from running. 'Is there anything to eat?'

After apologising to the customer, Sadie looked across at Lily. 'I'm just with a customer, why don't you go and dry yourselves off and I'll be with you in a moment?'

'Sorry. Okay. Come on, Georgia. Let's go and grab some towels.'

'Sorry.' Sadie smiled at the customer and took the card from her. 'Thank you. I'll pop this in the bouquet.'

'Thank you. Bye.' Taking a small umbrella out of her handbag, the lady opened it and stepped out into the street.

'Bye.' Waiting until the door had closed, Sadie walked to the bottom of the stairs. 'Lily!'

'Yes?' Lily came to the top of the stairs, rubbing a towel through her hair.

'I've got some cakes I picked up from the café earlier. When Poppy gets back, you can have one of those each, okay?'

'Oh yum. Thanks. Where is Poppy then? I assumed she was here?'

'No, she's still out on her BMX with Ed, Harry and his dad. I assume they'll be on their way back, judging by the look of you and the rate the rain's coming down now.' Although it had been raining lightly for some time, in the last twenty minutes or so the heavens had opened and it was pouring. She just hoped the council or the castle ground keeper, or whoever's job it was, had unblocked the drain further up the lane. She didn't fancy a repeat of the flooding.

'Harry and his dad aren't up there. We saw them as we were running back from the park.'

'Really?' Poppy knew not to stay up at the track without Harry's dad there. Lily must have been mistaken.

'Definitely. He drives that old blue minivan, doesn't he?'

'Yes.'

'It was him then. Harry waved at us too.'

Sadie slumped her shoulders. Harry and his dad usually cycled up to the tracks and back. For them to have been in the van, they must have left a while back.

'Is Poppy still up there then?'

'She must be.' Pulling her mobile out of her back pocket, Sadie scrolled down to Poppy's number. She was young to have a mobile, and Sadie had been against the idea when Max had bought them for the girls' last Christmas, but they certainly had their uses. Come on, Poppy, pick up.

'Is she not answering?'

'No.' Pressing the call button again, Sadie held the phone back to her ear and let the door to the stairs close behind her as she wandered towards the window. The rain was really heavy. The track would be completely bogged down by now. Even the tarmac track would be flooded or getting that way. Where was she?

'I'll try Ed.' Lily joined her mum at the window and scrolled through her mobile.

'Any luck?'

'Nothing.'

Stabbing the green button again, Sadie crossed her fingers. Pick up, Poppy. Pick up.

'Mum?' Finally. Poppy's voice sounded muffled and far away.

'Poppy, where are you? Harry and his dad aren't with you, are they? How many times have I told you that you need to stay with them? Are you with Ed?'

'I'm with Ed, but it's raining too much. We... we...' Poppy's voice wobbled.

'It's okay. I'll come and get you. Where are you?'

'We're at the...'

The phone buzzed with static in Sadie's ear. 'Poppy? Where are you?'

'...the mud started to slip and...'

'Okay. I'm on my way. Just tell me where you are.' Locking the front door, Sadie ran through to the back room. 'Poppy, where are you?'

'At the...' A faint scream carried down the line before it went quiet.

'Poppy? Poppy?' Pulling her phone away from her ear, Sadie stared at her mobile. Nothing. It had cut out.

'Is she okay?'

'I don't know. It sounds as though they're in trouble. I'm going to go up there.'

'I'll come.'

'No, you and Georgia stay here in case she comes back. Keep trying to ring her and if she answers let me know where she is, please?'

'Okay.' Lily rubbed her eyes.

'Hey, it's okay. She'll be fine. This is Poppy we're talking about. Try not to worry.' Pulling Lily towards her, she hugged her briefly before grabbing her car keys. 'Go back upstairs. I won't be long.'

Nodding, Lily left the room.

Letting the door bang shut behind her, Sadie raced to the car. What had happened? Why had Poppy screamed and why had the phone kept cutting out? Breathe, she needed to breathe and think. Poppy knew to go on to the tarmac track when it rained. That's where she'd be.

Yanking the car door open, Sadie slid into the seat and turned the ignition. Nothing. Come on. Not now. The car had been playing up for a few weeks, but it had still been going so she'd kept putting off booking it into the garage.

'Start, you stupid thing.' Wiping her now wet and matted hair from her eyes, she tried again. Nothing.

Getting out of the car, she kicked the tyre.

'Sadie, is everything all right?'

Looking across to the row of shops, Sadie spotted Alex. 'No, no, it's not. The car's not starting and Poppy's in trouble.'

Running across to his car which was parked next to hers, Alex pulled open the door. 'Get in. We'll take my car.'

'Buddy!'

Sadie looked back at The Flower Shop's back door, Lily was standing there shouting as Buddy ran towards Sadie. Looking at Alex and back to Lily, Sadie put her hand to her mouth. There wasn't time for this. They didn't have time to be messing around.

'He can come with us. It'll save time.' Alex opened the back door and Buddy jumped inside.

'Here.' Lily ran towards them, Buddy's lead in her hand.

'Thanks.' Taking the lead, Alex got into the car and indicated Sadie to do the same.

Slipping into the passenger seat, Sadie tried Poppy's phone again. Nothing.

'Where is she? What's happened?'

'She's up at the BMX tracks. She was meant to be there with Harry's dad. She knows to leave when he does. She should have left.'

'Is she in the woods or at the tarmac track?' Alex glanced at her as he pulled out of the car park.

'I assume at the tarmac track because it's raining, but her phone cut out.' Sadie looked out of the window, the rain lashing against the glass with a force she hadn't seen before. 'She screamed before the phone cut out.'

Keeping his eyes ahead, Alex took a deep breath. 'That doesn't mean anything. She was probably screaming because of the rain.'

'No, it wasn't. It wasn't like that. Something's happened to her. I know it has. I can feel it. She's in trouble.' She shouldn't have let her go up there. When she'd dropped her off, the clouds had looked dark and menacing. She should have just put her foot down.

'It's this one, isn't it?' Alex pointed to a lay-by at the side of the road.

'Yes. This one.'

The lay-by was deserted. As soon as the car pulled to a stop, Sadie jumped out, shortly followed by Alex, who grabbed his coat from the back seat and ran across to her.

'Here, put this on.'

Looking down, Sadie realised she'd left without her coat. Her thin, pale grey jumper was now dark in colour, the wool snagging at the bottom. Pausing to let Alex put it around her shoulders, Sadie did as she was told and put her arms through before pulling away and running down the narrow walkway which led between the trees. Following the signs, they turned right until they came to a field positioned at the side of the woods. Standing by the gate, Sadie held her hand above her eyes, trying to keep the rain from obscuring her vision and scoured the tarmac track which weaved through it. 'Poppy! Poppy! Ed!'

'Poppy! Ed!' Holding the gate open for her, Alex pointed to the left. 'You go that way, I'll go this. Shout when you find them.'

Nodding, Sadie began to run around along the track, up and down, over the small mounds and between the slopes. Where were they? 'Poppy!'

* * *

As she saw Alex running towards her, her heart sank. They weren't there. Poppy and Ed weren't there.

'No luck. Do you think they'd have stayed up at the tracks in the woods?'

'No, maybe. Poppy knows not to stay on those tracks when it's raining, though. They get too boggy. But they must be. They must be up there.'

'Come on, then.' Holding out his hand, Alex took Sadie's in his and together they ran back around the track and through the gate, Buddy fast on their heels.

'Which way is it?' Pausing at the entrance to the woods, Alex looked back at Sadie.

'Umm, it's that way. Straight up and to the right. The track starts up there.' As they ran, Sadie could see what the storm had done to the woods already. Branches had been blown down, and the ground was covered in a sheen of water, which mixed with the mud would make it lethal for anyone, let alone two kids on their BMXs.

As they neared the official beginning of the track, Sadie swallowed. As she'd feared, the dips were filled with rainwater and the hills streaming with water. The twists and turns in the track were a swamp of mud.

'Poppy! Ed! Where are you?' Even to herself, her voice didn't sound like hers, she didn't recognise the high-pitched panicked tones. Where were they? They hadn't been at the tarmac track, but there wasn't sight or sound of them here either. Where had they gone? She and Alex would have noticed if they'd left and had been making their way home, they would have seen them as they were driving here. They had to be here in the woods.

Unless... Sadie stopped, covering her eyes with her hands.

'You okay?'

'Where are they? What if they've been taken? Poppy screamed. She screamed before the line went dead. What if they'd been making their way home and someone had taken them?' Bile rose into her mouth. Her Poppy. Her little Poppy. She should never have let her out today. She should have made her stay at home.

'Listen.' Keeping his voice low, Alex cupped her elbows, forcing her to focus on his face as he spoke. 'If someone had taken them, we would have seen the bikes abandoned along the road. They're here. They're some-where and we'll find them. Sadie, okay?'

Sadie nodded. He was right. If someone had taken them, they would have seen their bikes. Yes, they would have. They were here. They had to be in the woods. Starting to run again, Sadie stopped just in time as a branch cracked and fell at her feet.

That was it. They were back at the beginning of the track again, and they hadn't seen them.

'Is that your phone ringing?' Alex pointed to Sadie's side.

Yes, yes, it was. It must be Poppy. She must be ringing to say she was okay. Trying to answer, she dropped her phone.

Alex bent down and retrieved it from a puddle at her feet, glancing at the screen as he passed it back to Sadie. 'It's Lily.'

Relief washed through her body. Lily was ringing to tell her Poppy was home. 'Lily? Is she back? Have you got her there?'

'Mum? No, I managed to get hold of her though. They're by the pond, there's been an accident.'

'Oh no.' With her hands shaking, Sadie plunged her phone into Alex's coat pocket and looked at him. 'They've had an accident. They're hurt. I know she's hurt.'

'Where is she?'

'The pond. At the pond.'

'Where's that? The one at the back of the woods?'

'Yes, they must have been coming home through the fields. Why would they have done that? Alex, she's hurt.' Sadie could barely feel her body shaking, barely acknowledge the tears streaming down her face mixing with the relentless rain.

'Right, it'll be quicker if we get back to the car and drive around. She'll be all right. She spoke to Lily, so she's okay even if she is hurt.'

Nodding, Sadie allowed herself to be led back through the trees and down the incline towards the car park. Yes, Poppy would be okay.

Back in the car, Sadie gripped hold of her phone as Alex pulled out of the lay-by, did a three-point turn in the middle of the road, and sped off in the direction they'd come.

* * *

About half-a-mile back towards the village, there was a narrow road which led to a small car park at the back of the woods. This was where the dog walkers and ramblers usually parked, well away from the BMX track by the main road. Farmers' fields surrounded a meadow which led to an area with a pond and entrance to the woods.

As Alex weaved the car around potholes and puddles on the road, Sadie tried Poppy's phone again. Still no answer. Why wasn't she picking up? As they neared, Sadie could see that the small car park was deserted and a large puddle had formed at the entrance.

Slowing the car down, Alex drove through the entrance, water splashing at the sides of the car. Putting his foot on the accelerator again, he drove to the edge of the car park and pulled the handbrake on.

As they jumped out of the car, Alex opened the back door and took Buddy's lead.

'This way.' Sadie led the way through to the meadow.

'Mind yourself, some of these parts are really deep.' As they ran through the flooding meadow, Alex pointed to a part where the water looked deeper than elsewhere.

Sadie's foot hit something under the surface of the water and she tripped, saving herself by putting her hands out.

'Are you okay?'

Shrugging Alex's hand and concerns away, Sadie pushed herself to standing and ran towards the hedgerow which surrounded the meadow. If she remembered correctly, there was a small wooden walkway about halfway down which led through the hedgerow, partitioning the small field with the pond from the meadow.

Just as they were coming up to the wooden walkway, Sadie's phone buzzed, its ringtone lost in the noise of the rain. Pulling it out, Sadie slowed and stopped. 'Poppy! Poppy, are you okay? We're in the meadow, where are you? We're coming.'

'Mum... Mum?' Her voice was barely audible. 'Mum, we're stuck. We can't get back. We're stuck.'

'Where? Where are you stuck?'

'Mum? Mum... I can't hear you... We're at...'

'Poppy? Poppy, where are you?' Pulling her phone from her ear, Sadie looked at it. Nothing. The connection was lost. Shaking her head, she looked across to Alex. 'She said they're stuck. They're stuck.'

'Okay. They must be nearby. Lily said she'd told her they were at the pond.'

Pausing at the wooden walkway, Sadie looked around her. The area with the pond was about half the size of the meadow they had just run through and was surrounded by trees on three sides, and the hedgerow on the fourth. A usually serene and slow-moving stream cut through the field in front of the trees along the back, which led into the main part of the woods. Apart from the small the wooden walkway between the hedges, there was a gap in the hedge further down for the service vehicles. Sadie looked across to the right where the pond sat, only she could hardly distinguish between pond and grass as the rain had all but covered the ground. The pond looked as though its shallow banks had burst and the gravel pathway which usually looped it had all but disappeared.

'Poppy? Ed?' Turning to Alex, Sadie pointed across towards the pond. 'I can't see them. She said they were here. She said they were at the pond.'

'Did they say at the pond or near it? They might be in the woods nearby.' Wiping his wet hair from his eyes, Alex scoured the tree line.

'How are we supposed to find them now?'

'Have you got FindMyPhone? Can you see if Poppy's location is showing?'

'I can do, but it's usually not very accurate. It won't pinpoint her exact location.' It was worth a try though, anything was. Pulling out her phone, Sadie scrolled through her apps, stopping every so often to wipe the raindrops from the screen.

Buddy barked and pulled against his lead, turning in circles.

'Buddy. No.'

Standing on his hind legs, Buddy propelled himself forward, tugging his lead from Alex's grasp. Lunging forward, Alex tried and failed to get hold of him again. Looking across at Sadie, Alex signalled her to follow. 'He may have picked up on Poppy's scent.'

As Buddy weaved this way and that way through the waterlogged field, Sadie and Alex splashed behind him, running as fast as they could through the water to keep up. Coming to an abrupt stop in front of them, it took Sadie a moment to realise that it was the stream that Buddy had stopped in front of. This too had escaped its banks and was flowing uncharacteristically fast. Barking, Buddy's gaze was fixed at the trees opposite.

'Poppy? Ed? Is that you? Are you over there?' Inching forward towards the stream, Sadie searched the trees opposite.

Alex gripped onto Sadie's arm and pointed with his other hand. 'Look, look over there.'

'Mum? Mum, is that you?' Poppy's voice was faint, but it was definitely her.

'Poppy!' Relief flooded through Sadie's body as she made out Poppy's small frame standing between two trees, a little further up the steep muddy bank.

'Ed is hurt. He slipped, and he's hurt his ankle. He can't walk on it.' Poppy's voice quivered as she pointed into the thicket behind her.

'Okay. Don't worry. We'll come to you. Just stay there.' Holding her hand up, Sadie indicated to Poppy to stay put before looking up and down the stream. She needed to find a way to get across. She needed to find a way to get to them. The water was flowing quickly, and because the stream had burst its banks there was no way to tell how deep it was.

'Here.' Running towards the trees to the left, Alex came back holding a branch. 'We can see how deep it is.'

'Good idea.'

Wading further into the running water, Alex slipped before throwing himself backwards. 'The bank dips down there.'

Sadie grabbed hold of his arm and pulled him back up to standing.

'Thanks.' Leaning forward once more, Alex tried to keep his footing as he leaned down and held the branch upright in the furthest point he could reach, without falling in again. 'It's about three foot, give or take.'

Sadie grimaced as the unmistakable rumble of thunder rolled across the sky.

'Mum!' Poppy's shout carried on the wind as she stood holding onto the trunk of a tree opposite.

'It's okay, sweetheart. One moment.'

'Even if we get across there without getting swept off our feet, there's no way we'll be able to carry Ed across if he can't walk.' Alex reached into his pocket and pulled out his phone. 'I'll give the emergency services a call and get someone out.'

Chewing on her bottom lip, Sadie knew that was probably the most sensible idea for everyone's safety, but to see Poppy obviously scared and distressed barely six metres away from her and not be able to do anything... She shook her head. There was no choice. 'Okay.'

Alex sighed. 'I haven't got any signal, have you?'

Sadie looked down at her phone and shook her head. 'Nothing.' What were they supposed to do now? 'We could go back and go through the woods from the lay-by. We might be able to get them that way.'

Alex ran his fingers through his drenched hair and looked across at Poppy. 'No, that would be a good couple of miles from the lay-by to them, and that's if there aren't any obstacles en route. Wait here.'

'Where are you going?' Too late, Alex had already started running back towards the walkway through the hedgerows.

'Mum, what's happening?'

'It's okay. Alex has just gone to get help. It won't be much longer now.' Inching forward, Sadie used her foot to locate the bank of the stream. She couldn't wait for help, Poppy looked terrified and poor Ed must be in an even worse state because he was in pain and couldn't even move around to warm himself up. He'd be sat there in his soaking wet clothes. Sadie swallowed. Maybe she could get across and just stay with them until help came. Yes, that would be better than her just standing and waiting around.

'Mum, Ed's shaking now and he's gone really pale.'

That was it. She needed to get across. She was a fairly good swimmer; she'd be able to swim against the current of flowing water. 'Don't worry, I'm coming.'

'Careful.'

'I will be, sweetheart.' Stepping forward, it didn't take long until she slipped on her back just as Alex had done, but instead of trying to get back, she wriggled herself forward along the ground. With her feet out in front of her, she felt along the ground until she could feel it dip further down. She must be at the edge of the stream, or where the stream had originally been, anyway. Now all she had to do was stand up and wade across. Placing her hands behind her, she used all her strength to push herself up, but every time she managed to get on her feet for a moment, the current was too strong and threatened to pull her over.

She couldn't get across, she couldn't get to Poppy and Ed.

'Mum! Are you okay?'

'I'm fine.' Briefly holding her hand up before plunging it back into the cold water again to find something to steady herself, she grinned. She needed Poppy to think she was in control. She couldn't do it. She couldn't get across. Twisting her body, she flipped herself onto her front and grabbed a handful of long grass in front of her, using it to pull herself up and out of the flowing water. Kneeling at the other side again, Sadie caught her breath. What now? What now?

A low rumble vibrated through the ground, and Sadie turned. What was that? Was that Alex in his car? Yes, he was driving through the gap in the hedgerow which the service team used. Pulling herself to standing, she watched as his car slid on the wet ground; the tyres struggling to grip the ground underneath the surface of the water. What was he doing?

As the car steadied again and Alex managed to regain control, she watched as he picked up speed as he drove towards her. What was he thinking? Why was he driving his car around here? He'd likely get stuck if he didn't back out soon. The closer he got, the faster the car became.

Peering through the windscreen as the car came forward, she could see determination etched across his face. He was going straight for the stream. How would that help?

'Alex! Careful! Stop!' He was going to end up wrapping it around a tree if he wasn't careful. Even though he seemed to have more grip now, he was going a bit quicker and the car was still weaving about unpredictably. Standing there, helpless, Sadie watched as he drove straight into the stream, the telltale red glow of the brake lights coming on as he hit the water.

As the car came to a thudding stop as it hit the opposite bank of the stream, Sadie ran towards him. Had he meant to do that, or had he lost control? Was he okay? 'Alex!'

She watched as Alex wound down the window and climbed out of the driver's side. Pulling himself up onto the roof, he slid down the windscreen and crawled across the bonnet before jumping down. Grabbing a low-hanging branch, he steadied himself before climbing the muddy incline up to where Poppy was waiting.

Standing there, Sadie watched as they disappeared into the trees. After what felt like half an hour but was probably barely a few minutes, they emerged again, this time holding up Ed between them as he hobbled forward. Pausing at the top of the incline, they lowered Ed back onto the ground before Alex indicated for Poppy to follow him. Holding her hand, they half slid and half stumbled back down towards the car.

Going towards the car, Sadie pulled herself up using the spare wheel which was strapped to the back and began crawling across the roof, holding on to the roof bars to stop herself from slipping. As she came towards the windscreen, she grabbed Poppy's hand and pulled her up.

'That's it, hold on.' Gripping Poppy's hand, they made their way across again and Sadie helped her climb down. Indicating her to stay, she made her way back across.

Waiting on the roof of the car, Sadie watched as Alex helped Ed towards her before helping him up onto the roof. Climbing down, Sadie held out her arms and helped Ed on the ground, before turning back and holding her hand out for Alex.

They were safe. They were all safe.

29

'And you seriously drove your car into the stream?' Lily sat wide-eyed on the floor and looked up at Alex as he drank his coffee on the sofa.

'There wasn't another way of getting your sister and Ed.' Alex shrugged.

'And where's your car now? Is it okay?' Georgia, who had decided to stay for a takeaway, looked over at him.

'It'll be fine.'

'When it gets pulled out of the stream and has its engine fixed, you mean?' Sadie dried her wet hair with a towel. After Poppy and Ed had been rescued, Sadie had run down the road until she'd managed to get a signal to call Ed's Dad who had come and picked them up. Although Ed would probably need an X-ray, he had hopefully just sprained his ankle badly. After going home for a shower and a change of clothes, Alex had popped round to check on Poppy, who had insisted he stayed for their takeaway.

'I'm sure the insurance will pay out if not.'

Sadie looked at him. She wasn't so sure the insurance would cover flooding an engine on purpose, but when she'd said she'd repay him, he'd dismissed her and said it had been his choice and that Poppy was his goddaughter. Sitting down on the opposite side of the sofa, with Poppy in-between, Sadie reached for her coffee. How could she ever repay him for what he had done?

'That's the doorbell! Our pizzas are here!' From where she was sat, in the middle of the sofa, snuggled under a blanket, Poppy grinned.

'I'll go.' Sadie stood up and headed downstairs.

* * *

Balancing the pizza boxes in her hand, Sadie paused at the door to the living room. Poppy was half asleep curled up in her pyjamas, Lily and Georgia were giggling over something on their phones and Alex was sat seemingly engrossed in the talent show on the TV and still drinking his coffee.

She could have lost her today. She could have lost her Poppy. Sadie blinked back the tears which were threatening to spill. She knew she was probably being overdramatic, but she'd feared the worst when they hadn't been able to find her and Ed, and the thought of someone having taken them, or the fact that they could have slipped and banged their heads or something... Sadie shook the thoughts from her head. She couldn't think like that. She didn't want to think like that. Poppy was home safe and sound and Ed was getting seen to in the hospital. They'd both be fine.

She still had so many questions to ask Poppy. She'd tried to glean as much information from her on their way home, as to why she and Ed hadn't gone home with Harry and his dad, but all she could get out of her had been apologies and the fact that she and Ed had decided to stay on for a bit. Apparently, they'd planned to leave shortly after Harry and his dad had, and then the downpour had come and Ed had fallen over and hurt his ankle.

Plastering a smile on her face in the hopes it would conceal how she was feeling, she walked into the living room and placed the boxes on the coffee table. 'Pizza! I'll just go and get some plates.'

In the kitchen, Sadie reached up into the cupboard to pull down the plates.

'I'll get those.' Walking up behind her, Alex reached and took them down, placing them on the work surface in front of her.

'Thanks.' She turned around; their faces were only inches apart.

'Are you okay?'

Taking a step back, Sadie busied herself getting glasses and a bottle of pop she'd found at the back of the cupboard. 'I'm fine. Thank you again for today. I don't know what I would have done without you.'

'Sadie.' Stepping towards her, Alex turned her to face him again. 'Are you sure you're okay?'

'Yes. No. I just keep thinking about what could have happened.' Looking down, she shrugged. It was silly, feeling like this. She should be grateful. She *was* grateful. It was just every time her mind wandered, she could just see Poppy, small and terrified, stuck on the other side of the stream. Pulling her towards him, Alex enveloped her in his arms and kissed the top of her head. His warmth, and the safety she felt in his arms, tipped her over and the tears rolled freely down her cheeks. 'It's silly, I know it is. I'm grateful, I'm happy she's fine but...'

'Hey.' Alex gently tipped her chin back with his forefinger, so they were looking into each other's eyes. 'It's normal to feel the way you are. It was a massive shock. I think if we weren't all affected by it, we'd be heartless. It was a horrible and scary situation.'

Nodding slightly, Sadie looked at him. 'You're right. I know you are.'

'I am.' Alex gave a cheeky grin. 'But, seriously, it's natural to feel the way you are. It's been a crazy day.'

'You can say that again.'

'It's been a crazy day!'

Frozen to the spot, Sadie could see every flicker of his eyes and feel his warm breath against her cheeks.

'Mum?'

Both Alex and Sadie pulled away at the same time just as Lily came through the door.

Pausing in the doorway, Lily looked at her mum and then to Alex and back again before shrugging. 'I was just going to come and get a drink.'

'Here, do you want to take these glasses in and I'll bring the plates and the pop?'

'Okay.' Taking the glasses from the work surface, Lily gave them both a strange look before turning around and heading back out.

'I'll take these.' Picking up the plates, Alex smiled and followed Lily through to the living room.

Sadie laid the palms of her hands to her cheeks. What had just happened? Had she imagined it, or had there been a moment? Would they have kissed if Lily hadn't walked in? Picking up the bottle of fizzy drink, Sadie shrugged. It hadn't happened. It had probably all been in her imagination, or if it hadn't then it was probably just a reaction to the day they'd shared.

30

'Okay, love you. Enjoy your day at school.' Hiding behind the hedge on the corner down from the bus stop, Sadie hugged Poppy. She had given her the option to have today off school, but Poppy had insisted she wanted to go in and tell everyone her weekend adventure.

'Love you too, Mum.' Grinning, Poppy pulled her rucksack higher up on her shoulder and walked around the corner.

As much as Sadie wanted to wait until the bus had come and wave her and Lily off, she knew she'd only embarrass them in front of their friends. Turning around, she almost walked straight into Harry's dad. 'Oh, sorry. I didn't see you there.'

'Hi.' Harry's dad waved Harry around the corner.

'I see you do the same then. You're not allowed to show your face around the corner?'

'No chance. Poor Harry would die of embarrassment! I'm glad I ran into you, actually. I heard what happened at the woods with Poppy and Ed and I can't help but feel responsible. You see, my wife's car had broken down, so we had to leave quickly to go and help. Poppy and Ed had assured me they were allowed to walk back by themselves.' Frowning, he shrugged. 'If I'd had even an inkling they were going to hang around, I would have insisted they walk back with me. I'm so sorry.'

'Oh no, it's not your fault. At all. Poppy, and I'm sure Ed too, knows not to stay over there on their own and not to stay in the woods when it's raining. It's so good of you to let them hang around with you and Harry. It's not your fault at all. They were just being kids and pushing the boundaries.' Sadie grimaced. 'I think they've both learnt their lesson now though.'

'Yes, I imagine they have. And thank you, I've been so worried that you and Ed's parents would view me as responsible.'

'Not at all. Besides, I told Poppy she could have today off school, but she's insisted on going in. She's got an adventure she needs to tell!' Sadie laughed.

'Ahh, it's all about adventures at that age.'

'It seems to be.' Hearing the bus arrive, they both started walking quickly in the opposite direction. 'And thank you so much for keeping an eye on them when they're up there with you.'

'No worries at all. They occupy Harry. I'd better get going, I've got a fair bit of travelling to do with work today.'

'Okay. Bye.'

'See you another time.' He jumped off the kerb and crossed the road, heading back towards his house.

Sadie checked her watch. She still had a few minutes before The Flower Shop needed opening up. Certainly enough time to pop to the café for a bacon butty and a latte.

Turning the corner towards the café, Sadie sighed. The queue was that long people were waiting outside. She shrugged. She had time to wait and now she'd thought about getting a latte, her body was craving one.

As she joined the end of the queue, she tucked her hands in her coat pockets, hiding them from the early morning chill. The café was often busy at this time. A lot of people from the village popped to grab breakfast or caffeinated drinks on the way to work, mix those with people passing through, and they had a good amount of early morning business.

As the queue shortened, she stepped into the warmth of the café. The aroma of coffee mixed with newly baked cakes made her stomach rumble.

'Sadie.'

Turning, she saw Alex standing next to an empty table. She hadn't seen him in the queue, he must have been that further ahead and inside when she'd joined it. 'Hi.'

Alex nodded his head towards the two cups and paper bags on the table. 'A latte and a bacon butty, right? I was going to pop by on my way to the office and drop these off for you.'

'Oh, thank you.' Stepping out of the queue, Sadie walked over to him.

'Look, I've even treated us both to a reusable takeaway cup, no more wasting plastic and cardboard for us. Are you impressed?'

She looked down at the silver metal takeaway cups and grinned. 'I am, actually. I'm very impressed. Thank you.'

'You're welcome.' Alex glanced down and ran his fingers through his hair. 'I...'

'Did... Sorry, you go first.' Sadie took a sip of latte.

'No, it's fine. What were you going to say?'

'Did the garage give your car the all clear?' After the barber kindly gave her car a jump-start yesterday, they'd gone back up to the woods to collect Poppy and Ed's bikes and to see to Alex's car. Miraculously, it had started, one of the perks of driving a 4x4 she supposed, but he'd said he'd take it to the garage to get it checked over.

'It's there now. They're going to give it a valet too.' He winked.

Sadie nodded and laughed. 'I can't imagine that'd be a nice job, the state we'd left it in.'

'No, but I'm sure they'll do a good job.'

'What were you going to say?'

'Oh, I was just going to...' Looking across at the queue and back to Sadie, Alex shifted on his feet. 'I just wanted to talk about...'

Tilting her head, she looked at him. He wasn't usually this hesitant about talking to her. 'Is everything okay?'

'Yes, I...' Chewing his bottom lip, he looked at her before gently taking her cup out of her hand and placing it firmly on the table. 'I wanted to ask...'

As he inched towards her, Sadie could feel the electricity between them. She leaned forward towards him as he placed his hand at the back of her neck, his skin warm against hers. When his lips finally met hers, she sank towards him, wrapping her arms around his neck. That's why he'd been acting so shy then. Smiling against his lips, she closed her eyes, the familiar rush of the feelings she felt towards him pulsing through her.

Leaning back, he licked his lips. 'I was going to ask if you'd forgive me for being an eejit the other day and if you'd have me back?'

'Of course, I will.'

EPILOGUE

Sadie pulled at the clasp in her hair. She'd put it in too tight in the rush of getting ready.

'Here, let me.' Leaning towards her, Alex loosened the clasp before kissing her on the lips. 'Have I told you today that I love you?'

She laughed. 'Just a couple of times!'

'Well, it's true.'

'I love you too.' Turning, she took hold of his hand and lifted it to her lips before lowering it and waving at Poppy and Lily. They looked so grown up, standing next to Rachel and her now-husband, Lance, on the church steps as the photographer ordered everyone to say 'cheese' as the photo was taken.

'Bride and bridesmaids, hold up those fabulous bouquets!' The photographer waved a hand in front of the camera lens.

'Did you hear that? Even the photographer thinks your creations are fabulous!' Wrapping his arms around her waist, Alex grinned at Lily and Poppy.

'Aw, I'm sure he says that about everything he photographs.'

'I very much doubt it. Plus, you've got that journalist coming to do a feature on The Flower Shop next week, you've got to admit your business has gone from strength to strength in the last few months.'

A flush of redness crept across her face. The Flower Shop *was* doing well, even if she didn't know if she'd have the confidence to show it off to the journalist from the local paper next Tuesday. It would be good for business if she could, though.

'Thank you! Let's have the maid-of-honour, sorry, the best man of the bride join us now, please? That's it, stay put bridesmaids, we need you too.' Barking his orders, the photographer ran towards the church steps, pulling one person this way and another that way, determined to get the best photograph possible.

'Hey, they look like they're having a good time?' Melissa weaved her way towards Sadie, Luke closely behind.

'They do, don't they? They were made up when Rachel asked them to be bridesmaids.'

'I bet.' Melissa leaned in closer. 'And things look like they're going well with Alex?'

Sadie grinned. 'Yes, they are. Things are going really well. We've even spoken about moving in together.'

'Ooh, that's exciting! What do the girls think?'

'They can't wait. We're going to move into Alex's house, to begin with anyway. They're looking forward to having a garden again and, apparently, I let them have more takeaways when Alex is about.' Sadie laughed.

'They've got their priorities sorted, I see.' Melissa grinned. 'I'm glad it's going so well for the both of you. You both deserve it.'

'Thanks.'

'Time to throw the bouquet. Gather round girls!' Jumping down from the steps, Rachel called across to her guests.

'Aw, now I've got to watch my hard work be thrown to the ground.' Sadie covered her eyes in mock despair.

'Go catch it then!'

'No, I'm not doing that.'

'Go on. You're not married, yet. Go catch your bouquet.'

'Come on, Mum! Let's go and catch the bouquet!' Poppy ran towards her and began pulling her towards the small gathering in front of Rachel.

'Yes, come on, Mum!'

'Not you too, Lily. I'm outnumbered here.' Laughing, Sadie looked from

Lily to Poppy and back to Rachel, who was still shouting at people to join the crowd. Looking across at Melissa, Sadie smiled, why not? She wouldn't catch it anyway, and it would be a fun thing to do with Lily and Poppy.

'I'll hold your handbag. This is serious business.'

Sadie did as she was told and passed her bag to Melissa, and allowed herself to be pulled in the direction of the group of women and children at the foot of the church steps.

'Right, I'm going to throw it on three. Ready? One, two, three.' Bending down, Rachel straightened herself and let go of the bouquet.

As the large bouquet was catapulted into the air, a collective gasp sounded from the ground and people rushed forward, their arms eagerly held out and upwards.

With Lily and Poppy by her side, Sadie lifted her arms and pretended to make an attempt to catch it. The bouquet, which was still spinning, came closer and closer. Blinking against the bright sunlight, Sadie grimaced. It was heading straight towards her. If there was one thing which would spoil this day, it would be watching that bouquet, which had taken two hours to complete, smash into the ground. There was no chance she was going to let that happen. Not today and not to Rachel's bouquet. Jumping up, she felt the stems against her skin and gripped.

'Yay! Mum, you did it. You caught the bouquet!' Lily grinned before taking her mobile from her bag and snapping photographs of her mum, standing, looking at the flowers in her hand.

She had actually caught it! She'd never caught anything in her life, she had always been the child who was picked last for the rounders teams because her classmates knew she wouldn't be able to catch a ball if her life depended on it, and now she'd caught a bouquet.

'Yay! Mum and Alex are getting married! Mum and Alex are getting married!' Dancing around in front of her, Poppy clapped her hands.

Lowering the bouquet, Sadie could feel the heat of embarrassment flush across her face as the wedding party applauded and cheered. What had she done? Catching Alex's eye, Sadie shrugged. 'It took me two hours to make, there was no chance I was going to let that go to waste.'

Alex winked and walked across to her as Rachel announced the reception at the pub across the road was about to start. 'That was one heck of a catch.'

'As I said, it took me two hours to make. It would have broken my heart if it had fallen to the ground.' Sadie looked down at the bouquet in her hand. She shouldn't have joined in the tradition.

'Come on, you lot. There are free drinks for the first hour!' Luke called back as he and Melissa joined the wave of guests crossing the road to the reception.

'We'll be over in a moment.' Alex waved at them. 'Lily and Poppy, you two wait with us, would you?'

'We'll miss our free drinks.' They were alone now, just the four of them, and the serenity of the churchyard surrounded them.

Clearing his throat, Alex took the bouquet from Sadie and passed it to Lily before taking Sadie's hands in his. 'Sadie, I've known you a long time and I love you more than I've ever loved anybody before, or could I ever imagine loving someone.'

With her hands in his grasp, Sadie could feel his hands becoming clammy. Looking up at him, she noticed his face had paled. 'Are you okay?'

Alex laughed nervously. 'I will be, hopefully. I want you to know how much I love you and the girls.' He looked across at Lily and Poppy. 'And I can't imagine my life without you three in it.' Getting down to one knee, he fished in his pocket for a small box.

Standing still, it was Sadie's turn to feel nervous. He was going to ask, wasn't he? He was actually going to ask!

'I had so much I'd planned to say and I hadn't planned on asking you today, but I've been carrying this around with me for days now, and since you caught the bouquet, it seems crazy not to use this opportunity...'

'Alex?'

As he pulled the small box open, a row of small diamonds glinted in the sunlight. 'Will you marry me?'

Bringing her free hand to her mouth, Sadie gasped. 'Yes. Yes, of course, I will.'

'Can I be a bridesmaid?' Poppy jumped up and down around them. 'You said I could, didn't you, Alex? Can I?'

'You two knew?' Looking across at Lily and Poppy, Sadie shook her head. How could they have kept this a secret from her?

'Of course, they knew. I couldn't very well ask their mum to marry me if I didn't have permission from the two most important people in your life.' Alex slipped the ring on Sadie's finger and leaned forward to kiss her.

ACKNOWLEDGEMENTS

Thank you, readers, for taking the time to read *The Flower Shop on Serendipity Lane*. I hope you've enjoyed reading about Sadie's journey to follow her dreams and her love with Alex as much as I enjoyed writing her story.

A huge thank you to my wonderful children, Ciara and Leon, who motivate me to keep writing and working towards 'changing our stars' each and every day. Also to my lovely family for always being there, through the good times and the trickier ones.

And a massive thank you to my amazing editor, Emily Yau, who reached out and believed in me – thank you.

Thank you also to Shirley for copyediting and proofreading *The Flower Shop on Serendipity Lane*. And, of course, Clare Stacey for creating the beautiful cover. Thank you to all at Team Boldwood!

ABOUT THE AUTHOR

Sarah Hope is the author of many successful romance novels, including the bestselling Cornish Bakery series. She lives in Central England with her two children and an array of pets, and enjoys escaping to the seaside at any opportunity.

Sign up to Sarah Hope's mailing list for news, competitions and updates on future books.

Follow Sarah on social media here:

f facebook.com/HappinessHopeDreams

X x.com/sarahhope35

instagram.com/sarah_hope_writes

BB bookbub.com/authors/sarah-hope

ALSO BY SARAH HOPE

Escape to...

The Seaside Ice-Cream Parlour

The Little Beach Café

Christmas at Corner Cottage

The Bramble Patch Craft Shop

Berry Grove Bed and Breakfast

The Flower Shop on Serendipity Lane

The Wagging Tails Dogs' Home Series

The Wagging Tails Dogs' Home

Chasing Dreams at the Wagging Tails Dogs' Home

A Fresh Start at the Wagging Tails Dogs' Home

LOVE NOTES

LOVE IN EVERY CHAPTER

WHERE ALL YOUR ROMANCE
DREAMS COME TRUE!

THE HOME OF BESTSELLING
ROMANCE AND WOMEN'S
FICTION

WARNING:
MAY CONTAIN SPICE

Boldwood

Boldwood Books is an award-winning fiction publishing company seeking out the best stories from around the world.

Find out more at www.boldwoodbooks.com

Join our reader community for brilliant books, competitions and offers!

Follow us
@BoldwoodBooks
@TheBoldBookClub

Milton Keynes UK
Ingram Content Group UK Ltd.
UKHW041815110224
437557UK00002B/13

9 781805 491392